Needle

Needle

Hal Clement

AN EQUINOX BOOK/PUBLISHED BY AVON BOOKS

AVON BOOKS
A division of
The Hearst Corporation
959 Eighth Avenue
New York, New York 10019

ISBN: 0-380-00635-9

First Equinox Printing, April, 1976

EQUINOX TRADEMARK REG. U.S. PAT. OFF. AND IN
OTHER COUNTRIES, MARCA REGISTRADA, HECHO EN
U.S.A.

Printed in the U.S.A.

Chapter I. CASTAWAY

EVEN ON THE earth shadows are frequently good places to hide. They may show up, of course, against lighted surroundings, but if there is not too much light from the side, one can step into a shadow and become remarkably hard to see.

Beyond the earth, where there is no air to scatter light, they should be even better. The earth's own shadow, for example, is a million-mile-long cone of darkness pointing away from the sun, invisible itself in the surrounding dark and bearing the seeds of still more perfect invisibility— for the only illumination that enters that cone is starlight and the feeble rays bent into its blackness by the earth's thin envelope of air.

The Hunter knew he was in a planet's shadow though he had never heard of the earth; he had known it ever since he had dropped below the speed of light and seen the scarlet-rimmed disk of black squarely ahead of him; and so he took it for granted that the fugitive vessel would be detectable only by instruments. When he suddenly realized that the other ship was visible to the naked eye, the faint alarm that had been nibbling at the outskirts of his mind promptly rocketed into the foreground.

He had been unable to understand why the fugitive should go below the speed of light at all, unless in the vague hope that the pursuer would overrun him sufficiently to be out of detection range; and when that failed, the Hunter had expected a renewed burst of speed. Instead, the deceleration continued. The fleeing ship had kept between his own and the looming world ahead, making it dangerous to overhaul too rapidly; and the Hunter was coming to the conclusion that a break back on the direction they had come was to be expected when a spark of red light visible to the naked eye showed that the other

5

had actually entered an atmosphere. The planet was smaller and closer than the Hunter had believed.

The sight of that spark was enough for the pursuer. He flung every erg his generators could handle into a drive straight away from the planet, at the same time pouring the rest of his body into the control room to serve as a gelatinous cushion to protect the *perit* from the savage deceleration; and he saw instantly that it would not be sufficient. He had just time to wonder that the creature ahead of him should be willing to risk ship and host in what would certainly be a nasty crash before the outer fringes of the world's air envelope added their resistance to his plunging flight and set the metal plates of his hull glowing a brilliant orange from heat.

Since the ships had dived straight down the shadow cone, they were going to strike on the night side, of course; and once the hulls cooled, the fugitive would again be invisible. With an effort, therefore, the Hunter kept his eyes glued to the instruments that would betray the other's whereabouts as long as he was in range; and it was well that he did so, for the glowing cylinder vanished abruptly from sight into a vast cloud of water vapor that veiled the planet's dark surface. A split second later the Hunter's ship plunged into the same mass, and as it did so there was a twisting lurch, and the right-line deceleration changed to a sickening spinning motion. The pilot knew that one of the drive plates had gone, probably cracked off by undistributed heat but there was simply no time to do a thing about it. The other vessel, he noted, had stopped as though it had run into a brick wall; now it was settling again, but far more slowly, and he realized that he himself could only be split seconds from the same obstacle, assuming it to be horizontal.

It was. The Hunter's ship, still spinning wildly although he had shut off the remaining drive plates at the last moment, struck almost flat on water and at the impact split open from end to end along both sides as though it had been an eggshell stepped on by a giant. Almost all its kinetic energy was absorbed by that blow, but it did not stop altogether. It continued to settle, comparatively gently now, with a motion like a falling leaf, and the Hunter felt its shattered hull come to a rest on what he realized must be the bottom of a lake or sea a few seconds later.

At least, he told himself as his wits began slowly to clear, his quarry must be in the same predicament. The abrupt stoppage and subsequent slow descent of the other machine was now explained—even if it had struck head-on instead of horizontally, there would have been no perceptible difference in the result of a collision with a water surface at their speed. It was almost certainly unusable, though perhaps not quite so badly damaged as the hunter's ship.

That idea brought the train of thought back to his own predicament. He felt cautiously around him and found he was no longer entirely in the control room—in fact, there was no longer room for all of him inside it. What had been a cylindrical chamber some twenty inches in diameter and two feet long was now simply the space between two badly dented sheets of inch-thick metal which had been the hull. The seams had parted on either side, or, rather, seams had been created and forced apart, for the hull was originally a single piece of metal drawn into tubular shape. The top and bottom sections thus separated had been flattened out and were now only an inch or two apart on the average. The bulkheads at either end of the room had crumpled and cracked—even that tough alloy had its limitations. The perit was very dead. Not only had it been crushed by the collapsing wall, but the Hunter's semiliquid body had transmitted the shock of impact to its individual cells much as it is transmitted to the sides of a water-filled tin can by the impact of a rifle bullet, and most of its interior organs had ruptured. The Hunter, slowly realizing this, withdrew from around and within the little creature. He did not attempt to eject its mangled remains from the ship; it might be necessary to use them as food later on, though the idea was unpleasant. The Hunter's attitude toward the animal resembled that of a man toward a favorite dog, though the perit, with its delicate hands which it had learned to use at his direction much as an elephant uses its trunk at the behest of man, was more useful than any dog.

He extended his exploration a little, reaching out with a slender pseudopod of jellylike flesh through one of the rents in the hull. He already knew that the wreck was lying in salt water, but he had no idea of the depth other than the fact that it was not excessive. On his home world

7

he could have judged it quite accurately from the pressure; but pressure depends on the weight of a given quantity of water as well as its depth, and he had not obtained a reading of this planet's gravity before the crash.

It was dark outside the hull. When he molded an eye from his own tissue—those of the perit had been ruptured—it told him absolutely nothing of his surroundings. Suddenly, however, he realized that the pressure around him was not constant; it was increasing and decreasing by a rather noticeable amount with something like regularity; and the water was transmitting to his sensitive flesh the higher-frequency pressure waves which he interpreted as sound. Listening intently, he finally decided that he must be fairly close to the surface of a body of water large enough to develop waves a good many feet in height, and that a storm of considerable violence was in progress. He had not noticed any disturbance in the air during his catastrophic descent, but that meant nothing—he had spent too little time in the atmosphere to be affected by any reasonable wind.

Poking into the mud around the wreck with other pseudopods, he found to his relief that the planet was not lifeless—he had already been pretty sure of that fact. There was enough oxygen dissolved in the water to meet his needs, provided he did not exert himself greatly, and there must, consequently, be free oxygen in the atmosphere above. It was just as well, though, to have actual proof that life was present rather than merely possible, and he was well satisfied to locate in the mud a number of small bivalve mollusks which, upon trial, proved quite edible.

Realizing that it was night on this part of the planet, he decided to postpone further outside investigation until there was more light and turned his attention back to the remains of his ship. He had not expected the examination to turn up anything encouraging, but he got a certain glum feeling of accomplishment as he realized the completeness of the destruction. Solid metal parts in the engine room had changed shape under the stresses to which they had been subjected. The nearly solid conversion chamber of the main drive unit was flattened and twisted. There was no trace whatever of certain quartz-shelled gas tubes; they had evidently been pulverized by the shock and washed away by the water. No living

8

creature handicapped by a definite shape and solid parts could have hoped to come through such a crash alive, no matter how well protected. The thought was some comfort; he had done his best for the perit even though that had not been sufficient.

Once satisfied that nothing usable remained in his ship, the Hunter decided no more could be done at the moment. He could not undertake really active work until he had a better supply of oxygen, which meant until he reached open air; and the lack of light was also a severe handicap. He relaxed, therefore, in the questionable shelter of the ruined hull and waited for the storm to end and the day to come. With light and calm water he felt that he could reach shore without assistance; the wave noise suggested breakers, which implied a beach at no great distance.

He lay there for several hours, and it occurred to him once that he might be on a planet which always kept the same hemisphere toward its sun; but he realized that in such a case the dark side would almost certainly be too cold for water to exist as a liquid. It seemed more probable that storm clouds were shutting out the daylight.

Ever since the ship had finally settled into the mud it had remained motionless. The disturbances overhead were reflected in currents and backwashes along the bottom which the Hunter could feel but which were quite unable to shift the half-buried mass of metal. Certain as he was that the hull was now solidly fixed in place, the castaway was suddenly startled when his shelter quivered as though to a heavy blow and changed position slightly.

Instantly he sent out an inquiring tentacle. He molded an eye at its tip, but the darkness was still intense, and he returned to strictly tactile exploration. Vibrations suggestive of a very rough skin scraping along the metal were coming to him, and abruptly something living ran into the extended limb. It demonstrated its sentient quality by promptly seizing the appendage in a mouth that seemed amazingly well furnished with saw-edged teeth.

The Hunter reacted normally, for him—that is, he allowed the portion of himself in direct contact with those unpleasant edges to relax into a semiliquid condition, and at the same moment he sent more of his body flowing into the arm toward the strange creature. He was a being

9

of quick decisions, and the evident size of the intruder had impelled him to a somewhat foolhardy act. He left the wrecked space ship entirely and sent his whole four pounds of jellylike flesh toward what he hoped would prove a more useful conveyance.

The shark—it was an eight-foot hammerhead—may have been surprised and was probably irritated, but in common with all its kind it lacked the brains to be afraid. Its ugly jaws snapped hungrily at what at first seemed like satisfying solid flesh, only to have it give way before them like so much water. The Hunter made no attempt to avoid the teeth, since mechanical damage of that nature held no terrors for him, but he strenuously resisted the efforts of the fish to swallow that portion of his body already in its mouth. He had no intention of exposing himself to gastric juices, since he had no skin to resist their action even temporarily.

As the shark's activities grew more and more frantically vicious, he sent exploring pseudopods over the ugly rough-skinned form, and within a few moments discovered the five gill slits on each side of the creature's neck. That was enough. He no longer investigated; he acted, with a skill and precision born of long experience.

The Hunter was a metazoon—a many-celled creature, like a bird or a man—in spite of his apparent lack of structure. The individual cells of his body, however, were far smaller than those of most earthly creatures, comparing in size with the largest protein molecules. It was possible for him to construct from his tissues a limb, complete with muscles and sensory nerves, the whole structure fine enough to probe through the capillaries of a more orthodox creature without interfering seriously with its blood circulation. He had, therefore, no difficulty in insinuating himself into the shark's relatively huge body.

He avoided nerves and blood vessels for the moment and poured himself into such muscular and visceral interstices as he could locate. The shark calmed down at once after the thing in its mouth and on its body ceased sending tactile messages to its minute brain; its memory, to all intents and purposes, was nonexistent. For the Hunter, however, successful interstition was only the beginning of a period of complicated activity.

First and most important, oxygen. There was enough

of the precious element absorbed on the surfaces of his body cells for a few minutes of life at the most, but it could always be obtained in the body of a creature that also consumed oxygen; and the Hunter rapidly sent sub-microscopic appendages between the cells that formed the walls of blood vessels and began robbing the blood cells of their precious load. He needed but little, and on his home world he had lived in this manner for years within the body of an intelligent oxygen-breather, with the other's full knowledge and consent. He had more than paid for his keep.

The second need was vision. His host presumably possessed eyes, and with his oxygen supply assured the Hunter began to search for them. He could, of course, have sent enough of his own body out through the shark's skin to construct an organ of vision, but he might not have been able to avoid disturbing the creature by such an act. Besides, ready-made lenses were usually better than those he could make himself.

His search was interrupted before it had gone very far. The crash had, as he had deduced, occurred rather close to land; the encounter with the shark had taken place in quite shallow water. Sharks are not particularly fond of disturbance; it is hard to understand why this one had been so close to the surf. During the monster's struggle with the Hunter it had partly drifted and partly swum closer to the beach; and with its attention no longer taken up by the intruder, it tried to get back into deep water. The shark's continued frenzied activity, *after* the oxygen-theft system had been established, started a chain of events which caught the alien's attention.

The breathing system of a fish operates under a considerable disadvantage. The oxygen dissolved in water is never at a very high concentration, and a water-breathing creature, though it may be powerful and active, never has a really large reserve of the gas. The Hunter was not taking very much to keep alive, but he was trying to build up a reserve of his own as well; and with the shark working at its maximum energy output, the result was that its oxygen consumption was exceeding its intake. That, of course, had two effects: the monster's physical strength began to decline and the oxygen content of its blood to decrease. With the latter occurrence the Hunter almost unconsciously increased his drain on the system, thereby starting a vicious circle that could have only one ending.

The Hunter realized what was happening long before the shark actually died but did nothing about it, though he could have reduced his oxygen consumption without actually killing himself. He could also have left the shark, but he had no intention of drifting around in comparative helplessness in the open sea, at the mercy of the first creature large and quick enough to swallow him whole. He remained, and kept on absorbing the life-bearing gas, for he had realized that so much effort would be needed only if the fish were fighting the waves—striving to bear him away from the shore he wanted to reach. He had judged perfectly by this time the shark's place in the evolutionary scale and had no more compunction about killing it than would a human being.

The monster took a long time to die, though it became helpless quite rapidly. Once it ceased to struggle, the Hunter continued the search for its eyes, and eventually found them. He deposited a film of himself between and around their retinal cells, in anticipation of the time when there would be enough light for him to see. Also, since the now-quiescent shark was showing a distressing tendency to sink, the alien began extending other appendages to trap any air bubbles which might be brought near by the storm. These, together with the carbon dioxide he produced himself, he gradually accumulated in the fish's abdominal cavity to give buoyancy. He needed very little gas for this purpose, but it took him a long time to collect it, since he was too small to produce large volumes of carbon dioxide very rapidly.

The breakers were sounding much more loudly by the time he was able to take his attention from these jobs, and he realized that his assumption of a shoreward drift was justified. The waves were imparting a sickening up-and-down motion to his unusual raft, which neither bothered nor pleased him; it was horizontal motion he wanted, and that was comparatively slow until the water became quite shallow.

He waited for a long time after his conveyance stopped moving, expecting each moment to be floated and dragged back into deep water again, but nothing happened, and gradually the sound of waves began to decrease slightly and the amount of spray falling on him to diminish. The Hunter suspected that the storm was dying out. Actually, the tide had turned; but the result was the same as far as he was concerned.

By the time the combination of approaching dawn and thinning storm clouds provided enough light for his surroundings to be visible his late host was well above the reach of the heaviest waves. The shark's eyes would not focus on their own retinas out of water, but the Hunter found that the new focal surface was inside the eyeball and built a retina of his own in the appropriate place. The lenses also turned out to be a little less than perfect, but he modified their curvature with some of his own body substance and eventually found himself able to see his surroundings without exposing himself to the view of others.

There were rifts in the storm clouds now through which a few of the brightest stars were still visible against the gray background of approaching dawn. Slowly these breaks grew larger, and by the time the sun rose the sky was almost clear, though the wind still blew fiercely.

His vantage point was not ideal, but he was able to make out a good deal of his surroundings. In one direction the beach extended a short distance to a line of tall, slender trees crowned with feathery tufts of leaves. He could not see beyond these, his point of observation being too low, though they were not themselves set thickly enough to obstruct the view. In the opposite direction was more debris-strewn beach, with the roar of the still-heavy surf sounding beyond it. The Hunter could not actually see the ocean, but its direction was obvious. To the right was a body of water which, he realized, must be a small pool, filled by the storm and now emptying back into the sea through an opening too small or too steep for the surf to enter. This was probably the only reason the shark had stranded at all—it had been washed into this pool and left there by the receding tide.

Several times he heard raucous screeching sounds and saw birds overhead. This pleased him greatly; evidently there were higher forms of life than fishes on the planet, and there was some hope of obtaining a more suitable host. An intelligent one would be best, since an intelligent creature is ordinarily best able to protect itself. It

13

would also be more likely to travel widely, thus facilitating the now-necessary search for the pilot of the other ship. It was very likely, however, as the Hunter fully realized, that there would be serious difficulty in obtaining access to the body of an intelligent creature who was not accustomed to the idea of symbiosis.

All that, however, would have to wait on chance. Even if there were intelligent beings on this planet they might never come to this spot; and even if they did, he might not recognize them for what they were in time to get any good out of the situation. It would be best to wait, several days if need be, to observe just what forms of life frequented this locality; after that he could make plans to invade the one best suited to his needs. Time was probably not vital; it was as certain as anything could be that his quarry was no more able to leave the planet than was the Hunter himself, and while he remained on it the search would be decidedly tedious. Time spent in careful preparation would undoubtedly pay dividends.

He waited, therefore, while the sun rose higher and the wind gradually died down to a mild breeze. It became quite warm; and he was aware before long of chemical changes going on in the flesh of the shark. They were changes which made it certain that, if a sense of smell were common to many of the creatures of this world, he was bound to have visitors before too long. The Hunter could have halted the process of decay by the simple expedient of consuming the bacteria that caused it, but he was not particularly hungry and certainly had no objection to visitors. On the contrary!

Chapter II. SHELTER

THE FIRST visitors were gulls. One by one they descended, attracted by sight and smell, and began tearing at the carcass of the shark. The Hunter withdrew to the lower parts of the body and made no attempt to drive them off, even when they pounced upon the eyes of the great fish and speedily deprived him of visual contact with the outside world. If other life forms came he would know it anyway; if they didn't, it was just as well to have the gulls there.

The greedy birds remained undisturbed until midafternoon. They did not make too much progress in disposing of the shark—the tough skin defied their beaks in most places. They were persistent, however, and when they suddenly took wing and departed in a body, it was evident to the Hunter that there must be something of interest in the neighborhood. He hastily extruded enough tissue from one of the gill slits to make an eye and looked cautiously about him.

He saw why the gulls had left. From the direction of the trees a number of much larger creatures were coming. They were bipeds, and the Hunter estimated with the ease of long practice that the largest weighed fully a hundred and twenty pounds, which, in an air-breather, meant that the addition of his own mass and oxygen consumption was unlikely to prove a serious burden. Much closer to him was a smaller four-legged creature running rapidly toward the dead shark and uttering an apparently endless string of sharp yelping sounds. The Hunter placed it at about fifty pounds and filed the information mentally for future use.

The four bipeds were also running, but not nearly so rapidly as the smaller animal. As they approached, the hidden watcher examined them carefully, and the more

15

he saw the more pleased he was. They could travel with fair speed; their skulls were of a size that gave promise of considerable intelligence, if one could safely assume that this race kept its brain there; their skins seemed almost entirely unprotected, giving promise of easy access through the pores. As they slowed up and stopped beside the hammerhead's body, they gave another indication of intelligence by exchanging articulate sounds which unquestionably represented speech. The Hunter, to put it mildly, was delighted. He had not dared hope for such an ideal host to appear so quickly.

Of course there were problems still to be solved. It was a fairly safe bet that the creatures were not accustomed to the idea of symbiosis, at least as the Hunter's race practiced it. The alien was sure he had never seen members of this race before, and was equally sure he knew all those with whom his people normally associated. Therefore, if these beings actually saw him approaching, they would almost certainly go to considerable lengths to avoid contact; and even if this proved futile, forcible entry on the Hunter's part would create an attitude highly unlikely to lead to future co-operation. It seemed, therefore, that subtlety would have to be employed.

The four bipeds remained looking down at the shark and conversing for only a few minutes, then they walked off a short distance up the beach. Somehow the Hunter got a vague impression from their attitudes that they found the neighborhood unpleasant. The quadruped remained a little longer, examining the carcass closely; but it apparently failed to notice the rather oddly placed eye which was following its movements. A call from one of the other creatures finally attracted its attention, and as the Hunter watched it bounded off in the direction they had taken. He saw with some surprise that they had entered the water and were swimming around with considerable facility. He marked down the fact as another point in their favor; he had seen no trace of gills in his rather careful examination of their bodies, and as air-breathers they must have had a considerable margin between their ability to absorb oxygen and their actual need for it to remain under water as long as he saw one of them do. Then he realized that there was another good

16

point: he could probably approach them much more easily in the water.

It was evident from their behavior that they could not see very well, if at all, under water—they invariably raised their heads above the surface to orient themselves, and did this with considerable frequency. The quadruped was even less likely to see him approaching, as it kept its head above water at all times.

The thought led to instant action. A threadlike pseudopod began groping rapidly toward the pool an inch or two under the sand. The eye was kept in operation until most of the jelly-like body had crossed the four-yard gap, then another was formed at the water's edge, and the Hunter drew the rest of his body into a compact mass just below it. The operation had taken several minutes; winding among sand grains had been an annoyingly devious mode of travel.

The water was quite clear, so it was not necessary to keep an eye above the surface to direct the stalk. The mass of jelly quickly molded itself into an elongated, fishlike shape with an eye in front, and the Hunter swam toward the boys as rapidly as he could. In one way, he reflected, it was really easier to see under water. He could use a concave lens of air, held in shape by a film of his own flesh, which was far more transparent than an optical system composed entirely of the latter substance.

He had intended to swim right up to one of the boys, hoping his approach would not be noticed and his efforts at contact marked by swirling water or his subject's friends —they were indulging in acts of considerable violence as they swam and plunged. However, it speedily became evident that only luck would bring him in contact with one of the creatures, since they swam much more rapidly than the Hunter could; and, realizing this, he found what seemed to be an excellent means of making an undercover approach. He suddenly noticed beside him a large jellyfish, bobbing rather aimlessly along after the manner of its kind; and with his attention thus diverted, he saw that there were quite a number of the things in the vicinity. Evidently the bipeds did not consider them dangerous or they would not be swimming here.

Accordingly, the Hunter altered his form and method of locomotion to agree with those of the medusae and approached more slowly the area in which the boys were playing. His color was slightly different from that of any of the other jellyfish but these, in turn, differed among themselves, and he felt that shape must be a more important criterion than shade. He may have been right, for he got almost up to one of the bipeds without apparently causing any alarm. They were fairly close together at the moment, and he had high hopes of making contact—he did, in fact, with a cautiously extended tentacle, discover that the varicolored integument covering a portion of their bodies was an artificial fabric—but before he could do any more, the subject of his investigation slid to one side and moved several feet away. He gave no sign of alarm, however, and the Hunter tried again. The approach ended in precisely the same fashion, except that this time he did not get so close.

He tried each of the other boys in turn, with the same annoying near-success. Then, puzzled by a phenomenon which seemed to be exceeding the generous limits of the law of chance, he drifted a short distance away and watched, trying to learn the reason for it. Within five minutes he realized that, while these creatures seemed to have no actual fear of jelly-fish, they sedulously avoided physical contact with them. He had chosen an unfortunate camouflage.

Robert Kinnaird avoided jellyfish almost without conscious thought. He had learned to swim at the age of five, and in that and each of the nine subsequent years of his life he had enough first-hand experience with their stinging tentacles to assure his avoiding their company. He had been fully occupied in ducking one of his companions when the Hunter had first touched him, and even though he had dodged hastily on noticing the lump of jelly in the water beside him he had not really thought about the matter—if he did, it was merely a brief reflection that he was lucky not to have been stung. He forgot the incident promptly, but his attention had been sufficiently diffused by it to prevent the thing's again approaching so closely.

About the time the Hunter realized what was wrong, the boys grew tired of swimming and retired to the beach. He watched them go in mounting annoyance, and continued to watch as they ran back and forth on the sand playing some obscure game. Were the mad creatures never still? How in the Galaxy could he ever come in contact with such infernally active beings? He could only watch, and ponder.

Ashore, once the salt had dried on their sun-browned hides, the boys did finally begin to quiet down and cast expectant glances toward the grove of coconut palms between them and the center of the island. One of them seated.himself, facing the ocean, and suddenly spoke.

"Bob, when are your folks coming with the grub?"

Robert Kinnaird flung himself face downward in the sun before replying. " 'Bout four or half-past, Mother said. Don't you ever think of anything but eating?"

The redheaded questioner mumbled an inarticulate reply and subsided flat on his back, gazing up into the now cloudless blue sky. Another of the boys took up the conversational ball.

"It's tough, you having to go tomorrow," he said. "I kind of wish I was going with you, though. I haven't been in the States since my folks came out here. I was only a kid then," he added serenely.

"It's not so bad," returned Bob slowly. "There are a lot of good fellows at the school, and there's skating and skiing in the winter that you don't get here. Anyway, I'll be back next summer."

The talk died down and the boys basked in the hot sunshine as they waited for Mrs. Kinnaird and the food for the farewell picnic. Bob was closest to the water, lying stretched in full sunlight; the others had sought the rather inadequate shade of the palms. He was already well tanned but wanted to get the last possible benefit out of the tropical sun, which he would miss for the next ten months. It was hot, and he had just spent an active half-hour, and there was nothing at all to keep him awake . . .

The Hunter was still watching, eagerly now. Were the peripatetic things really settling down at last? It looked as though they were. The four bipeds were sprawled on the sand in various positions which they presumably found comfortable; the other animal settled down beside one of them, letting its head rest on its forelegs. The conversation, which had been almost incessant up to this point, died down, and the amorphous watcher decided to take a chance. He moved rapidly to the edge of the pool.

The nearest of the boys was about ten yards from the water. It would not be possible to maintain a watch from the Hunter's present position and at the same time send himself under the sand to a point below the now-motionless body of his intended host. He must, however, keep the other in sight. Once more camouflage seemed indicated, and once more the ever-present jellyfish seemed to fill the need. There were a number of them lying on the sand motionless; perhaps if he moved slowly and emulated their shape the Hunter could escape notice until he was close enough for an underground attack.

He may have been excessively cautious, since none of the creatures was facing his way and all were nearly if not entirely asleep, but caution is never really wasted, and the Hunter did not regret the twenty minutes he took getting from the water's edge to a point some three yards from Robert Kinnaird. It was uncomfortable, of course, since his skinless body had even less protection from the hot sun than the jellyfish it was imitating; but he stood it, and eventually reached a point which his earlier experience suggested was close enough.

Had anyone been watching the large medusa lying apparently helpless a few feet from the boy at that moment he might have noticed a peculiar diminution in its size. The shrinking itself was not remarkable—it is the inevitable fate of a jellyfish on a hot beach—but the more orthodox members of the tribe merely grow thinner until only a cobwebby skeleton remains. This specimen dwindled not only in thickness but in diameter, and there were no remains whatsoever. Until it was almost completely gone, of course, there was an odd little lump in the center which preserved its size and shape while the body vanished around it; but this at last went, too, and no trace remained except a shallow depression in the sand—a depression which that careful observer might have noticed extended all the way from the water's edge.

The Hunter kept the eye in use during most of the underground search. His questing appendage at last reached sand that was more closely compacted than usual and, advancing very cautiously now, finally encountered what

20

could only be living flesh. Robert's toes were buried in the sand, since he was lying on his stomach, and the Hunter found that he could operate without emerging at all to the surface. With that fact established, he dissolved the eye and drew the last of his mass out of sight below the sand—with considerable relief as the sunlight was cut off.

He did not attempt to penetrate until his whole body had been drawn through the sand and was wrapped about the half-buried foot. He surrounded the limb with extreme care, bringing himself into contact with the skin over several square inches. Then and only then did he commence interstition, letting the ultra-microscopic cells of his flesh slide through pores, between skin cells, under toenails—into the thousands of openings that lay unguarded in this, to his way of thinking, singularly coarse organism.

The boy was sound asleep, and remained so; but the Hunter worked as fast as possible nevertheless, for it would have been extremely awkward to have the foot move while he was only partly inside. Therefore, as swiftly as was compatible with extreme caution, the alien organism flowed smoothly along the bones and tendons in foot and ankle; up within the muscle sheaths of calf and thigh; along the outer wall of the femoral artery and through the tubelets within the structure of the thigh bone; around joints, and through still other blood vessels. It filtered through the peritoneum without causing sensation or damage; and finally the whole four pounds of unearthly life was gathered together in the abdominal cavity, not only without harming the boy in the least but without even disturbing his slumber. And there, for a time, the Hunter rested.

He had a bigger oxygen reserve this time, having entered from air rather than water. It would be some time before he needed to draw on his host for more. He was hoping, if it were possible, to remain exactly where he was for an entire day, so that he could observe and memorize the cycle of physiological processes which this host undoubtedly performed differently from any he had known before. At the moment, of course, the creature was asleep, but that would probably not be for long. These beings seemed pretty active.

Bob was aroused, like the other boys, by the sound of his mother's voice. She had come silently, spread a blanket in the shade, and arranged the food on it before speaking; and her first words were the ancient "Come and get it!" She would not stay to help them eat it, though cordially and sincerely pressed to do so by the boys, but went back through the palm grove to the road that led to their home.

"Try to be back by sundown," she called to Bob over her shoulder as she reached the trees. "You still have to pack, and you'll have to be up early in the morning." Bob nodded, with his mouth full, and turned back to the food-laden blanket.

After disposing of the meal, the boys sat, talked, and dozed for the standard hour after eating; then they returned to the water, where they indulged further in games of violence; and at last, realizing that the abrupt tropical night would soon be upon them, they gathered up the blanket and started for the road and their respective dwellings. They were rather silent now, with the awkwardness natural to their ages when faced by a situation which adults would treat either emotionally or with studied casualness. The farewells, as they passed their respective dwellings, were brief and accompanied by reiterated and reciprocated promises to "write as soon as you can."

Bob, proceeding at last alone to his own house, felt the mixture of regret and pleasurable anticipation which he had come to associate with these occasions. By the time he reached home, though, the latter feeling had gained the ascendant, and he was looking forward with considerable eagerness to meeting again the school friends he had not seen for more than two months. He was whistling cheerfully as he entered the house.

The packing, done with the tactful assistance of his mother, was quickly completed, and by nine o'clock he was in bed and asleep. He himself considered the hour rather early, but he had learned the value of obedience at certain times very early in life.

The Hunter was able to remain quiescent, as he had hoped, for some hours—till well after Bob was asleep, in fact. He could not, however, last an entire day; for no matter how quiet he remained, the mere fact of living used up some energy and consequently some oxygen.

Eventually he realized his store was growing low, and he knew it would be necessary to establish a supply before the need became desperate.

He knew, of course, that his host was asleep, but this in no way decreased his caution. He remained for the time being below the diaphragm, not wishing to disturb in any way the heart he could feel beating just above it; but he was able to find without effort a large artery in the abdomen which offered no more resistance to penetration than had any other part of the human organism thus far. He discovered, to his intense satisfaction, that he could draw enough oxygen from the red cells (he did not think of them by color, since he had not yet seen them) to supply his needs without seriously diminishing the quantity that passed through the vessel. He checked this fact very carefully. His whole attitude in the present exploration was utterly different from that which had directed his actions within the body of the shark, for he had come to look upon Robert in the light of a permanent companion during his stay on the earth, and his present actions were ruled by a law of his kind so ancient and so rigid as to assume almost the proportions of an instinct.

Do nothing that can harm your host!

Chapter III.   OUT OF PLAY

Do nothing that can harm your host! For the majority of the Hunter's kind even the desire to break that law never existed, since they lived on terms of the warmest friendship with the beings whose bodies harbored theirs. The few individuals who proved to be exceptions were regarded with the liveliest horror and detestation by their fellows. It was one of these whom the Hunter had been pursuing at the time of his crash on the earth; and that being, he well knew, must still be found—if only to protect this native race from the inroads of the irresponsible creature.

Do nothing that can harm your host! From the moment of the Hunter's arrival the swarming white cells in the boy's healthy blood had been aroused. He had avoided the most serious contacts with them up to now by keeping clear of the interiors of blood vessels, though there were enough of them wandering free in the lymphatics and connective tissue to be a nuisance. His body cells were not naturally immune to their powers of absorption, and only by constant evasive action had he been able to avoid serious damage to himself. He knew this could not go on indefinitely; for one thing, he must occasionally direct his attention to other matters, and, for another, the continuation of such a misunderstanding, whether he persevered in evasive action or began to fight back, would mean an increase in the number of white cells and probably some sort of illness to his host. Therefore, the leucocytes must be pacified. His race had, of course, worked out long since a general technique for solving this problem, but care still had to be taken in individual cases—particularly unfamiliar ones. By a trial-and-error process carried out with as much speed as was practical, the Hunter determined the nature of the chemical clue by which the white cells differentiated invading organisms from legitimate members of the human body; and after prolonged and still extremely careful effort he exposed every one of his cells to sources of the appropriate chemicals in his host's blood stream. A few molecules of the desired substance were absorbed on the surface of each cell, and this, to his relief, proved to be sufficient. The leucocytes ceased to bother him, and he could use the larger blood vessels safely as avenues of exploration for his questing pseudopoda.

Do nothing that can harm your host! He needed food as well as oxygen. He could have consumed with relish and satisfaction any of the various forms of tissue surrounding him, but the law made selection necessary. There were certainly intruding organisms in this body—besides himself—and they were the logical food source, for by consuming them he would be eliminating their menace to his host and thereby helping to earn his keep. Identifying them would be easy; anything a leucocyte attacked would be legitimate prey for the Hunter. Probably the local microbes would not keep him fed for long, small as his needs were, and it would also be necessary to tap the digestive tract at some point; but that need not cause damage, unless a slightly increased appetite on the part of the host came under that heading.

For many hours the cautious exploration and adjustment continued. The Hunter felt his host awaken and resume activity, but he made no effort to look outside. He had one problem which must be carefully and accurately solved; and, although his dodging the attentions of thousands of leucocytes at once, as he had done for a time, may seem evidence to the contrary, his power of attention was limited. That had simply been an automatic action roughly comparable to a man's carrying on a conversation while he climbs stairs.

Filaments of the Hunter's flesh, far finer than human neurons, gradually formed an all-inclusive network throughout Bob's body from head to toe; and through those threads the Hunter came gradually to know the purpose and customary uses of every muscle, gland, and sense organ in that body. Throughout this period most of his mass remained in the abdominal cavity, and it was more than seventy-two hours after his first intrusion that he

25

felt secure enough in his position to pay attention once more to outside affairs.

As he had done with the shark, he began to fill the spaces between the boy's retinal cells with his own body substance. He was actually able to make better use of Bob's eyes than their proper owner could, for the human eyes see in maximum detail only those objects whose images fall within an area of retina less than a millimeter across. The Hunter could use the whole area on which the lens focused with reasonable sharpness, which was decidedly larger. In consequence, he could examine with Bob's eyes objects at which the boy was not looking directly. This was likely to be a help, since many of the things in which the hidden watcher was most interested would be too commonplace to the human being to attract his direct gaze.

The Hunter could hear dimly even within the human body, but he found it helpful to establish direct physical contact with the bones of the middle ear. Thus, hearing as well as seeing better than his host, he felt ready to investigate the planet on which chance had marooned him and his quarry. There was no further reason—he thought—for delay in searching for and destroying the criminal of his own race now free on the world. He began to look and listen.

The search itself he had never regarded as more than a routine job. He had had similar problems before. He had expected to look around from the vantage point of Bob's body until he found the others, leave and eliminate his opponent by standard means—regardless of the fact that all his equipment was at the bottom of the sea. He had had, in short, a viewpoint which is excusable in a space navigator but not in a detective: he had been regarding a planet as a small object and thinking his search was practically over when he had narrowed it down to one world.

He was rudely jolted out of this attitude as he took his first look around since meeting Bob Kinnaird. The picture that fell on their common retinas was that of the interior of a cylindrical object vaguely suggestive of his own space ship. It was filled with several rows of seats, most of them occupied by human beings. Beside the watcher was a window through which Bob was looking at the moment; and the suspicion that had entered the Hunter's mind was instantly confirmed by the view through that window. They were on board an aircraft, traveling at a considerable altitude with a speed and in a direction which the alien was in no position to estimate. Start looking for his quarry? He must first look for the right continent!

The flight lasted for several hours and had probably already consumed several. The Hunter quickly gave up the attempt to memorize landmarks over which they passed. One or two of them did stick in his mind and might give a clue to direction if he could ever identify them later; but he put little trust in this possibility. He must keep track of time rather than position, and when he was more familiar with human ways find out where his host had been at the time of his own intrusion.

The view itself, though, was interesting, even if the landmarks were lacking. It was a beautiful planet, from his alien viewpoint; mountains and plains, rivers and lakes, forests and prairies were all visible at various times, now clearly through miles of crystal atmosphere and now in glimpses between billowing clouds of water vapor. The machine he rode was also worthy of attention; from Robert's window he could not see very much of it, but that little told him a great deal. A portion of a metal wing was visible, bearing attachments which evidently contained engines, as rapidly rotating air foils were visible ahead of them. Since the craft was presumably symmetrical, the Hunter decided there must be at least four of these engines. He could not tell with accuracy how much of their energy was wasted in heat and sound—for one thing, he suspected that the cabin in which he rode was quite effectively sound-proofed. The machine as a whole, however, suggested that this race had evidently attained a considerable degree of mechanical advancement, and a new idea blossomed from that: might he not attempt to enter into communication with this being which was his host and secure its active co-operation in his search? It was a point well worth considering.

There was plenty of time for thought before the airplane gradually began to descend. The Hunter could not see directly ahead, and it happened that they entered a solid cloud layer almost immediately, so he was unable to get any idea of their destination until just before the landing. He chalked up another point for the race: they either had senses he lacked, or were very competent and ingenious instrument makers, for the descent through the clouds was as smooth as any other part of the flight.

After some time spent letting down through the gray murk, the machine broke out into clear air. As it banked into a wide turn the Hunter saw a large city built around a great, crowded harbor; then the faint drone of the engines increased in pitch, a large double wheel appeared below one of the nacelles, and the craft glided easily downward to contact with a faint jar a broad, hard-surfaced runway located on a point of land across the harbor from the largest buildings.

As Robert disembarked he glanced back at the airplane, so the Hunter was better able to form an estimate of its size and construction details. He had no idea of the power developed by the four bulky engines, and could not, therefore, guess at the speed; but he could see the quivering in the air above the huge nacelles that told of hot metal within and knew at least that they were not the phoenix converters used by his race and its allies. Whatever they were, though, it had already become evident that the machine could put a very respectable fraction of the planet's circumference behind it without having to descend for fuel.

After alighting from the airplane the boy went through the usual formalities incident to reclaiming his baggage, took a bus around the harbor to the city, walked about for a while, and visited a movie. This the Hunter also enjoyed; his vision persistence involved about the same time lapse as the human eye, so he saw the show as a movie rather than a set of separate pictures. It was still daylight when they emerged and walked back to the bus station, where Bob reclaimed the luggage he had checked, then they boarded another bus.

This turned out to be quite a long ride; the vehicle took them far outside the city and through several smaller towns, and the sun was almost down when it finally left them by the roadside.

A smaller side road, with broad, well-kept lawns on either side, led off up a gentle slope, and at the top of this slope was a large, sprawling building, or group of buildings—the Hunter was not sure which from his viewpoint. Robert picked up his bags and walked up the hill toward this structure, and the alien began to hope that the journey had ended, for the time being at least. He was far enough from his quarry already. As it turned out, his hopes for once were fulfilled.

To the boy the return to school, assignment to a room, and meeting with old acquaintances were by now familiar, but to the Hunter every activity and everything he saw and heard were of absorbing interest. He had no intention, even yet, of making a really detailed study of the human race, but some subconscious guide was beginning to warn him that his mission was not to be quite the routine job he had expected and that he might possibly have use for all the earthly knowledge he could get. He didn't know it yet, but he had come to the best possible place for knowledge.

He looked and listened almost feverishly as Bob went to his room, unpacked, and then wandered about the dormitory meeting friends from former terms. He found himself trying almost constantly to connect the flood of spoken words with their meanings; but it was difficult, since most of the conversation concerned events of the vacation just past, and the words usually lacked visible referents. He did learn the personal names of some of the beings, however, among them that of his host.

He decided, after an hour or two, that it would be best to turn his full attention to the language problem. There was nothing whatever at the moment that he could do about his own mission, and if he understood the speech around him he might be able to learn when his host was to return to the place where they had met. Until he did return, the Hunter was simply out of play—he could do nothing at all toward locating and eliminating his quarry.

With this idea finally settled upon he spent Robert's sleeping hours organizing the few words he had learned, trying to deduce some grammatical rules, and developing a definite campaign for learning more as quickly as possible. It may seem odd that one who was so completely unable to control his own comings and goings should dream of planning anything, but the extra effective width of his vision angle must be remembered. He was to some

29

extent able to determine what he saw and therefore felt that he should decide what to look for.

It would have been far simpler, if he could only control his host's movements in some way or other, or interpret and influence the multitudinous reactions that went on in his nervous system. He had controlled the perit, of course, but not directly; the little creature had been trained to respond to twinges administered directly to its muscles, as a horse is trained to respond to the pressure of the reins. The Hunter's people used the perits to perform actions which their own semiliquid bodies lacked the strength to do, and which were too delicate for their intelligent hosts to perform—or which had to be performed in places which had brought the Hunter to earth.

Unfortunately for this line of thought Robert Kinnaird was not a perit and could not be treated as one. There was no hope, at present, of influencing his actions at all, and any such hope in the future must rest on appeals to the boy's reason rather than on force. At the moment the Hunter was rather in the position of a movie spectator who wants to change the plot of the film he is seeing.

Classes began the day after their arrival. Their purpose was at once obvious to the unlisted pupil though the subjects were frequently obscure. The boy's course included, among other subjects, English, physics, Latin, and French; and of those four, oddly enough, physics proved most helpful in teaching the Hunter the English language. The reason is not too difficult to understand.

While the Hunter was not a scientist, he knew something of science—one can hardly operate a machine like a space ship without having some notion of what makes it work. The elementary principles of the physical sciences are the same anywhere, and while the drawing conventions accepted by the authors of Bob's textbooks differed from those of the Hunter's people, the diagrams were still understandable. Since the diagrams were usually accompanied by written explanations, they were clues to the meanings of a great many words.

The connection between spoken and written English was also cleared up one day in a physics class, when the instructor used a heavily lettered diagram to explain a problem in mechanics. The unseen watcher suddenly understood the connection between letter and sound and within a few days was able to visualize the written form of any new word he heard—allowing, of course, for the spelling irregularities that are the curse of the English language.

The learning process was one which automatically increased its speed as time went on, for the more words the Hunter knew, the more he could guess at from the context in which he met them. By the beginning of November, two months after the opening of school, the alien's vocabulary had the size, though not the precise content, of an intelligent ten-year-old's. He had a rather excessive store of scientific terms and many blanks where less specialized words should have been. Also, the meanings he attached to many terms were the strictly scientific ones—for example, he thought work meant "force times distance," and only that.

By this time, however, he had reached a point where tenth-grade English had some meaning to him, and the opportunities to judge word meanings from context became very frequent indeed, ignorant as the Hunter was of human customs.

About the beginning of December, when the strange little being had almost forgotten everything in the pleasure of learning, an interruption occurred in his education. It occurred, the Hunter felt, through his own negligence and restored him to a better sense of duty. Robert Kinnaird had been a member of the school football team during the fall. The Hunter, with his intense interest in the health of his host, somewhat disapproved of this, though he understood the need of any muscled animal for exercise. The final game of the school season was played on Thanksgiving Day, and when the Hunter realized it *was* the final one, no one gave more thanks than he. However, he rejoiced too soon.

Bob, reconstructing one of the more exciting moments of the game to prove his point in an argument, slipped and twisted an ankle severely enough to put him to bed for several days. The Hunter felt guilty about it because, had he realized the danger even two or three seconds in advance, he would have "tightened up" the net of his tissue that existed around the boy's joints and tendons. Of course his physical strength being what it was, this would not actually have been much help, but he regretted not

31

trying. Now that the damage had actually been done, there was nothing whatever he could do—the danger of infection was already nil without his help, since the skin had not been broken.

The incident, at any rate, recalled him not only to his duties to his host but also those he had as a police agent; and once again he started thinking over what he had learned that could bear on his police problem. To his astonishment and chagrin this turned out to be nothing at all; he did not even know where the boy had been at the time of his own arrival.

He did learn, from a chance remark passed between Bob and one of his friends, that the place was an island, which was one of the few bright spots in the picture—his quarry, if it had landed at the same place, must either still be there or have left by some traceable means. The Hunter remembered too vividly his own experience with the shark to believe that the other could escape successfully in a fish, and he had never heard of a warm-blooded air-breather that lived in the water. Seals and whales had not come up in Bob's conversation or reading, at least not since the Hunter had been able to understand it.

If the other were in a human being, that person could leave the island only in some sort of craft, and that should mean that his movements would be traceable. It was a comforting thought, and one of the few the Hunter was to have for some time to come.

It remained to learn the location of the island, as a preliminary step to getting back to it. Bob received frequent letters from his parents, but for some time the Hunter did not recognize these as clues, partly because he had a good deal of trouble reading script and partly because he did not know the relationship of the boy to the senders of the letters. He had no particular scruples about reading the boy's mail, of course; he simply found it difficult. Robert did write to his parents as well, at somewhat irregular intervals, but they were not his only correspondents, and it was not until nearly the end of January that the Hunter found that by far the greater number of the boy's letters were going to and coming from one particular address.

The discovery was helped by the youngster's receipt of a typewriter as a Christmas present. Whether his parents meant this as a gentle hint is hard to say, but at least it greatly facilitated the Hunter's reading of the outgoing mail, and he quickly learned that most letters went to Mr. and Mrs. Arthur Kinnaird. He already knew, from his reading, the custom of family names descending from father to offspring, and the salutations removed any doubt there might have been about their identity. The deduction seemed defensible that the boy would spend the summer with his parents, and if that were the case, then the Hunter had the name of the island from the address on the letters.

He still did not know where it was, or how to get there; he could only be sure, from the duration of his airplane ride, that it was a long way from his present location. Bob would presumably be going back at the time of the next vacation, but that gave the fugitive another five months to get under cover—as if the five he had already enjoyed were not enough.

There was a large globular map of the planet in the school library and almost a plethora of flat maps and charts on the walls and in the various books in the school. Robert's persistent failure to bestow more than a passing glance at any of them promised quickly to drive the Hunter mad; and the alien, as time went on, was tempted more and more strongly to attempt to overcome the comparatively tiny muscles controlling the direction of his host's eyes. It was a bad and dangerous idea, but being intelligent does not mean that one's emotions are any the less powerful, as many men have demonstrated.

He controlled himself, therefore—partially. At least he controlled his actions; but as his patience wore ever thinner he began to look more and more favorably on what had at first seemed a mad notion—that of actually getting into communication with his host and enlisting the human being's aid. After all, the Hunter told himself, he might ride around seeing the world from Bob's eyes for the rest of the boy's life, which would probably be a long one with the alien to fight disease, without either getting a clue to his quarry's whereabouts or a chance to do anything even if the other were located. As things now stood, the other could appear in public and perform the amoeboid equivalent of thumbing his nose at the

Hunter without any risk to itself. What could the little detective do about it?

With the beings who normally served the Hunter's kind as hosts, communication eventually reached a high level of speed and comprehensiveness. The union took place with the host's full knowledge and consent; it was understood that the larger being furnished food, mobility, and muscular strength, while the other protected him from disease and injury as far as possible. Both brought highly intelligent minds into the partnership, and the relationship was one of extreme friendliness and close companionship in nearly all cases. With this understood by both parties, literally anything the symbiote did to affect his host's sensory organs could be utilized as a means of speech; and as a rule, over a period of years, multitudes of signals imperceptible to anyone else but perfectly clear to the two companions would develop to bring their speed of conversation to almost telepathic levels. The symbiote could administer twinges to any and all muscles, build shadow images directly on the retina of his host's eye, move the fur with which the other race was thickly covered—there was no limit to the various means of signaling.

Of course Bob did not have this background, but it was still possible to affect his senses. The Hunter dimly realized that there might be some emotional disturbance when the boy first learned of his presence, but he was sure he could minimize that. His own race had practised symbiosis for so long that they had practically forgotten the problems incident to establishing the relationship with a being *not* accustomed to the idea. All that the Hunter really thought about, once he had made up his mind to communicate, was the apparent fact that circumstances were playing into his hands.

There was the "protective" net he had constructed over Bob's muscles; and there was the typewriter. The net could be contracted, like the muscles it covered, though with far less power. If a time arrived when Bob was sitting at the typewriter without particular plans of his own, it might be possible for the Hunter to strike a few keys in his own interest. The chances of success for the experiment depended largely on the boy's reaction when he found his fingers moving without orders; the Hunter managed to make himself feel optimistic about that.

Chapter IV. *SIGNAL*

Two nights after the Hunter made his decision to act the opportunity occurred. It was a Saturday evening, and the school had won a hockey game that afternoon. Bob had come through it without injury, to the Hunter's surprise and relief, and had managed to cover himself with a certain amount of glory, and the combination of institutional and personal triumph proved sufficient stimulus to cause the boy to write to his parents. He went to his room immediately after supper—the other occupant was not in at the time—and pounded off a description of the day's events with very fair speed and accuracy. At no time did he relax sufficiently to give an opportunity for control, in the alien's opinion; but with the letter finished and sealed, Robert suddenly remembered a composition which his English teacher had decreed should be turned in the following Monday. It was as foreign to his nature as to that of most other schoolboys to get his work done so early, but the typewriter was out, and the hockey game offered itself as a subject which he could treat with some enthusiasm. He inserted a fresh piece of paper in the machine, typed the standard heading of title, pupil's name, and date, and then paused to think.

The alien wasted no time whatever. He had long since decided on the wording of the first message. Its first letter lay directly under the boy's left middle finger, and the net of unhuman flesh about the appropriate muscle promptly tugged as hard as it could on the tendon controlling that finger. The finger bent downward obediently and contacted the desired key, which descended—halfway. The pull was not powerful enough to lift the type bar from its felt rest. The Hunter knew he was weak compared to human muscles but had not realized he was that weak; Bob's manipulation of the keys had seemed so completely effortless. He sent more of his flesh flowing into the net which was trying to do the work of a small muscle and tried again—and again and again. The result was the same: the key descended far enough to take up the slack in its linkage, and stopped.

All this had attracted Bob's attention. He had, of course, experienced the quivering of muscles abruptly released from a heavy load, but there had been no load here. He pulled the offending hand away from the keyboard, and the suddenly frantic Hunter promptly transferred his attention to the other. As with a human being his control, poor enough in the beginning, grew worse with haste and strain, and the fingers of Robert's right hand twitched in a most unnerving fashion. The boy stared at them, literally terrified. He was more or less hardened to the prospect of physical injury at any time, as anyone who plays hockey and football must be, but there was something about nervous disorder that undermined his morale.

He clenched both fists tightly, and the quivering stopped, to his intense relief; the Hunter knew he could never overcome muscles opposed to his own attempts. However, when the fists cautiously relaxed after a few moments, the detective made another try—this time on the arm and chest muscles—in an effort to bring the hands back to the typewriter. Bob, with a gasp of dismay, leaped to his feet, knocking the chair back against his roommate's bed. The Hunter was able to deposit a much heavier net of his flesh about these larger muscles, and the unwilled tug had been quite perceptible to the boy. He stood motionless, now badly frightened, and tried to decide between two courses of action.

There was, of course, a stringent rule that all injuries and illnesses must be reported promptly to the school infirmary. Had Bob suffered damage such as a cut or bruise he would have had no hesitation in complying with this order, but somehow the idea of owning to a nervous disorder seemed rather shameful, and the thought of reporting his trouble was repugnant. He finally decided tentatively to put it off, in the hope that matters would be improved by morning. He put the typewriter away, took out a book, and settled down to read. At first he felt decidedly uneasy, but as the minutes passed without further misbehavior on the part of his muscular system he gradually calmed down and became more absorbed in the reading matter. The increasing peace of mind was not, however, shared by his unsuspected companion.

The Hunter had relaxed in disgust as soon as the writing machine had been put away, but he had no intention of giving up. The knowledge that he *could* impress himself on the boy's awareness without doing him physical damage was something gained; and even though interference with the youngster's muscles produced such a marked disturbance, there were other methods which suggested themselves to the alien. Perhaps they would prove less disconcerting, and he knew they could be equally effective as means of communication. The Hunter may have had a smattering of the psychology peculiar to the races he knew, but he was certainly failing to analyze properly the cause of his host's disturbance.

His race had lived with others for so many hundreds of generations that the problems of starting the relationship had been forgotten much as man has forgotten the details surrounding his mastery of fire. Nowadays children of the other race grew up expecting to find a companion of the Hunter's kind before they passed adolescence, and the Hunter failed completely to realize how a person not brought up with that conditioning might be expected to react.

He put down Bob's disturbance to the particular method he had employed, rather than to the very fact that he had interfered. He did, in consequence, the worst thing he could possibly do: he waited until his host seemed to be over the shock of the first attempt, and then promptly tried again.

This time he worked on Bob's vocal cords. These were similar in structure to those he had known, and the Hunter could alter their tension mechanically in the same way he had pulled at muscles. He did not, of course, expect to form words; that would have required control of diaphragm, tongue, jaw, and lips, as well as the vocal cords, and the symbiote was perfectly aware of the fact; but if he did his pulling while the host was exhaling air, he could at least produce sound. He could control it only in an off-and-on fashion, so he could hardly send an articulate message that way; but he had an idea in mind for

37

proving that the disturbance was being produced deliberately.

He could use bursts of sound to represent numbers and transmit series—one and its square, two and its square, and so on. No one, surely, hearing such a pattern of sound, could suppose it originated naturally. And now the boy was calmed down again, reading, fully absorbed, and breathing slowly and evenly.

The alien got further than any human being, knowing the facts, would have believed possible, principally because Bob was just finishing a yawn as the interruption started and was not able to control his own breathing right away. The Hunter was busily engaged in producing a set of four rather sickly croaks, having completed two and paused, when the boy caught his breath and an expression of undiluted terror spread across his face. He tried to let out his breath slowly and carefully, but the Hunter, completely absorbed in his work, continued his unnerving operation regardless of the fact that he had been interrupted. It took him some seconds to realize that the emotional disturbance of his host had reappeared in full force.

His own emotional control relaxed at this realization, for, recognizing clearly that he had failed again, knowing perfectly that his young host was almost frantic with terror that robbed him of most of his control, the alien nevertheless not only failed to desist from his attempts but started still another system of "communication." His third method involved cutting off the light from his host's retinas in patterns corresponding to letters of the English alphabet—in utter disregard of the fact that by this time Robert Kinnaird was rushing down the hallway outside his room, bound for the dispensary, and that a rather poorly lighted stairway lay ahead.

The inevitable results of interference with his host's eyesight under such circumstances did not impress themselves upon the Hunter's mind until Bob actually missed a step and lunged forward, grasping futilely for the rail.

The alien recovered his sense of duty rapidly enough. Before the hurtling body touched a single obstacle he had tightened around every joint and tendon with his utmost strength to save Robert a serious sprain. Moreover, as a sharp, upturned corner of one of the metal cleats which held the rubber treads on the stairs opened the boy's arms from wrist to elbow, the Hunter was on the job so fast that practically no blood escaped. Bob felt the pain, looked at the injury which was being held closed under an almost invisible film of unhuman flesh, and actually thought it was a scratch that had barely penetrated the skin. He turned the corner of the cleat down with his heel and proceeded to the dispensary at a more moderate pace. He was calmer when he got there, since the Hunter had been sobered into discontinuing his efforts to make himself known.

The school did not have a resident doctor, but did keep a nurse on constant duty at the dispensary. She could make little of Robert's description of his nervous troubles, and advised him to return the next day at the hour when one of the local doctors normally visited the school. She did examine the cut on his arm, however.

"It's clotted over now," she told the boy. "You should have come here with it sooner, though I probably wouldn't have done much to it."

"It happened less than five minutes ago," was the answer. "I fell on the stairs coming down to see you about the other business; I couldn't have brought it to you any faster. If it's already closed, though, I guess it doesn't matter."

Miss Rand raised her eyebrows a trifle. She had been a school nurse for fifteen years and was pretty sure she had encountered all the more common tales of malingerers. What puzzled her now was that there seemed no reason for the boy to prevaricate; she decided, against her professional knowledge, that he was probably telling the truth.

Of course some people's blood *does* clot with remarkable speed, she knew. She looked at the forearm again, more closely. Yes, the clot was extremely fresh—the shiny, dark red of newly congealed blood. She brushed it lightly with a fingertip, and felt, not the dry, smooth surface she had expected, or even the faint stickiness or nearly dry blood, but a definite and unpleasant *sliminess*.

The Hunter was not a mind reader and had not foreseen such a move. Even if he had, he could not have withdrawn his flesh from the surface of Robert's skin; it would be many hours, more probably a day or two, before the edges of that gash could be trusted to hold themselves together under normal usage of the arm. He had to stay, whether he betrayed himself or not.

He watched through his host's eyes with some uneasiness as Miss Rand drew her hand away sharply and leaned over to look still more closely at the injured arm. This time she saw the transparent, almost invisible film that covered the cut, and leaped to a perfectly natural but completely erroneous conclusion. She decided the injury was not so fresh as Robert had claimed, that he had "treated" it himself with the first substance he had found handy—possibly model airplane dope—and had not wanted the fact to come out since it constituted a violation of the school rules.

She was doing a serious injustice to the boy's common sense, but she had no means of knowing that. She was wise enough to make no accusations, however, and without saying anything more took a small bottle of alcohol, moistened a swab with it, and began to clean away the foreign matter.

Once again only his lack of vocal cords kept the Hunter silent. Had he possessed the equipment, he would have emitted a howl of anguish. He had no true skin, and the body cells overlying the cut on his host's arm were unprotected from the dehydrating action of the alcohol. Direct sunlight had been bad enough; alcohol felt to him as concentrated sulphuric acid feels to a human being—and for the same reason. Those outer cells were killed almost instantly, desiccated to a brownish powder that could have been blown away, and would undoubtedly have interested the nurse greatly had she had a chance to examine it.

There was no time for that, however. In the shock of the sudden pain the Hunter relaxed all of the "muscular" control he was exerting in that region to keep the wound closed; and the nurse suddenly saw a long, clean slash some eight inches from end to end and half an inch deep in the middle, which started to bleed freely. She was almost as startled as Robert, but her training showed its value; she quickly applied compresses and bandages, though she was surprised also at the ease with which she managed to stop the bleeding. With that accomplished she reached for the telephone.

Robert Kinnaird was late getting to bed that night.

Chapter V.   ANSWER

THE BOY was tired, but he had trouble in getting to sleep. The local anesthetic the doctor had used while sewing up the gash was beginning to wear off, and he was becoming progressively more aware of the wound as the night wore on. He had almost forgotten the original purpose of his visit to the dispensary in the subsequent excitement; now, separated by a reasonable time from the initial fright, he was able to view the matter more clearly. There had been no recurrence of the trouble; maybe he could let it go. Besides, if nothing more were going to happen, how could he show anything to the doctor?

The Hunter also had had time to alter his viewpoint. He had left the arm entirely when the anesthetic was injected and busied himself with his own problem. He had finally realized that *any* disturbance of a sense organ or other function of his host was going to result in emotional trouble, and he was beginning to have a shrewd suspicion that the mere knowledge of his own presence might be as bad, even though he did not actually make himself felt. Equally bad, nothing originating in the boy's own body was ever going to be interpreted by him as an attempt at communication. The idea of symbiosis between two intelligent life forms was completely foreign to this race, and the Hunter was slowly coming to realize just what that meant in terms of mental attitudes. In his own mind he was berating himself for not recognizing the situation much earlier.

He had been blinded to any idea save that of communication from within by at least two factors: lifelong habit, and a reluctance to leave his present host. Even now he found himself trying to evolve a plan which would not involve his departure from Robert's body. He had realized from the beginning what his chance of return would be if the boy saw him coming; and the thought of being barred from the home to which he had become so well adjusted, of sneaking about as an almost helpless lump of jelly in an alien and unfriendly world, seeking host after host as he worked his way stepwise back toward the island where he had landed, seeking unaided for traces of a fugitive almost certainly as well hidden as was the Hunter himself right now—it was a picture he put from his mind.

Yet communicate he must, and he had demonstrated to his own satisfaction the futility of trying it from within. Therefore he must—what? How could he get into intelligent conversation with Robert Kinnaird, or any other human being, from outside? He could not talk, he had no vocal apparatus, and even his control over his own shape would be overstrained by an attempt to construct a replica of the human speech apparatus from lung to lip. He could write, if the pencil were not too heavy; but what chance would he get? What human being, seeing a four-pound lump of gelatinous material trying to handle writing materials, would wait around for legible results— or would believe, if he stayed to read?

Yet there might be a way, at that. Every danger he had envisioned was a provisional one: he could not get back into the boy's body *if* Bob saw him coming; no human being would take his senses seriously *if* he saw the Hunter writing; no human being would believe a message written by the Hunter without seeing him—*if* the Hunter could not furnish substantial evidence of his existence and nature. Although the last two difficulties seemed to possess mutually exclusive solutions, the puzzled detective suddenly perceived an answer.

He could leave Bob's body while the boy slept, compose a written message, and return before he awakened. It seemed too simple all at once. No one would see him in the darkness; and as for the authenticity of the note— Robert Kinnaird, of all people on the planet, would be the one to have to take such a message seriously. To him alone, as things were at the moment, was the Hunter in a position to prove both his existence and, if desirable, his whereabouts. If he did decide to tell where he was, at least the boy need not *see* him, and the knowledge might not have such an emotional impact.

The idea seemed excellent, though admittedly there were a few risks. A good policeman is seldom too reluctant to take chances, however, and the Hunter had little difficulty in deciding to adopt the plan. With a course of action thus firmly in mind he once more began paying attention to his surroundings.

He could still see. The boy had his eyes open then, and must still be awake. That meant delay and still more strain on the Hunter's patience. It was annoying, this night of all nights, that Bob should take so long to go to sleep—annoying, even though the alien could guess the cause and hold himself at least partly responsible. It was nearly midnight, and the Hunter was having trouble holding his temper in check by the time respiration and heartbeat gave definite proof that his host was asleep and he dared begin his planned actions. He left Bob's body as he had entered, through the pores of the skin in his feet— he was well enough acquainted with the boy's sleeping habits to know that these were least likely to be moved during the process. The maneuver was accomplished successfully, and without delay the detective flowed downward through sheet and mattress and reached the floor under the bed.

Although the window was open and the shade up, it was too dark to see very well; there was no moon and no bright light at all close to the dormitory building. He could, however, make out the outlines of the study table, and on that table there were, he knew, always writing materials. He moved toward it in a smooth, amoeboid flow, and a few moments later was among the books and papers that littered the table top.

Clean paper was easy to find; a scratch pad was lying by itself at the edge of the table in front of one of the chairs. There were pencils and pens as well; but after a few minutes of experimentation the Hunter found them unmanageable because of their weight and length. He found a remedy, however. One of the pencils was a cheap variety of the mechanical type, which the Hunter had previously seen refilled, and he was able to work the lead out of it with a few minutes of prying. He found himself with a thin, easily manageable stick of the usual clay-graphite writing compound, soft enough to make a visible mark even with the feeble pressure the Hunter could apply.

He set to work on the scratch pad. He printed slowly but neatly. The fact that he could barely see what he was doing made no difference, since he had disposed his body over the whole sheet and could feel perfectly well the position of the pencil point and the shallow groove it left behind it. He had spent considerable time planning just what the note was to say, but was aware that it might not be too convincing.

"Bob," the note began—the Hunter did not yet realize that certain occasions call for more formal means of address—"these words are to apologize for the disturbance I caused you last night. I must speak to you; the twitching of your muscles and the catching of your voice were my attempts. I have not space here to tell you who and where I am, but I can always hear you speak. If you are willing for me to try again, just say so. I will use the method you request; I can, if you relax, work your muscles as I did last night, or if you will look steadily at some evenly illuminated object I can make shadow pictures in your own eyes. I will do anything else within my power to prove my words to you, but you must make the suggestions for such proofs. This is terribly important to both of us. Please let me try again."

The Hunter wanted to sign the note but could think of no way to do so. He had no personal name, actually; "Hunter" was a nickname arising from his profession. In the minds of the friends of his former host he was simply the companion of Jenver the Second of Police; and he judged that to use such a title in the present instance would be unwise. He left the message unsigned, therefore, and turned his attention to the problem of where to leave it. He did not want Bob's roommate to see it, at least until after his host had done so; therefore, it seemed best to carry the paper back to the bed and place it on, or under, the covers.

This the Hunter started to do, after he had succeeded in working the sheet loose from the pad to which it had been attached. Getting a better idea on the way across the room, however, he left it in one of the boy's shoes, and returned successfully to the interior of his body, where he proceeded to relax and wait for morning. He did not have to sleep in that environment—Bob's circulatory system was amply capable of taking care of the visitor's metabolic wastes as fast as they were formed. For the first time the Hunter found himself regretting this fact; sleep would have been a good way to pass the hours which would have to elapse before Bob read the note. As it was, he simply waited.

When the reveille buzzer sounded in the corridor outside—the mere fact that it was Sunday was not considered an excuse for remaining in bed—Bob slowly opened his eyes and sat up. For a moment his actions were sluggish; then, remembering that it was his turn, he sprang barefooted across the floor, slammed down the window, and leaped back to the bed where, more leisurely, he began to dress. His roommate, who had enjoyed his privilege of remaining under the covers until the window was closed, also emerged and began groping for articles of clothing. He was not looking at Robert, so he did not see the momentary expression of surprise that flickered across Kinnaird's face as he saw the sheet of paper loosely rolled up and thrust into one of his shoes.

He pulled out the note, scanned it quickly, and thrust it into a pocket. His immediate thought was that someone —probably his roommate—was up to some sort of trick; and it was in his nature immediately to decide to deny the perpetrator the satisfaction of the expected reaction. For half the morning he drove the Hunter nearly mad by his indifference, but he had not forgotten the note.

Bob had simply been waiting until he was alone and could count on being so for a while. In his room, with the other boy away, he took out the note and read it again carefully. His initial opinion remained unchanged for a moment, then a question occurred to him. Who would have known about his troubles the night before?

Of course he had told the nurse; but neither she nor the doctor, it seemed to him, would indulge in a practical joke of this nature—nor would they tell anyone who might. There might be other explanations—there probably were, but the easiest to check at the moment was that which took the note at face value. He looked outside the door, in the closet, and under the bed, being normal enough not to wish to be caught falling for a practical joke; then he seated himself on one of the beds, looked at the blank wall opposite the window, and said aloud, "All right, let's see your shadow pictures."

The Hunter obliged.

There is a peculiar pleasure in producing cataclysmic results with negligible effort. The Hunter felt it now; his only work was in thickening by a fraction of a millimeter some of the semitransparent body material already surrounding the rods and cones in his host's eyeball so as to cover those sensitive nerve endings and cut off some of the incoming light in a definite pattern. Accustomed as he was to the maneuver, it was almost completely effortless, but it produced results of a very satisfying magnitude. Bob started to his feet, staring; he blinked repeatedly, and rubbed his eyes, but persistence of vision carried the rather foggy word "thanks," which had apparently been projected on the wall, until he opened them again. The word tended to "crawl" a little as he watched. Not all the letters were on the fovea—the tiny spot of clearest vision on the human retina—and when he turned his eyes to see them better, they moved too. He was reminded of the color spots he sometimes saw in the dark, on which he could never turn his eyes properly.

"Wh—who are you? And where are you? And how—?" His voice died out as questions flooded into his mind faster than he could utter them.

"Sit quietly and watch, and I will try to explain." The words flowed across his field of vision. The Hunter had used this method before, with many other written languages, and he held the rate of letter change at that value, since if he either speeded up or slowed down the boy's eyes started to wander.

"As I said in my note, it is hard to explain who I am. My job corresponds to that of one of your police agents. I have no name in the sense that you people have, so you had best think of me as the Detective, or the Hunter. I am not a native of this world, but came here in pursuit of a criminal of my own people. I am still seeking him. Both his ship and mine were wrecked when we arrived, but circumstances made me leave the scene of the landing before I could begin an orderly search. That fugitive represents a menace to your people as well as mine, and for that reason I ask your help in locating him."

"But where do you come from? What sort of person are you? And how do you make these letters in front of my eyes?"

"All in good time." The Hunter's limited English reading had made him rather fond of clichés. "We come from a planet of a star which I could point out to you but whose name I do not know in your language. I am not a person like yourself. I fear you do not know enough biology to permit a good explanation, but perhaps you know some of the differences between a protozoan and a virus. Just as the big, nucleated cells which make up your body evolved from protozoan-type creatures, so did my kind evolve from the far smaller life forms you call viruses. You have read about such things, or I would not know your words for them; but perhaps you do not remember."

"I think I do," Bob replied aloud. "But I thought viruses were supposed to be practically liquid."

"At that size, the distinction is minor. As a matter of fact, my body has no definite shape—you would think of one of your amoebae if you were to see me. Also, I am very small by your standards, although my body contains thousands of times as many cells as yours."

"Why not let me see you? Where are you, anyway?"

The Hunter dodged the question.

"Since we are so small and flimsy in structure, we frequently find it awkward and sometimes dangerous to travel and work by ourselves, and we have formed the habit of riding larger creatures—not in the sense you probably take that word, but living inside their bodies. We are also able to do that without harming them, since we can adjust our shapes to the available space and can even make ourselves useful by destroying disease germs and other unwelcome organisms, so the animal enjoys better health than it otherwise might."

"That sounds interesting. You found it possible to do the same with an animal of this planet? I should think it would have been too different for you. What kind are you using?"

That brought the question about as close to home as it could get. The Hunter tried to postpone the evil hour by answering first questions first. "The organism was not too different from——" He got no further, for Bob's memory had started to function.

"Wait a minute! Wait—a—minute!" The boy sprang up his feet again. "I think I see what you've been leading up to. You don't mean you *ride* other animals, you go into

48

partnership with them. And that trouble last night——
So that's what held that cut closed! What made you let
go?"

The Hunter told him, filled with relief. The boy had realized the truth sooner than the alien had really wanted,
but he seemed to be reacting well—he was more interested
than shocked. At his request the symbiote repeated the
muscle-pulling effects that had caused so much disturbance the previous evening, but he refused to show himself. He was too relieved by the present state of affairs to
want to take any chances with Bob's feelings.

Actually, he had made an incredibly lucky choice of
hosts. A much younger or less well-educated child could
not have begun to understand the situation and would
have been frightened out of its senses; an adult would
probably have headed at top speed for the nearest psy-
chiatrist's office. Bob was old enough to understand at
least some of what the Hunter had told him and young
enough not to blame the whole thing on subjective phenomena.

At any rate he listened—or, rather, watched—steadily
and soberly as the Hunter unfolded the series of events
which had brought him first to earth and then halfway
around it, to a Massachusetts boarding school. The alien
explained the problem which lay before him and the reason why Bob should interest himself in it. The boy understood that clearly enough: he could easily envision the
mischief of which his guest would be capable in his present location if he did not possess a strong moral sense,
and the thought of a similar organism running loose
among the human race uninhibited by any such restric-
tion made him shudder.

Chapter VI. *PROBLEM ONE*

BOB TURNED to practical considerations even before the Hunter started to bring them up. "I suppose," he said thoughtfully, "that you want to get back to the place where you found me and start scouting among the islands for your friend. How can you be sure he got ashore at all?"

"I can't, until I find traces of him," was the answer. "Did you say islands? I was hoping there would be only one within reasonable distance. How many are there in that region?"

"I don't know; it's quite a large group. The nearest to my own that I know of is about thirty-five miles to the northeast. It's a smaller one, but they have a power station there too."

The Hunter pondered. He had been almost exactly in the line of flight of the other ship up to the time he had gone out of control; as nearly as he could remember, they had both come nearly straight "down," so that even after his ship began spinning he should not have left that line by far. It had been his close-range screen that showed the other sinking after it had struck water; their points of landing could not be more than two or three miles apart. He explained this to Bob.

"Then if he got ashore at all, it's most likely on my island. That gives us about a hundred and sixty people to check, if he's still there. Are you sure he'll use a human body, or do we have to check everything alive?"

"Any creature large enough to spare the food and oxygen we use will serve. For a warm-blooded air-breather like yourself I should guess that the animal that was with you the day we met was about the smallest likely. However, I should expect him to use a human being, eventually if not at first. You represent, as far as I know, the only intelligent race on this world; and it has long been recognized by my people that an intelligent creature is the most satisfactory host. Even though this creature will not be seeking companionship, the fact that a man is probably the safest host available will guide him, I am sure."

"That is, if he is ashore yet. All right, we'll devote most of our attention to people. It's just as well, I guess; we have a needle in a haystack as it is." The Hunter was familiar with Bob's expression from his reading.

"That describes it well, except that the needle is camouflaged as a wisp of hay," was his answering comment.

They were interrupted at this point by Bob's roommate, returning to prepare for dinner, and there was no further chance for conversation that day. Bob saw the doctor about his arm during the afternoon, and, since the Hunter possessed no miraculous healing powers, the doctor considered its progress normal. It was pleasantly free from all signs of infection, "in spite," the doctor remarked, "of that silly trick of yours. What did you try to close it with, anyway?"

"I did nothing to it," replied the boy. "It happened when I was on my way to the dispensary, anyway, and I thought it was just a scratch until the nurse started cleaning it and everything let go." He saw the doctor did not believe him, and decided there was little use pursuing the argument. Nothing had actually been said between him and his guest about keeping the latter's presence a secret, but it had occurred to the boy that if knowledge of the alien spread too far—assuming his story were believed, of course—it might have a serious effect on their chances of success, so he let the doctor finish his lecture on first aid and left as soon as he could.

Shortly after the evening meal he found an opportunity to get off by himself, and at once put a question to the Hunter.

"What do you plan to do about getting back to the island? Normally, I won't be going until the middle of June, nearly six months from now. Your fugitive has already had about that much time to get under cover, or out of the way. Do you plan to wait and let him bury himself deeper, or have you thought of some means of getting us there sooner?" The Hunter had been expecting the question and had an answer ready—one designed to teach him more about the boy's personality than he had been able to guess.

"My motions, from now on, are wholly dependent on yours. To leave you would be to waste much of the work of the last five months; true, I know your language, which would help me anywhere, but I suspect that securing the co-operation of anyone else would be a lengthy job. You are the only human being on whom I can count for understanding help. At the same time, it is true that the sooner I get back to the island the better it will be, so it seems best that you should come as well. I know that you are not completely free to control your own actions, but if you could devise some means of getting us back there, it would be a great help. I can be of little assistance in the matter; you have grown up in this environment and can judge more accurately the chances of any given plan. All I am qualified to do is advise about the actions and nature of our quarry and what to do when we really start looking for him. What valid reason could you offer your people for returning immediately to the island?"

Bob did not answer at once. The idea of taking such a matter into his own hands was rather new to him; but inevitably it grew more attractive as he thought about it. Of course he would miss a lot of school, but that could be made up later. If the Hunter were telling the truth, this matter was much more important; and Robert could see no reason why his guest should deceive him. The alien, then, was right: he must solve the problem of getting home at once.

Simply disappearing was not to be thought of. Apart from the purely practical difficulties of crossing the continent and a good part of the Pacific without assistance, he had no desire to cause his parents anxiety if it could be avoided. That meant that a *good* excuse for the journey must be found, so that it could be undertaken with official approval.

The more he thought about it the clearer it seemed that only illness or physical injury would serve. Homesickness had been known to produce results in one or two cases, but Robert remembered what he had thought of the individuals involved and decided he didn't want that reputation. It would be nice to acquire an injury in some manner which would reflect credit on himself—through a heroic rescue or some similar adventure—but he had sense enough to realize that the opportunity was small and the actual merit of the idea nil. Of course the hockey season was still on; anything might happen of its own accord.

As for illness, that could not very well be acquired at will. He could perhaps imitate something well enough to fool friends and teachers, but he did not for an instant deceive himself into thinking he could fool a doctor for any length of time. Faking seemed out, therefore. The usual run of ideas, such as false telegrams requesting his presence, pretense of bad news from home, and all their variations ran through his mind, for he had read his share of the more melodramatic literature; but none of them satisfied the objections which his sound common sense at once raised. He found himself in a complete quandary, and told the Hunter so after many minutes of thought.

"This is the first time I have regretted choosing such a young host," answered the alien. "You lack the freedom of travel that an adult would take for granted. However, I am sure you have not exhausted your fund of ideas. Continue to think, and let me know if I can help in any of your plans." That terminated the conversation for the time. Bob left the room moodily.

He brightened up presently, however, shelved his worries for the moment, and presently was engaged in a game of ping-pong with one of his classmates in the recreation room next to the gym. The relaxation allowed his subconscious mind to work on the problem, and in the middle of the first game he had another idea—as luck would have it, at a time when he could neither tell the Hunter nor secure his views on the matter. He became so preoccupied with the plan that the game, which had been going well for him up to this point, deteriorated almost to a slaughter. He managed to pull himself together for the next game only by reminding himself that it was certain to be some time before he could get in touch with his guest, even if he stopped playing. Also, this early he was developing an exaggerated fear of doing anything abnormal least his secret should be suspected; and there was nothing normal about his being beaten so thoroughly as he had just been.

It was indeed quite a time before he managed another

talk with the Hunter. When he returned to his room, the other occupant was already there, and his presence prevented conversation not only until "lights out" but throughout the night, as Bob was not sure how much disturbance it would take to wake the fellow. Anyway, he could not very well see the Hunter's answers in the dark. The next day was Monday, with classes, and he was not alone until after supper, when, in near desperation, he took some books and went in search of an empty classroom. There, talking in a low tone to escape notice from anyone passing the door, he finally managed to unbottle the repressed questions. He started, however, with a point other than his idea.

"Something will have to be done about this," he said. "You can talk to me whenever I'm not actually doing something else, but I can't say anything to you when anyone's around without having them think I'm crazy. I've had an idea since last night and have been wondering when I could tell you."

"The conversation problem should not be difficult," answered the Hunter. "If you simply talk in an inaudible whisper—even keep your lips closed if you wish—I think I can learn quite easily to interpret the motions of your vocal cords and tongue. I should have thought of it long ago but gave no particular attention to the need for secrecy with which we are faced. I shall start practice at once. It should not be hard; I understand many of your people become quite adept at lip reading, and I have more than lips to go by. What was the idea that was worrying you so?"

"I can see no way of getting to the island, except through feigning sickness and being ordered to take an early vacation. I can't possibly fake an illness well enough to fool a doctor, but you are in a position to give me all sorts of symptoms—enough to drive them crazy. How about it?"

The Hunter was hesitant in his answer.

"It is certainly a possibility, but there are objections. You, of course, cannot realize how deeply bred into us is the repugnance to the idea of doing anything that can harm our hosts. In an emergency, with a being whose physical make-up I knew completely, I might carry out your plan as a last resort; in your case I could not be sure that no permanent harm was going to result from my actions. Do you see?"

"You have lived in my body for more than five months, you say. I should think you must know me as well as you ever will," Bob objected.

"I know your structure but not your tolerances. You represent a completely new species to me, of which I have data on only one individual. I do not know how long given cells can do without food or oxygen; what constitutes the limiting concentration of fatigue acids in your blood; what interference your nervous and circulatory systems can stand. Those things obviously I could not test without harming and possibly killing you. There are, I suppose, a few things I might do in the line you suggest, but I certainly would not like it; and, in any case, how do you know that you would be sent home in case of illness? Would they not be more likely to hospitalize you here?"

The question silenced Bob for several seconds; that possibility had not occurred to him.

"I don't know," he said at last. "We'll have to find something that calls for a rest cure, I guess." His features wrinkled in repugnance at the idea. "I still think you could do something about it without having a nervous breakdown."

The Hunter was willing to concede that point but was still reluctant to interfere with his host's vital processes. He said he would "think it over," and advised the boy to do the same—also to produce another idea, if possible.

This Robert agreed to do, though he felt the chances of success were small. The Hunter was not sanguine, either. Little as he knew of human psychology, he was pretty sure that Bob could not really work on another plan until his present one was proved impossible rather than merely undesirable. The boy still liked the plan and had no real conception of the way it affected the Hunter's feelings.

Consequently, the only real progress made in the next few days was in communication. As the detective had expected and hoped, he was able quickly to interpret the motions of the boy's vocal cords and tongue, even when he kept his lips nearly closed and spoke in a whisper audible to no one but himself. Answering was easy, provided Bob's current occupation left him free to turn his eyes on some relatively blank space. Also, a few mutually understood abbreviations began to creep in, so that their exchange of ideas speeded up noticeably. Neither, however, produced another idea for getting the boy away from school.

An observer during those few days, familiar with the course of events not only between Bob and his guest but in the offices of the school officials, would have been amused. On the one hand, the Hunter and his host were concentrating on trying to find an excuse for leaving; on the other, the headmaster and his staff were wondering volubly about the cause of the boy's suddenly developed inattention, listlessness, and general failure to measure up to his earlier standards; more than one of them remarked that it might be well to get the youngster back to his parents' hands for a time. The Hunter's mere presence—or rather, Bob's knowledge of it—was producing conditions bound in the end to lead to the very situation they wanted. He was, of course, doing the boy no physical damage, but the preoccupation with the current problem and a number of too-public conversations with the concealed alien constituted a behavior pattern only too noticeable to those responsible for Bob's well-being.

The doctor was eventually consulted on the matter. He reported the boy's health sheet clean, with no illness whatever this term and only two minor injuries. He examined the still-healing arm again, on the chance that an unsuspected infection might be responsible, but of course found nothing. His report left the masters mystified. Bob had changed from a normally pleasant and gregarious youngster to a solitary and at times almost sullen individual. At their request the doctor had a private interview with Robert.

He learned nothing concrete this time, either, but he gained the impression that Bob had a problem on his mind which he did not wish to share with anyone. Being a doctor, he formed a perfectly justified but quite erroneous theory on the nature of the problem, and recommended that the boy be returned to the care of his parents for a few months. It was as simple as that!

The headmaster wrote a letter to Mr. Kinnaird, explaining the situation as the doctor saw it, and stating that, if there were no objections, he planned to send Robert home immediately until the opening of the fall term.

Bob's father rather doubted the doctor's theories. He knew his son well, considering the relatively small amount he had seen of him in recent years; but he concurred with Mr. Raylance's suggestion. After all, if the kid were not doing well at school it was a waste of time to have him there whatever the reason for the trouble. There was a perfectly good doctor and—though Mrs. Kinnaird had her doubts—a perfectly good school on the island, and it would be easy to fill the gap in his education while a more careful study of the situation was being made. Also, quite apart from these reasons, Mr. Kinnaird would be glad of the chance to see more of his son. He cabled the school authorizing Bob's return, and prepared for his arrival.

To say that Robert and the Hunter were surprised at the news is a distinct understatement. The boy stared wordlessly at Mr. Raylance, who had called him into his office to inform him of the imminent journey, while the Hunter strove unsuccessfully to read a few papers which were exposed on the headmaster's desk.

Eventually Bob recovered the use of his voice. "But what is the reason, sir? Has anything happened at home?"

"No, everything is all right. We felt that you might be better off there for a few months, that's all. You haven't been hitting your usual mark lately, have you?"

To the Hunter, this remark explained the situation with crystal clarity, and he metaphorically kicked himself for not having foreseen it; to Bob, understanding came more slowly.

"You mean—I'm being kicked out of school? I didn't think it was that dad—and it's only been a few days."

"No, no, nothing of the sort." The headmaster missed the implications of Bob's last remark. "We notice that you seemed to be having trouble, and the doctor thought you needed a little time off. We'll be glad to have you back next fall. If your like, we can send along a study outline with you, and the teacher on the island can help you keep up with it. You can spread that work through the whole summer and will probably be able to stay with your class when you come back. Is that all right? Or"—he smiled— "is it just that you don't want to go home?"

Bob returned the smile rather lamely. "Oh, I'll be glad

enough to go, all right. I mean——" He paused, rather embarrassed as he realized another possible construction of his words.

Mr. Raylance laughed aloud. "All right, Bob. Don't worry—I understand what you mean. You'd better get packed and say good-by to your friends; I'll try to get you a reservation for tomorrow on the usual air route. I'm sorry you're going; the hockey team will certainly miss you. However, the season is nearly over, and you'll be back in time for football. Good luck."

They shook hands, and Bob dazedly went to his room and began to pack. He said nothing to the Hunter; it was not necessary. He had long since given up taking the statements of his elders at face value simply because they were his elders, but try as he might he could find no ulterior motive lurking behind the words and actions of the headmaster. He decided, for the time being, to take his luck without question and leave the next step to the Hunter.

That individual had ceased to worry from the time he had realized the import of Mr. Raylance's words. The removal of a source of anxiety affected him just as it frequently does a human being—he tended to feel, for a time, as though troubles were a thing of the past. It might be too much to say that he felt his job was as good as done; but there would have been some excuse if he had felt that way. He was a good detective. He had, of course, some failures against his record, but not one of them had occurred while he had the advantage of an intelligent and co-operative host to supply the physical powers his own body lacked. Bob was not Jenver, but he had come to feel strongly attached to the youngster.

This atmosphere of self-congratulation continued during Bob's packing and even through part of the trip. Mr. Raylance was successful in obtaining the reservation, and the next day Bob took the bus to Boston and caught the noon plane to Seattle, where they were to change to the TPA plane. During the ride and flight the boy talked with his guest whenever possible, but the conversation was purely about the events and scenes of the trip. They did not turn to business until they were over the Pacific, for Bob always accepted without any particular thought the

Hunter's ability to take care of things once they reached the scene of action.

"Say, Hunter, just how are you going to find this friend of yours? And what will you do to him then? Have you some means of getting at him without hurting his host?"

It was a shock. For once the Hunter was glad that his method of speech was less easily used than Bob's. Had it been otherwise, he would almost certainly have started talking before he realized he had nothing to say. In the next five seconds he wondered whether he might not have left behind somewhere the mass of tissue that normally served him for a brain.

Of course his quarry had long since hidden—must by now be established in another body, just as the Hunter himself was. That was nothing unusual. Normally, however, such a being—undetectable by sight, sound, smell, or touch—was detected by chemical, physical, and biological tests, with or without the co-operation of the being acting as host. He knew all those tests; he could administer them, in some cases, so rapidly that while merely brushing against a suspected organism he could tell if one of his own people were present, and even make a good guess at his identity. There were something like a hundred and sixty people on the island, Bob had said. They could be covered in a few days' testing—*but he could not make the tests!*

All of his equipment and supplies had gone with his ship. Even with the fantastic assumption that he could find the hulk again it would be folly to suppose that instruments had remained unbroken and chemical containers sealed through the crash and the five subsequent months under salt water.

He was on his own, as few policemen had ever been before; hopelessly isolated from the laboratories of his own world, and the multitudinous varieties of assistance his own people could have given him. They did not even know where he was, and with a hundred billion suns in the Milky Way system . . .

He remembered, wryly, that Bob had actually brought up the question days before and the cavalier manner in which he had disposed of it. Now it was bitterly clear that the summary they had made of the situation on that occasion had been glaringly accurate. They *were* looking

59

for a needle in a haystack—a haystack whose human straws numbered more than two billion; and that deadly, poisoned needle had thoughtfully crawled inside one of them!

Bob got no answer to his question.

Chapter VII. *STAGE . . .*

THE GREAT plane bore them from Seattle to Honolulu; from there to Apia; in a smaller machine they flew from Apia to Tahiti; and at Papeete, twenty-five hours after leaving Boston, Bob was able to point out to the Hunter the tanker which made the rounds of the power islands and on which they would make the last lap of their trip. It was a fairly typical vessel of its class and far from new, though the Hunter could not see many details as they passed overhead. That opportunity came a couple of hours later, when Bob had made sure that all his luggage was still with him and was being transferred to the harbor.

Baggage and boy—Robert was the only listed passenger —eventually found their way onto a small lighter, which chugged its way out into the harbor to deposit them on the ship that they had seen from the air.

Even the Hunter could see that she was designed for cargo rather than speed. She was very broad for her length, and the entire midship section was occupied by tanks, which rose only a few feet above the water line. Bow and stern were much higher, and were connected by catwalks crossing above the tanks. From these, ladders dropped at frequent intervals, giving access to the valve and pump machinery; and the tall, brown-skinned mate who saw Bob climbing the companionway glanced at these and groaned inaudibly. He knew from past experience the impossibility of keeping the boy off the oil-slick rungs, and lived in fearful anticipation of the day he would have to deliver a collection of compound fractures to the elder Kinnaird.

"Hi, Mr. Teroa!" Bob yelled as he reached the level of the bridge. "Think you can stand me for a day or so?"

The mate smiled. "I guess so. It seems you're not the worst possible nuisance, after all." Bob opened his eyes wide, in mock astonishment, and shifted to the hodge-podge of French and Polynesian dialects used among the islands.

"You mean someone has turned up who causes more trouble? You must introduce me to this genius."

"You know him—or, rather them. My Charlie and young Hay sneaked aboard a couple of months ago and managed to stay out of sight until it was too late to put 'em off. I had quite a lot of explaining to do."

"What were they after—just the trip? They must have seen everything on your run long ago."

"It was more than that. Charlie had some idea of proving he could be useful, and getting a steady job. Hay said he wanted to visit the Marine Museum in Papeete without a lot of older folks telling him what to look at. I was kind of sorry to have to keep him on board until we got home."

"I didn't know Norman was a natural-history bug. This must be something new; I'll have to see what he's up to. I've been gone five months, so I suppose he could have got started on anything."

"That's right, you have. Come to think of it, I wasn't expecting you back this soon, either. What's the story? Get heaved out of school?" The suggestion was made with a grin which removed offense.

Bob grimaced. He had not worked out a story in any detail, but judged correctly that if he himself could not understand the school doctor's motive there would be nothing odd in his being unable to explain it.

"The doc at school said I'd do better at home for a while," he replied. "He didn't tell me why. I'm O. K. as far as I know. Did Charlie get the job he wanted?" Bob thought he knew the answer, but wanted the subject changed if at all possible.

"Strangely enough, he's getting it, though you needn't tell him just yet," the mate answered. "He's a pretty good seaman already, and I figured if he was going to pull stunts like that I'd better have him in sight, so I applied for him, and I think it's going through. Don't you get the idea that you can do the same by stowing away, though!" and Teroa gave the boy a friendly push toward the cat-walk that led aft to the limited passenger accommodations.

62

Bob went, his mind for the moment completely away from his main problem. He was absorbed in memories of his friends and speculations about what they had done during his absence (as usual, there had been very few letters exchanged while he was at school). The island itself he regarded as "home," though he spent so little time there; and for the moment his thoughts were those of any moderately homesick fifteen-year-old.

The Hunter's question—projected against the blue of the harbor as Bob leaned over the stern rail—could hardly have been better timed to fit in with the boy's mood. The alien had been thinking hard. He had come to one conclusion, about his own intelligence, but that was not really constructive; and he realized that much more data were going to be needed before he could trace his enemy. His host could certainly furnish some of that information.

"Bob, could you tell me more about the island—its size, and shape, and where people live? I am thinking that our job will be one of reconstructing the actions of our friend rather than locating him directly. Once I know more about the scene of action, we can decide where he is most likely to have left a trail."

"Sure, Hunter." Bob was more than willing. "I'll draw you a map; that will be better than words. I think there's some paper with my things." He turned from the rail, for the first time in many trips ignoring the vibration that swelled from below as the great Diesels pounded into action. His "cabin" was a small room in the sterncastle containing a bunk and his pile of luggage—the ship was definitely not designed for passengers. After some search Bob found a piece of paper large enough for his purpose, and, spreading this out on a suitcase, he began to draw, explaining as he went.

The island, as it took shape under the boy's pencil, was shaped rather like a capital L, with the harbor formed by the interior angle facing north. The reef that surrounded it was more nearly circular, so that the enclosed lagoon was very broad on the north side. There were two main openings, apparently, in the reef; Bob, pointing at the more westerly, said that it was the regular entry, as it had been deepened by blasting away the coral until the tanker could enter at any time.

"We still have to knock brain corals out of the channel

every so often. The other way we don't bother with—small boats can go through, but you have to be careful. The lagoon is shallow, not more than about fifteen feet, and the water is always warm. That's why the tanks were built there." He indicated a number of small squares penciled on the area of the lagoon. The Hunter thought of asking just what the tanks were for, but decided to wait until Bob finished.

"In here"—the boy pointed to the bend of the L—"most of the people live. It's the lowest part of the island—the only part where you can see from one side to the other. There're about thirty houses sort of scattered there, with big gardens around them so they're not very close together—nothing like the towns you've seen."

"Do you live in that area?"

"No." The pencil sketched a narrow double line almost the whole length of the island, close to the lagoon side. "That is a road that goes from Norm Hay's house near the northwest end down to the storage sheds in the middle of the other leg. Both branches have a row of hills—the low place where the houses are is a sort of saddle in the row—and several families live on the north slope up here. Hay is at the end, as I said; and coming back down the road you pass Hugh Colby's house, Shorty Malmstrom's, Ken Rice's, and then mine. Actually, that whole end of the island isn't used much, and is grown over except right around the houses. The ground is all cut up and hard to mow, so they grow the stuff for the tanks at the other end, where it's a lot smoother. We practically live in jungle—you can't even see the road from my house and it's the closest of the five. If your friend has decided to pass up his chances at a human host and simply hide in there, I don't know how we'd ever find him."

"About how large is the island? There is no scale on your map."

"The northwest branch is about three and a half miles long, the other about two. This causeway out to the dock in the middle of the lagoon is about a quarter mile or a little more—maybe nearly half. It's about the same from the shore end of it to the road—that's another paved one, leading from the causeway to the main road—reaches it practically in the middle of the village. It's a mile and a half from the junction to my house, and about as far from there to the end, where Norm lives." The pencil traveled somewhat erratically around the chart as Bob spoke and as his enthusiasm ran further and further ahead of his sense of order.

The Hunter followed the racing point with interest, and decided it was time to seek an explanation of the tanks to which the boy had referred more than once. He put the question.

"They call 'em culture tanks. They have bugs—germs—growing in them; germs that eat pretty near anything, and produce oil as a waste product. That's the purpose of the whole business. We dump everything that's waste into the tanks, pump oil off the top, and every so often clean the sludge out of the bottom—that's a nasty job, believe me. People were howling for years about the danger of the oil wells giving out, when any good encyclopedia would tell 'em that the lights they saw in marshes were caused by the burning of gases produced from things rotting under the swamp. Someone finally got bright enough to connect the ideas, and the biologists bred special bugs that would produce heavier oils instead of marsh gas. The island waste isn't enough to keep the five big tanks going, so the northeast end of the island is always getting the vegetation shaved off it to feed them. The sludge goes back to the same ground to serve as fertilizer. That's another reason, besides the smoothness of the ground, that we use only that end of the island for that —it's downwind from the settled part, and the sludge is awfully smelly when it's fresh. There are pipelines connecting the big tanks to the loading dock, so we don't have to cart the oil around the island, but there's a special fertilizer barge."

"Does no one live on the south side of the hills?"

"No. On our leg of the island that's the windy side, and every so often that means a lot. Maybe you'll see a real hurricane before you're through. On the other leg it's usually in fertilizer, and I can't see anyone wanting to live there."

The Hunter made no comment on this, and after a moment the tour went on. He got a good idea—better than Bob had, owing to his much greater knowledge of biology —about the workings of the island's principal industry, though he was not sure how useful the knowledge would be. He learned, from Bob's eager descriptions of past excursions, to know the outer reef and its intricacies almost well enough to find his way around it himself. He learned, in short, about all anyone could without actually journeying personally over the patch of rock, earth, and coral that was Bob's home.

When they came on deck again Tahiti's central peak alone was visible behind them. Bob wasted little time looking at it; he headed for the nearest hatch and descended to the engine room. There was only one man on duty, who reached for the phone switch as though to call assistance when he saw the boy, and then desisted, laughing.

"You back again? Keep off the plates in those shoes—I don't want to have to unwrap you from the shaft. Haven't you seen all you want of my engines yet?"

"Nope. Never will." Bob obeyed the injunction to say on the catwalks, but his eyes roved eagerly over the dials in front of the engineer. He could interpret some of them, and the engineer explained others; their power to attract faded with their mystery, and presently the boy began prowling again. Another crewman had come in and was making a standard inspection round, looking and listening for oil leaks, faulty bearings, and any of the troubles which plague power plants with and without warning. Bob tagged along, watching carefully. He knew enough to make himself useful before he was considered a nuisance, and ran several errands during the trip; so presently he found himself, unrebuked, down by the shaft well while his companion worked on a bearing. It was not a safe neighborhood.

The Hunter did not fully realize the danger, strangely enough. He was used to less bulky machines whose moving parts—when they had any—were very securely cased while in operation. He saw the nearly unguarded shaft and gears, but it somehow never struck him that they might be dangerous until a stream of rather lurid language erupted from under the shaft housing. At the same instant Bob jerked his hand back sharply, and the Hunter felt as well as his host the abrupt pain as a dollop of hot oil struck the boy's skin. The man had reached in a little too far in the semidarkness and allowed his oil gun to touch the shaft. The abrupt jerk had caused him to tighten on the trigger, releasing an excessive amount of lubricant onto the bearing he was checking. It had needed the oil, running hot as it was, but had flung off the excess with rather painful results.

The crewman backed out of his cramped position, still giving vent to his feelings. He had been scalded in several places by the oil, but when he saw Bob another thought took precedence. "Did you get hurt, kid?" he asked anxiously. He knew what was likely to happen if Bob *were* injured in his company—there were stringent orders from the bridge dealing with the things the boy was and was not to be allowed to do.

Bob had equally good reasons for not wanting to get in trouble where he was, so he held the scorched hand as naturally as possible and replied, "No, I'm O. K. What happened to you? Can I help?"

"You can get some burn ointment from the kit. These ain't bad, but I can sure feel 'em. I'll slap it on here; no sense in bothering anyone else."

Bob grinned understandingly and went for the ointment. On his way back with it he started to put a little of the stuff surreptitiously on his own burn; but a thought struck him, and he refrained.

The idea bothered him while he was helping the crewman apply the ointment; and as soon thereafter as he could, he left the engine room and made his way back to his quarters. He had a question to ask, which grew more urgent as the pain in his hand grew more intense.

"Hunter!" He spoke as soon as he was sure no one was around to distract his attention from the answer. "I thought you were able to protect me from injury of this sort! Look what you did to that cut." He indicated the nearly healed slash on his arm.

"All I did there was prevent bleeding and destroy dangerous bacteria," replied the Hunter. "Stopping pain would demand that I cut nerves in this case—burns are not cuts."

"Well, why not cut 'em? This hurts!"

"I have already told you that I will not willingly do anything to harm you. Nerve cells regenerate slowly, if at all, and you need a sense of touch. Pain is a natural warning."

"But what do I need it for if you can fix up ordinary injuries?"

"To keep you from getting such injuries. I don't fix

them—I simply prevent infection and blood loss, as I said. I have no magical powers, whatever you may have thought. I kept this burn from blistering by blocking the leakage of plasma, and the same act is making it much less painful than it would otherwise be, but I can do no more. I would not stop the pain if I could; you need something to keep you from getting careless. I expect trouble enough, since blocking minor cuts stops most of the pain, as you have found out. I have not mentioned this before, as I hoped the occasion would not arise, but I must insist that you be as careful in your everyday activities *as though I were not here;* otherwise you would be like a person who ignores all traffic rules because someone has guaranteed him free garage service. I cannot put that too strongly!"

There was one other thing the Hunter had done, which he did not mention. A burn, of all injuries, is one of the most likely to produce shock—the condition in which the great abdominal blood vessels relax, dropping the blood pressure so that the sufferer turns pale, loses his temperature control, and may become unconscious. The Hunter, feeling this condition start almost immediately after the accident, had tightened around the blood vessels as he had before around Bob's muscles, save that this time he administered the pressure intermittently—timing the squeezes to synchronize with the beating of Bob's hart; and his host had never even felt the nausea which is one of the first warnings of shock. This job was done at the same time as the Hunter was sealing the burned tissue against plasma leakage with more of his own flesh, but he did not mention it.

It was the first time there had been anything like strong words between the symbiote and his host. Fortunately Bob had sense enough to see the reason behind the Hunter's statements and sufficient self-control to hide the slight annoyance he could not help feeling at the Hunter's refusal to relieve his pain. At least, he told himself, shaking the throbbing hand, nothing dangerous could come of it.

But he had to revise his idea of life with the Hunter. He had been visualizing the period during the search as a sort of Paradise—not that he ever was bothered seriously by minor injuries, colds, and the like, but it would have been nice not to have to consider them. Mosquitoes and sand flies, for example—he had wanted to ask the Hunter what he could do about pests like those, but now he felt rather uncomfortable at the thought. He would have to wait and see.

The night which finally closed in on them was calm. Bob, making the most of his lack of supervision, stayed late on the bridge, sometimes silently watching the sea and sometimes talking with the man at the wheel. Around midnight he left the bridge and made his way aft. For a little while he leaned over the stern railing, watching the luminous wake of the tanker and thinking of the resemblance between the trackless breadth of the ocean and the planet which the Hunter might have to search. Finally he sought his bunk.

The wind picked up during the night, and when Bob arose in the morning the sea was rather high. The Hunter had opportunity for research into the causes and nature of seasickness, eventually reaching the conclusion that he could do nothing about it without doing permanent damage to his host's sense of balance. Fortunately for Bob the wind died down after a few hours, and the waves subsided almost as speedily; the tanker had barely touched the edge of the storm area.

He quickly forgot his annoyance once he could associate with the crew again, however, for, as he knew from previous experience, his home island should become visible shortly after noon. For the latter half of the morning he practically vibrated between bow and bridge, gazing eagerly ahead over the long swells toward family, friends, and—danger, though he did not fully appreciate the last.

Chapter VIII. *SETTING . . .*

THOUGH the island was "high" in the local terminology —that is, the submarine mountain which formed its base actually projected above the surface of the sea, rather than merely approaching it closely enough to serve as foundation for a coral superstructure—its highest point was only about ninety feet above sea level; so the tanker was comparatively close before Bob could point out anything to his invisible guest. The Hunter, finally seeing his hunting ground actually before him, thought it was time to call the meeting to order.

"Bob," he projected, "I know you enjoy this, but we really cannot see much as yet, and we will be ashore in a couple of hours. If you don't mind, I should like to see your map again."

Although the alien had no means of expressing emotion in his writing, Bob caught the undercurrent of seriousness in his words. "All right, Hunter," he answered, and went aft to the cabin where he had left the map. When the sheet was spread out in front of them, the detective went right to the point.

"Bob, have you thought about how we are going to catch this being? I never answered your question before."

"I was wondering, when you didn't. You people are so queer—to me, that is—that I decided you must be able to smell him out or something. You certainly can't see him, if he's like you. Do you have some sort of gadget that will find him for you?

"Don't rub it in." The Hunter did not explain his phrase. "I have no apparatus whatever. This is your planet; how would *you* go about it?"

Bob pondered for a few moments. "If you actually go into a body, I suppose you can tell if there's another of your people there." This was more a statement than a

70

question, but the Hunter made the brief sign which Bob had come to accept as an affirmative. "How long would such a search take? Could you get through the skin far enough while I was shaking hands with someone, say?"

"No. It takes many minutes to enter a body like yours without giving warning. The openings in your skin are large, but my body is much larger. If you let go of the other person's hand while I was still partly in both bodies, it would be very embarrassing for all concerned. If I left you entirely and worked at night while people were asleep, I suppose I could cover the whole island eventually; but I would be very much restricted in speed, and would be in an extremely awkward position when I found him. I will undoubtedly have to make the final check that way, but I should very much like to be pretty sure of my ground before testing anyone. I still want your ideas."

"I don't know any of your standard methods," Bob said slowly. "And I can't, right now, think of means for checking people for company; but we might try to trace his course from the time he landed, and find what people he *might* have got at. Could that be done?"

"With the addition of one word, yes. We can trace his *possible* course. There is likely to be little or no evidence about his actual path, but I can judge, I think, with considerable accuracy what he would do in any given situation. Of course I'll have to know a lot about the situation: all you can tell me, and all I can see for myself."

"I can see that," answered Bob. "All right, we'll have to start with the time he reached the island—if he did. Any ideas?"

"We'll have to start sooner than that. Before we can guess where he landed, we must judge where he crashed. Will you point out on your map the place where I found you?

Bob nodded, and his finger indicated a point on the paper. At the northwest tip of the island—the end of the longer branch of the L—the land tapered to a blunt point; and from this point the reef extended, first northward and then curving to the east and back to the south to enclose the lagoon. Bob was indicating the west side of this point.

"This," he said, "is the only real sea beach on the island. It's the only part of the shore not protected by the reef.

You see south of the tip there's a few hundred yards before the reef starts again and keeps the breakers from the whole south shore. It's the place the fellows and I like best, and it's where we were swimming the day you arrived. I remember that shark."

"Very well." The Hunter took up the conversation. "Up until shortly before we reached the earth's atmosphere I was tracking him on automatic control, so that I was within a few feet of his line of flight. When I realized how close we were to the planet I went on manual and tried to drive straight away, but it was along the same line. Even allowing for the disturbance your atmosphere caused on our lines of flight, I don't think we could have struck the water more than a mile or two apart. I can check that; I was watching him on the bow scanner, which has only a ten-degree field of vision.

"Also, I could not have crashed far offshore. Do you know how rapidly the water deepens off the island?"

"Not in feet. I know it's steep, though; large ships can come quite close to the reef."

"That's what I thought; and I was in shallow water. We crashed, we will say, within a two-mile radius of this point." The Hunter momentarily shaded, on Bob's retina, a point a little way off the shore from the beach. "And much of that can be eliminated. He certainly did not crash on shore; my instruments showed him sinking after the initial check. I am equally sure he did not land in the lagoon, since you say it is very shallow, and he must have struck hard enough to reach its bottom instantly—at a guess, he must have had over fifty feet of water; I certainly did, though not much over, I should say.

"We can, then, act on the assumption that he landed in the two-mile semicircle to the west of the island, centered just off-shore from your beach. I admit that is not an absolute certainty, and it may be hard to prove, but it gives us something to start on. Have you any other ideas?"

"Just questions. How long would it have taken him to get ashore?"

"Your guess is as good as mine. If he had the luck I did, a few hours. If he was in very deep water, with even less oxygen than I, and a stronger sense of caution, he might have spent days or weeks crawling along the bottom to shore. I myself would never have attacked that shark, or ventured to swim out of touch with the bottom, unless I had been very sure I was near shore."

"How would he have known the right direction? Maybe he's still crawling around down there."

"Maybe. However, with the storm that night he could have determined the direction of the breakers as easily as I did; and if the bottom slopes as steeply as you think, it would have furnished another clue for him. I don't think that problem would have been serious. Of course he is known to be a coward; that may have kept him with the wreckage of his ship for quite a while."

"Then in order to go any farther we'll have to explore the reef for a mile or so each way from the beach, to see if he left any traces. Is that right? And if he has, what do you suppose he will have done after landing—same as you?'

"Your first guess is right. As for the question, that depends. He would certainly want to find a host as soon as possible; but whether he simply waited for one where he landed, or went in search of something suitable, is hard to say. If he landed at a spot where any artificial structures are visible, he would probably have made his way to them, on the theory that intelligent beings were bound to come to them sooner or later. It's something that can't be predicted exactly, that's why I said I would have to know *all* the circumstances to guess his actions."

Bob nodded slowly, digesting this. Finally he asked, "What sort of traces are you likely to find at his place of landing? And if you don't find any, what will we do?"

"I don't know." There was no indication which question was being answered; and Bob finally grew tired of waiting for further explanation. It bothered him, for even he could see that the methods they had just outlined were not very promising. He thought intently for a time, half hoping his guest would come out with some supplementary technique from his own science. Suddenly an idea struck him.

"Hunter! I just thought of something! Remember the only time you could get to me, that day on the beach, was when I fell asleep?" The alien expressed assent. "Well, won't the same be true of this other fellow? He couldn't catch a person, or at least couldn't do it without being seen. You said yourself that it would take several minutes to get right inside; and even if this fellow doesn't care about the feelings or health of his host, he still wouldn't want to be seen. So it ought to narrow things down a bit if I found out who had been sleeping near the water in the last few months. There aren't any houses near the sea —Norm Hay's is the closest, and there shouldn't be too many people who made picnics the way we did that day. How about it?"

"You may have a point there. It is certainly worth trying; but remember, there is no part of the island that he could not reach given time enough, and everybody sleeps at some time or other—though he mightn't know that, come to think of it. Certainly anyone who has slept near the shore is, as you say, suspect."

A change in the rhythm of the engines interrupted the thoughtful silence that followed this remark, and Bob went back on deck, to find that the tanker had slowed and was turning to line up for the entrance to the western passage through the reef. A hasty trip along the catwalks took them to the bow, from which an unobstructed view could be had of the north reef and lagoon.

The reef, it seemed to the Hunter, was not too encouraging a field of search. Certainly no human being could have hidden there for long; and while his quarry could undoubtedly remain concealed, life in such a place would not be pleasant. Long sections of the barrier were barely visible above water, their position betrayed mostly by the breakers. Some portions were higher and had accumulated enough soil to support sparse vegetation—even coconut palms in one or two places. As the tanker nosed into the narrow passage, he realized that, in spite of this, searching the reef for clues might not be easy; it was never possible for a person to travel more than a few rods on foot, as he could see from the broken-up nature of the barrier; and on the outer side at least boating would be extremely dangerous—the endless breakers crashing through the openings in the coral created fierce and unpredictable currents and eddies almost certain to sweep any small craft against the rock-hard roughness of the reef. Even the tanker, big as she was and with plenty of steerage way, kept to the center of the marked channel while Bob and the Hunter watched the coral slip by on either side.

Even inside the lagoon they stayed carefully between the buoys, the Hunter noticed; and he recalled what Bob had said about the shallowness of the water here. On either side of them, scattered over the several square miles between reef and island proper, were angular concrete bulks that the Hunter assumed to be the culture tanks. These were from two to three hundred feet on a side, but their walls did not extend more than five or six feet above the water. The nearest was too far away for small details to be made out, but the Hunter was pretty sure it was covered by a roof consisting mostly of glass panes, while small square superstructures at various points were connected by catwalks to each other and to a diminutive landing stage on the side toward the channel.

Ahead of them was a larger structure, rather different in detail, and as they approached its purpose became evident. Like the tanks, it was rectangular in shape, but it rose much higher out of the water—almost as high as the tanker's bridge for the central portions. The "deck" level was lower but still considerably above that of the culture tanks. This surface was covered with various structures, some obviously storage tanks and pumps, others more obscure in nature. On the side toward the approaching vessel were great mooring cables and even bigger hoses, with twenty or thirty men visible working around them. The structure obviously was the dock to which Bob had referred and which was used to store and transfer the fuel oils which were the chief product of the island.

Both watchers looked through Bob's eyes with interest as the tanker glided in to the dock and settled against the fenders. More lines snaked across and were pulled aboard, drawing the hoses after them; and in a remarkably short time the thudding of pumps showed that the last eight days' production was flowing into the tanker. It took a hail from the bridge to distract them from the process.

"Bob! You'll need some help with your stuff, getting it ashore, won't you?" Teroa was calling down to the boy.

"Yes, thanks," Bob called back. "I'll be right there." He took one more quick look around, and his grin broadened at something he saw; then he was speeding over the catwalks to the stern. Partly visible around the corner of the

75

dock from where he had been standing was the long causeway that connected the structure with the shore; and along that causeway he had seen a jeep driving furiously. He knew who the driver of that vehicle would be.

The baggage was tumbled out onto the dock in record time, but the jeep had squealed around the corner and come to halt beside the hoses some minutes before Bob and the mate came down the plank with the last piece between them. Bob dropped his end of the foot locker and ran to meet the man standing beside the little car. The Hunter watched with interest and some sympathy.

Even he was sufficiently familiar with human faces by now to detect the resemblance between father and son. Bob still had six or seven inches of height to pick up, but there was the same dark hair and blue eyes, the same straight nose and broad, easily smiling mouth, and the same chin.

Bob's greeting had the exuberance natural to his age; his father, while equally delighted, maintained an under-current of gravity that went unnoticed by the boy but which was both seen and understood by the Hunter. The alien realized he had one other job—it was going to be necessary to convince Mr. Kinnaird that there was nothing actually wrong with his son, or the latter's freedom of action might be seriously curtailed. He filed that thought for the moment, however, and listened with interest to the conversation. Bob was overwhelming his father with a flood of questions that threatened to involve the doings of the entire population of the island. At first the Hunter was minded to criticize his host's action in starting the investigation so early; but he presently realized that the search was far from the boy's mind. He was simply trying to fill a five-month gap. The detective stopped worrying and listened carefully to Mr. Kinnaird's answers in the hope of finding some useful information; and he was human enough to be disappointed when the man cut off the flood of questions with a laugh.

"Bob boy! I don't know what *everyone's* been up to since you left; you'll have to ask them. I'm going to have to be here until they finish loading; you'd better take the jeep up to the house with your luggage—I expect your mother could stand seeing you, if you can spare the time. Your friends won't be out of school yet, anyway. Just a minute." He rifled through the jeep's toolbox recklessly, finally extracting a well-cased set of calipers from the collection of center punches, cold chisels, and wrenches.

"Oh, my gosh, that's right; I'll have to see about school myself, won't I? I'd forgotten I wasn't coming back for vacation this time." He looked so sober for a moment that his father laughed again, not realizing the cause of his son's sudden thoughtfulness. Bob recovered quickly, however, and looked up again. "Okay, Dad, I'll get the stuff home. See you at supper?"

"Yes, provided you get that jeep back here as soon as you've finished with it. And no remarks about my needing exercise!"

Bob grinned, good humor completely restored. "Not until I'm dressed to go swimming," he replied.

The loading was quickly accomplished, and Bob, sliding under the wheel, sent the little vehicle rapidly along the causeway to the shore. From here, as he had told the Hunter, a paved road led straight inland for a quarter of a mile, where it joined the main thoroughfare of the island at right angles. There was a large cluster of corrugated-iron sheds flanking the short road, and when they reached the turn the Hunter could see that these extended to the left, up the shorter arm of the island. He could also see the white concrete of at least one more culture tank peering around the corner of the hill in that direction and resolved to ask Bob at the first opportunity why these were not built in the water like the others.

Just at the turning where the two roads met, the dwelling houses started to replace the storage sheds. Most of the former were on the shoreward side of the main road, but one, surrounded by a large garden, lay on their right just before the turning. A tall, brown-skinned youth was busy in the garden. Bob, seeing him, braked the jeep quickly and emitted an ear-hurting whistle through his front teeth. The gardener looked up, straightened, and ran over to the road.

"Bob! Didn't know you were coming back so early. What have you been doing, kid?" Charles Teroa was only three years older than Bob, but he had finished school and was apt to use a condescending tone to his juniors who had not. Bob had given up resenting it; besides, he now had ammunition if there was to be a contest of repartee.

"Not as much as you have," he answered, "from what your father tells me."

The younger Teroa grimaced. "Pop would tell. Well, it was fun, even if that friend of yours did back out."

"Did you really expect them to give work to someone who spends half his days sleeping?" Bob gibed, mindful of the order to keep the job a secret for the present.

Teroa was properly indignant. "What do you mean? I never sleep when there's work to do." He glanced at a patch of grass in the shade of a large tree which grew beside the house. "Just look; best place in the world for a nap, and you found me working. I'm even going back to school."

"How come?"

"I'm taking navigation from Mr. Dennis. Figured it would help next time I tried."

Bob raised his eyebrows. "Next time? You're hard to discourage. When will that be?"

"Don't know yet. I'll tell you when I think I'm ready. Want to come along?"

"I donno. I don't want a job on a ship, that's certain. We'll see how I feel when you make up your mind. I've got to get this stuff home, and get the jeep back to Dad, and get to the school before the fellows get out; I'd better be going."

Teroa nodded and stepped back from the side of the jeep. "Too bad you're not one of those things we learned about in school, that splits in two every so often. I was wishing I was a little while ago, then part of me might have gotten away with that stunt."

Bob, on occasion, was a quick thinker. This time, at least, he managed to conceal the jolt Charles's words had given him; he repeated the farewells, started the vehicle, swung around the corner to the right, and stepped on the gas. For the half mile the road ran among the houses and gardens he said nothing, except at the very end, when he pointed out a long, low building on their left as the school. A short distance beyond this, however, he pulled to the side of the road and stopped. They were out of sight of the rest of the island, having driven with startling suddenness into the densely overgrown section Bob had mentioned.

"Hunter," the boy said tensely as soon as they were stopped, "I never thought of it, but Charlie reminded me. You folks are like amoebae, you said. Are you entirely like them? I mean—is there any chance of—of our having more than one of your people to catch?"

The Hunter had not understood the boy's hesitance and did not understand the question until he had digested it a moment.

"You mean, might our friend have split in two, as your amoebae do?" he asked. "Not in the sense you mean—we are slightly more complicated beings. It would be possible for him to bud off an offspring—separate a portion of his flesh to make a new individual, but that one would be at least one of your years reaching full size. He could, of course, release it at any time, but I don't think he would, for a very good reason.

"If he tried it while in the body of a host, the new symbiote would have no more knowledge than a newborn child of your own race; it would certainly kill the host in its blind search for food, or simply while moving around in ignorance of its surroundings. While it is true we know more biology than your race, we are not born with the knowledge; learning to live with a host takes time and is one of the chief phases of our education.

"Therefore, if our quarry does reproduce at all, he will do it from purely selfish motives—to create a being which will almost certainly be quickly caught and destroyed, so that the pursuers he expects will think he himself has been killed. It was a good point, of course—I had not considered the possibility myself—but it is true that a creature such as we are pursuing would probably not hesitate to do such a thing—if he thinks of it. Of course his first care will be to find a hiding place; and if that turns out to be a satisfactory host, I doubt whether he would take the chance of leaving for the purpose you suggested."

"That's some relief." Bob sighed. "For a few minutes there I was thinking that the last five months might have given us a whole tribe to chase down."

He restarted the jeep and drove the short remaining distance to his home without interruption. The house lay some distance up the hill from the road, at the end of a drive completely roofed in by trees. It was a fairly large, two-storied dwelling in the midst of the jungle—the heavy growths had been cleared away for only a few yards around it, so that the first-floor windows were shaded most of the time. In front, where the drive emerged, an extra amount of labor had made a sun porch possible, though even this Mrs. Kinnaird had found better to shade with flowering creepers. The temperature of the island was not excessively high, because of the surrounding water, but the sun was frequently intense and shade something to be ardently sought.

She was waiting on the porch. She had known of the ship's arrival, and had heard the jeep coming up the drive. Bob's greeting was affectionate, though less boisterous thán the one on the dock, but Mrs. Kinnaird could find nothing wrong either with her son's appearance or his behavior. He did not stay long, but she did not expect that; she simply listened happily to his almost endless talk as he unloaded the jeep, dragged the luggage up to his room, changed out of his traveling clothes, found his bicycle and loaded it into the car, and departed. She was fond of her son and would have liked to see more of him, but she knew that he would not enjoy sitting around talking to her for any length of time; and she was wise enough not to regret the fact particularly. As a matter of fact, if he had gone so much out of character as to do some such thing she would have been worried; as it was, the load that the school communication had put on her mind was partly lifted as she watched and listened. She was able to turn to her housework with a lighter heart, when the jeep bounced back down the drive on its way to the dock.

Bob met no one and stopped for nothing on this trip. He parked the jeep in its accustomed place beside one of the tanks, unloaded his bicycle, and started to mount. There was a slight delay, caused by his having forgotten to check the tires before leaving home, then he was pedaling back along the causeway. There was excitement and anticipation written large on his face, not merely because he was to rejoin his friends after a long absence, but because an exciting play was, from his point of view, about to start. He was ready. He knew the stage—the island on which he had been born, and whose every square yard he was sure he knew. The Hunter knew the setting—the habits and capabilities of the murderous being they sought, and only the characters were left. A trace of grimness tinged the excitement on Bob's face as he thought of that; he was far from stupid, and had long since realized that, of all the people on the island, the most likely ones to have afforded refuge to his quarry were those who spent the most time near the shore and in the water—in short, his best friends.

Chapter IX. *THE PLAYERS*

BOB TIMED his arrival well; the school was dismissed only a minute or two after he reached it, and he was immediately surrounded by a riotous crowd of acquaintances. The school-age population of the island was a rather large fraction of the total. When the station had been established some eighteen years before only young married couples were accepted for positions there. Consequently there was a great deal of chatter, handshaking, and mutual inquiry before the group finally broke up and left Bob surrounded by a few of his closest friends.

Only one of these could the Hunter recognize as a member of the group who had been swimming together the day he met Bob. He had not, at the time, been very familiar with the distinguished criteria of human features, but Kenny Rice's mop of flame-colored hair was hard to forget. The alien quickly learned from the conversation which of the others had belonged to the swimming party: they were boys named Norman Hay and Hugh Colby—presumably the ones to whom Bob had already referred in describing the layout of the island. The other one he had mentioned, Kenneth Malmstrom, was the only other member of the present group; he was a blond fifteen-year-old approximately six feet tall who had come by his nickname in the usual manner—he was distinguished by the inevitable sobriquet of "Shorty." These four, together with Bob, had been companions ever since they were old enough to go out of sight of their neighboring houses. It was more than coincidence that the alien had found most of them swimming at the point where he first came ashore; any islander, knowing the point where he had landed, would have been perfectly willing to bet that the Hunter would make one of the five his first host. They were born beachcombers. None of them, therefore, thought it strange when Bob quickly brought the conversation around to such matters.

"Has anyone been poking around the reef lately?"

"We haven't," replied Rice. "Hugh stepped through the bottom of the boat about six weeks ago, and we haven't been able to find a plank that would fix it so far."

"That bottom had been promising to go for months!" Colby, ordinarily an extremely quiet and retiring youngster—he was the youngest of the five—came stoutly to his own defense. Nobody saw fit to dispute his statement.

"Anyway, we've got to go the long way around to the south shore now if we take a boat," added Rice. "There was a lallapalooza of a storm in December, and it shifted a brain coral bigger than the boat into the gate. Dad has been promising to dynamite it ever since for us, but he hasn't got around to it yet."

"Can't you persuade him to let us do it even yet?" asked Bob. "One stick would be enough, and we all know how to handle caps."

"Try to convince him of that. His only answer has been, 'When you're older' ever since I was old enough to pronounce the word."

"Well, how about the beach, then?" asked Bob. There were many beaches on the island, but the word had only one meaning to this group. "We could walk part of the south shore and grab a swim as we went around. I haven't been in salt water since I left last fall." The others agreed, and dispersed to collect the bicycles which were leaning against the school building.

The Hunter made good use of Bob's ears and eyes during the ride. He learned little from the conversation, but he did clarify considerably his mental picture of the island. Bob had not mentioned the small creek which wound down to the lagoon a couple of hundred yards from the school, and he had not noticed it himself on the trip to the boy's house; but this time the well-made wooden bridge which carried them over it caught his attention. Almost immediately after they passed the spot where Bob had stopped the jeep, then, three quarters of a mile from the school, the other boys stopped and waited while Bob pedaled up the drive to get his bathing suit. A quarter of a mile farther Rice did the same; then there was another small creek, this time carried under the road through a concrete culvert. The Hunter gathered from several remarks made at this point that the boat to which Rice had referred was kept at the mouth of this watercourse.

Malmstrom and Colby in turn deposited their books and collected swimming trunks; and finally the group reached the Hay residence, at the end of the paved road and somewhat more than two miles from the school. Here the bicycles were left, and the group headed westward on foot around the end of the ridgelike hill which formed the backbone of the island and on which all their houses were built.

Half a mile of traveling, partly along a trail through the jungle-thick growth of the ridge and partly through a relatively open grove of coconut palms, brought them to the beach; and the Hunter at last found a spot on earth that he recognized. The pool in which his shark had stranded was gone—storm and tide had done their usual work on the sandbanks—but the palm grove and the beach were the same. He had reached the spot where he had met Bob—the spot from which his search for the fugitive should have started had it not been for some incredibly bad luck; and the spot from which, without further argument, it *would* start.

Detectives and crime were far from the minds of the group of boys, however. They had wasted no time in getting into swimming costume, and Bob was already dashing toward the surf, ahead of the rest, his winter-bleached skin gleaming in odd contrast to the well-tanned hides of his young friends.

The beach, though largely composed of fine sand, contained many fragments of sharp coral, and in his haste the boy stepped hard on several of these before he could bring himself to a stop. The Hunter was doing his duty, so Bob saw no evidence of actual damage when he inspected the soles of his feet; he decided that he was simply oversensitive from several months in shoes, and resumed his dash for the water. Naturally he could not show that he had gone soft before his friends. The Hunter was pardonably annoyed—wasn't one lecture enough?—and administered the muscular twinges he had been accustomed to give his former host as a signal that he was going too far; but Bob was too tensed up to feel the signal and would not have known its meaning in any case. He churned into an incoming breaker, the others at his heels. The Hunter gave up his attempts at signaling, held the cuts closed, and seethed quietly. Granting that his host was young, he still should have better self-control, and should not throw the entire burden of maintaining his health on the Hunter. Something would have to be done.

The swim was short; as Bob had said, this was the only part of the island unprotected by the reef, and the surf was heavy. The boys decided in a few minutes that they had had enough. They emerged from the water, bundled their clothes into their shirts, and set off southward down the beach carrying the garments. Before they had gone very far the Hunter took advantage of Bob's gazing momentarily out to sea to advise him in strong terms to don his shoes. The boy allowed his common sense to override minor considerations of vanity and did so.

After the first few hundred yards the reef appeared again at the shore line and gradually drew farther away, so the amount of jetsam on the beach naturally decreased; but in spite of this they had one piece of good fortune—a twelve-foot plank, fourteen inches wide and perfectly sound, had somehow found its way through the barrier and been cast up on the sand (the boys carefully refrained from considering the possibility that it might have been washed around from the construction work on the other end of the island). With the damaged boat foremost in their minds they delightedly dragged the treasure above high-water mark, and Malmstrom wrote his name in the sand beside it. They left it there, to pick up on their return.

Aside from this the "south shore"—the nearly straight stretch of beach that extended for some three miles along the southwest side of the island's longer branch—yielded little of interest or value to any of the youthful beachcombers. Near the farthest point of their walk they encountered a stranded skate, and Bob, remembering how the Hunter had come ashore, examined it closely. He was joined by Hay; but neither got much for his trouble. The creature had evidently been there for some time, and the process of examination was not too pleasant.

"A good way to waste time, as far as we are concerned," the Hunter remarked as Bob straightened up. For once he had correctly guessed the boy's thoughts. Bob almost agreed aloud before he remembered that they were not alone.

Bob returned to his home late for supper. The plank had been borne, by their united efforts, to the mouth of the creek where the boat was kept, so the only concrete souvenir of the afternoon's activities that he brought home with him was the beginning glow of a very complete sunburn. Even the Hunter had failed to appreciate the danger or detect the symptoms early enough to get the boy back into his clothes before the damage had been done.

The alien, unlike Bob, was able to see one good point in the incident. It might be more effective than lectures in curing the boy's unfortunate increasing tendency to leave the care of his body to the Hunter. He said nothing this time, and let the sufferer do his own thinking as he lay awake that night trying to keep as much of himself as possible out of contact with the sheets. Bob was, as a matter of fact, decidedly annoyed with himself; he had not been so careless for years, and the only excuse he could find for himself was the fact that he had come home at such an odd time. Even he could see that this was not a very good one, which made it more annoying.

The several square feet of bright red skin that descended to breakfast the next morning enclosed an exceedingly disgruntled youth. He was angry with himself, somewhat annoyed at the Hunter, and not too pleased with the rest of the world. His father, looking at him, was not sure whether it would be safe to smile, and decided not to. He spoke with some sympathy instead.

"Bob, I was going to suggest that you go down to school today to get straightened out on enrollment, but maybe you'd better cool off first. I don't imagine it will hurt to leave it till Monday."

Bob nodded, though not exactly in relief—he had completely forgotten school. "I guess you're right," he answered. "I wouldn't get much from school this week anyhow; it's Thursday already. Anyway, I want to look over the place for a while."

His father glanced at him sideways, "I'd think twice before going outdoors with that hide of yours," he remarked.

"He won't, though," cut in Mrs. Kinnaird. "Even if he is your son." The head of the family made no reply, but turned back to Bob,

"Be sure you keep yourself covered, anyway, and if you must explore, it might be a good idea to concentrate on the woods. At least it's shady there."

"It's just a case of having him carved or cooked, if you ask me," Mrs. Kinnaird said. "If he's cooked, at least his clothes are all right; usually after a session in the woods both his hide and his clothes are a lot the worse for thorns." The smile on her face belied the heartless implication in her words, and Bob grinned across the table at her.

"O.K., Mother, I'll try to hit a happy medium."

He went back up to his room after breakfast and donned an old long-sleeved khaki shirt of his father's instead of the T-shirt he had originally worn, came back and helped his mother with the dishes—his father had already driven off—spent a while fighting the ropy jungle growth which persistently threatened to overwhelm the house, and finally put away clippers and hormone spray and vanished into the tangle south of the dwelling.

His course carried him gradually farther from the road and distinctly uphill. He traveled as though with a definite purpose in mind, and the Hunter forbore to question him—the background of jungle was not very suitable for his method of communication anyway. Shortly after leaving the house they crossed a brook, which the detective correctly judged to be the same watercourse that was bridged by the road a little lower down. A fallen tree, whose upper surface bore signs of frequent use, crossed it here.

Mrs. Kinnaird had not exaggerated the nature of the jungle. Few of the trees were extremely tall, but the ground between them was literally choked with smaller growths, many of them, as she had said, viciously thorned. Bob threaded his way around these with a speed and skill that suggested long experience. A botanist might have been puzzled by many of the plants; the island bore a botanical and bacteriological laboratory in which work was constantly in progress to improve the oil-making bacteria and to breed better plants to feed the tanks. Since what was desired was very rapid growth with a minimum of demand on the mineral content of the soil, the test plants occasionally got out of hand.

The place Bob intended to go was barely eight hundred yards from the house, but the journey took more than half an hour. Eventually they reached the edge of the jungle and the top of the hill, and found themselves looking down toward the settled portion of the island. Where the jungle had been stopped by hormone sprays to make room for the gardens was a tree, taller than any they had seen in the jungle itself, though not so high as the coconut palms near the shore. Its lower branches were gone, but the trunk was ringed with creepers that made a very satisfactory ladder, and Bob went up without difficulty.

In the upper branches was a rough platform that indicated to the Hunter that the boys had used the place before; and from here, well above the general level of the jungle, practically the entire island was visible. Bob let his eye rove slowly around the full circle, to give the Hunter every chance to fill in details that had been lacking on the map.

As the Hunter had thought from his glimpse up the road the day before, there were some tanks on shore on the northeast end of the island as well. These, Bob said when questioned, housed bacteria which worked so much better at high temperature that it was worth while to have them up in the sunlight and accept the fact that their activity would stop at night.

"There seem to be more of them than there used to be," he added. "But, then, they're always doing work of one kind or another. It's hard to be sure—most of them are on the far slope of the northeast hill, which is about the only part of the place we can't see very well from here."

"Except objects in and near the edge of this jungle," remarked the Hunter.

"Of course. Well, we couldn't expect to find our friend from a distance, anyway; I came up here to give you a better idea of the layout. We'll have to do a good deal of our searching in the next three days; I certainly can't put off school longer than Monday." He nodded at the long building down the hill. "We could go looking over the reef now if the boat were in shape."

"Are there no other boats on the island?"

"Sure. I suppose we could borrow one, though it's not too smart to poke around the reef alone. If anything happens to the boat, or a person bashes himself falling on the coral, it's apt to be too bad. We usually go in boatloads."

"We might at least look over some of the safer portions, if you can get a boat. If not, can any parts near your beach be reached on foot?"

"No, though it wouldn't take much of a swim to get to the nearest part. I'm not going to swim today, though, unless you can do a good deal more about sunburn than you have done."

He paused a moment, and went on, "How about the other fellows? Did you see anything about them yesterday that might make it worth while to try firsthand testing?"

"No. What would you expect me to see?"

Bob had no answer to that, and after a moment's thought slowly descended the tree. He hesitated for a moment more at the bottom, as though undecided between two courses of action, then he headed downhill, threading his way between garden patches and slanting gradually toward the road. He explained his hesitancy with:

"Guess it isn't worth the trouble to get the bike."

They reached the road about two hundred yards east of the school and kept going in that direction, Bob glancing at the houses they passed as though estimating his chances of borrowing such a thing as a boat from the occupants. Presently he reached the road which led down to the dock, with the Teroa house at the corner, and Bob quickened his steps.

He walked around to the shoreward side of the dwelling, rather expecting to find Charles working in the garden, but the only people there were the two girls of the Teroa family, who said that their brother was inside. As Bob turned toward the house the door was flung open and Charles burst out.

"Bob! You doubting Thomas! I've got it!" Bob looked slightly bewildered and glanced around at the girls, both of whom were grinning widely.

"Got what?"

"The job, fathead! What were we talking about yesterday? A radiogram came this morning. I didn't even know there was an application in it—I thought I'd have to try all over."

"I knew." Bob grinned. "Your father told me."

"And you didn't tell me?" Teroa reached out for him and Bob moved back hastily.

"He said not to—you weren't supposed to know. Anyway isn't this better than sweating it out?"

Teroa relaxed, laughing. "I suppose so. Anyway, that red-headed friend of yours will be mad—it's what he gets for backing out!"

"Redhead? Ken? What has he to do with it? I thought it was Norman went with you."

"It was, but it was Rice's idea, and he was supposed to come along. He got cold feet or something and never showed up. Can I razz him now!" He turned suddenly serious. "Don't you tell him about this job. I want to!" He started to walk toward the dock, then turned back. "I'm going out to Four to collect something Ray borrowed a while back. Want to come along?"

Bob looked at the sky, but the Hunter expressed no opinion, and he had to make up his own mind. "I don't think so," he said. "The barge is a little ripe for my taste." He watched as the brown-skinned eighteen-year-old disappeared among the storage sheds, then turned slowly back up the road.

"That was our only real chance for a boat," he said to the Hunter. "We'll have to wait until the fellows get out of school. As a group, we stand a better chance of borrowing one—or maybe it won't take long to fix our own. I didn't have time to look at it very closely when we took the plank down yesterday."

"Was that boy going to use his own boat?"

"Yes. You heard him say he was going out to Four—that's Tank Four—to get something. The person he mentioned works on the barge they use for carrying the tank wastes. Charlie wants to collect from him before he leaves the island."

The Hunter was instantly alert. "Leaves the island? You mean the bargeman?"

"No—Charlie. Didn't you hear what he was saying?"

"I heard him talk about a job, but that was all. Is it taking him away?"

"Of course! Charlie's the son of the mate of that ship

—the one who stowed away, hoping to get a job on her! Don't you remember—his father told us the first night, on the ship!"

"I remember your talking to an officer on the tanker," the Hunter replied, "but I did not and do not know what you said. You were not talking English." Bob stopped short and whistled.

"I forgot all about that!" He paused a moment to marshal his thoughts, and told the story as briefly and clearly as he could. The Hunter thought for a time after he had finished.

"Then this Charles Teroa has left the island once since my arrival and is shortly to leave it again. Your friend Norman Hay has also left once. For Heaven's sake, if there are any others you've heard about, tell me!"

"There aren't, unless you want to count Charlie's father, and I don't suppose he's been ashore here much. What does it matter about the other trip? They never got ashore, you know, and I'm sure they didn't sleep in port, so if our friend was with them he couldn't have left except at sea."

"You may be right, but that will no longer be true for this one you just saw. He must be examined before he leaves! Start thinking, please."

For the first time that day Bob completely forgot his sunburn as he walked back up the road.

Chapter X. MEDICAL REPORT

BOB MANAGED to hide his concern at lunch; his mother had thought of something during the morning to take his mind off the new problem. She had been wondering how to persuade her son to have a checkup by the island doctor, and had realized just after he disappeared what a splendid excuse the sunburn provided. She had no opportunity to discuss it with her husband, since Bob had arrived home first, but he would probably have agreed with her anyway. She brought up the subject as they finished the meal.

She did not really expect to win without argument; she knew Bob was ashamed of having acquired the sunburn and did not want more people than were strictly necessary to know about it. She was therefore somewhat astonished when her son agreed without a murmur to the suggestion that he drop into the doctor's office that afternoon, though she had the control and presence of mind not to show it.

The fact of the matter was that Bob had been thinking about the Hunter's failure to answer certain of his questions, particularly those which dealt with the details of how he was to recognize his quarry and still more, what he was to do after the creature was found. If the Hunter knew, well and good; but the suspicion that his invisible guest did *not* know was growing. It followed that Bob must get some ideas of his own; and for such ideas to be any use, he must learn more about the Hunter's species. The alien had said he resembled a virus. Very well. Bob would find out about viruses, and the logical place to do that was in a doctor's office. He had known it would be somewhat out of character for him to make the suggestion himself, but it did not occur to him to wonder that his mother should have done so; he simply accepted it as a piece of luck.

Dr. Seever knew Bob very well—as he knew every other person born on the island. He had read the communication from the school doctor, and agreed with Mr. Kinnaird's opinion of it; but he was glad of the chance to see the boy himself. Even he, however, was a little startled when he saw the color of Bob's skin.

"Good heavens! You really celebrated getting back here, didn't you?"

"Don't rub it in, Doc. I really know better."

"I should think so. Well, we'll tan your hide for you—not the way it ought to be done, but you'll be more comfortable." The doctor set briskly to work, talking steadily the while. "You certainly aren't the fellow you used to be. I can remember when you were one of the most thoughtful and careful people here. Have you been sick lately at that school of yours?" Bob had not expected the question so soon or in just this form, but he had made plans for putting it to his own use when it came.

"Certainly not. You can look me over all day and won't find any germs at work."

Dr. Seever looked over his glasses at the boy. "That's certainly possible, I know, but is hardly assurance that nothing is wrong. It was not germs that caused that sunburn, you know."

"Well, I sprained an ankle and had a cut or two, but they don't count. You were talking about *sickness,* and you could find out about that with your microscope, couldn't you?"

The doctor smiled, conceiving that he knew what the boy was driving at. "It's nice to find someone with such touching faith in medical science," he said, "but I'm afraid I couldn't. Just a minute and I'll show you why." He finished applying the sunburn material, put the container away, and brought an excellent microscope out of its cabinet. Some searching among rather dusty slide files found what he wanted, and he began slipping the bits of glass onto the stage one after another as he talked.

"This one we can see, and recognize, easily. It's protozoan—an amoeba, of the type that causes a disease called dysentery. It's big, as disease-causing organisms run."

"I've seen them in bio class at school," Bob admitted, "but I didn't know they caused disease."

"Most of them don't. Now this"—the doctor slipped another slide under the objective—"is a good deal smaller. The other wasn't really a germ at all. This causes typhoid fever when it gets a chance, though we haven't had a case in a long time. The next is smaller still and is the cause of cholera."

"It looks like a sausage with the string still on one end," Bob remarked as he raised his head from the instrument.

"You can see it better with the high-powered objective in place," Dr. Seever remarked, turning the turret at the lower end of the instrument and sinking back into his chair while Bob looked once more.

"That's about as far as this gadget can go. There are many smaller bacteria—some of them harmless, some not. There is a class of things called Rickettsia which are smaller still and may not be bacteria at all, and there are viruses."

Bob turned from the microscope and attempted the difficult feat of looking interested without showing that the conversation had finally reached the point he wished.

"Then you can't show me a virus?" he asked, knowing the answer perfectly well.

"That's what I'm getting at. A few of them have been photographed with the aid of the electron microscope—they seem to look a little like that cholera bug I showed you—but that's all. As a matter of fact, the word 'virus' was simply a confession of ignorance for a long time; doctors were blaming diseases which seemed to be life-caused for one reason or another, but for which they could find no causative organism such as I've shown you, on what they called 'filterable viruses'—so named because no matter how fine a filter you squeezed the juice from a diseased creature through, the cause seemed to go through with it. They even found ways to separate the virus stuff chemically and crystalize it; it would still cause the same disease when the crystals were dissolved in water again. They devised a lot of very pretty experiments to guess at the sizes of the things, and their shapes, and other such matters long before they saw 'em. Some scientists thought —and still think—they are single molecules; big ones, of course—even bigger than the albumin ones—that's the white of egg, you know. I have read several darn good books on the subject; you might like to do the same."

"I would," replied Bob, still trying not to seem too eager. "Do you have any of them here?" The doctor got out of his chair and rummaged through another cabinet, eventually emerging with a thick volume, through which he leafed rapidly.

"There's a good deal here but I'm afraid it's a bit technical. You may take it if you want, of course. I had another that was much better in every way from your standpoint, but I guess I've already let it out."

"Who has it?"

One of your friends, as I recall—young Norman Hay. He's been getting interested in biology lately. Maybe you heard about his trying to get to the museum on Tahiti. I don't know whether he's after my job or Rance's over at the lab. He's had the book quite a while—several months, I think; if you can get it from him, take it."

"Thanks; I will." Bob meant the statement earnestly. "You couldn't tell me offhand more about the chemical separation you mentioned, could you? It sounds funny, identifying a living creature by chemistry."

"As I said, there's some doubt as to whether we should call the viruses living creatures. However, there's nothing unusual about the tests you mention. Haven't you ever heard of serums?"

"Yes, but I thought they were stuff that you used to make a person immune to some disease."

"That is frequently the case. However, a better way of looking at them is more or less as chemical fingerprints. The tissues of one type of creature try to fight off serums made from the tissues of another. You can get an animal used to human serum, for example, and then tell from the reaction between the serum of that animal and some unknown substance whether the substance contained human tissues or not. The details vary, of course, but that's one way of telling whether a bloodstain or other organic trace came from a man or some other animal."

"I see—I guess." Bob's eyes were narrowed in thought. "Does this book have anything about that?"

"No. I can give you something on it, but I warn you it's

95

a little beyond high-school chemistry. Whose job are *you* after?"

"What? Oh, I see. Not yours, anyway. There was a problem I ran across, and I'd like to solve it myself if I can. If I can't, I'll be back for more help, I expect. Thanks, Doc."

Seever nodded and turned back to his desk as Bob went out; and for several minutes the doctor meditated.

The boy was certainly more serious than he had been. It would be nice to know just what his problem was. Very possibly—even probably—it accounted for the personality change that had worried the school authorities. That, at least, would be a comforting report to give the boy's father; and that, later in the afternoon, was just what the doctor did.

"I don't think you need worry at all, Art, if you were. The kid's gotten himself interested to the hilt in something that appears to have a scientific flavor—young Hay did the same a few months ago—and will simply soak it into his system. You probably acted the same, the last time you learned something big. He's presumably going to change the world, and you'll hear about it in due time."

Bob had no intention of changing the world to any great extent, not even the human portion of it. However, some problems which had arisen in the course of the afternoon's talk might make changes to individuals necessary, and once out of the doctor's office he wasted no time in putting them up to the Hunter.

"Can we use that serum trick of the doc's?"

"I doubt it. I am familiar with the technique, and know that since I have been with you so long your own blood serum might serve if it were not for one fact; but we would still have to decide where to use it. If we could do that, I could make the exploration faster by personal contact."

"I suppose that's true. Still, you wouldn't have to leave me—I might be able to make the check myself."

"You have a point there. We will bear the possibility in mind. Have you any idea about getting at young Teroa? When will he be leaving?"

"The tanker comes every eight days, which means it's due back a week from today. I suppose he'll be going then; certainly not any sooner. I don't think the *Beam* is around."

"The *Beam?*"

"She's a yacht owned by one of the company bigwigs, who sometimes comes to look things over. I left on her last fall—that's why we were so far from the island when you first looked around. Come to think of it, I know she's not near; she went into drydock in Seattle last fall, to get some sort of diving gear built into her bottom, and is there yet. I suppose you were going to ask who could have left on her while we were gone."

"Correct. Thanks for settling the question so quickly." The Hunter would have smiled had he been able.

Bob had no watch but was pretty sure it was nearly time for school to be dismissed, so he headed in that direction. He was early, and had to wait outside; but presently his friends came pouring out, giving vent to expressions of envy as they saw him.

"Never mind about how lucky I am not to be in school," Bob said. "Let's get to work on that boat. I've got to go back to school myself on Monday, and I'd like to have some fun first."

"You've brought us luck, anyhow," said Hay. "We'd been looking for a plank for weeks and didn't find one until you got here. What say, fellows? Hadn't we better get that thing into the boat while the luck holds?" There was a chorus of agreement and a general movement to collect bicycles. Bob rode on Malmstrom's handle bars—he had walked to the doctor's—as far as his own house, where he picked up his own machine and some tools. They waited at the culvert while Malmstrom and Colby went onto their respective dwellings for equipment; when they returned, the bicycles were left, shoes removed, and trousers rolled up. There was a path from the road down to the place the boat was kept, but it ran through the shallower parts of the creek in spots to avoid the undergrowth, and the boys had never bothered to construct bridges.

Splashing and crashing through water and bushes, they finally dumped their collection of tools at the point where the little watercourse emptied into the lagoon. The boat was there drawn up on the sand, with the plank beside it. The boys were relieved to see the latter; there had been no risk of anyone's borrowing the boat, of course, even had it not been in its present condition, but the wood was another matter. The statement that Colby had stepped through the floor of the boat had been no exaggeration—a strip of planking four inches wide and more than two feet long was missing from the flat bottom.

The boys were not professional carpenters, but they had the boat turned over and the defective plank removed from its full length in record time. They found, however, that replacing the plank from the enormous board they had found was not such an easy matter. The first attempt came out too narrow in several places, because of their inability to saw straight near the line of the grain. The second try was started too wide, and after a good deal of labor with the plane was eventually reduced to a good fit. They had carefully salvaged the screws from the former piece and succeeded in attaching the replacement securely enough to satisfy them.

They immediately dragged the boat down to the water, brought the oars from the bushes, and the entire party piled in. The idea of letting the new plank soak for a while in order to swell, or at least to permit a guess at the seaworthiness of the new joints, occurred to them, but they were all excellent swimmers and much too impatient to hold up for any such consideration. There was some leakage at the seams, but it did not amount to more than the coconut-shell bailers could handle. The two youngest boys wielded these while Bob and Shorty rowed and Rice handled the tiller.

Bob suddenly realized that the figure which usually occupied the bow on these occasions was missing. Thinking back, he realized that this had been the case ever since his return. He spoke to Rice, who was facing him. "What's become of Tip? I haven't seen him since I got back."

"No one knows." The redhead's face clouded over. "He just disappeared quite a long time ago—well before Christmas. We've looked all over the place for him. I'm afraid he must have tried to swim over to the islet where Norm has his tank—we sometimes went there without him—and got picked off by a shark, though it doesn't seem very likely. The swim would be only a few yards, and I've never seen a live shark that close to shore. He just vanished."

"That's queer. Have you looked in the woods?"

"Some. You can't search there very well. Still, if he'd been there alive, he'd have heard us; and I can't think of anything that would hurt him there."

Bob nodded, and spoke half to himself. "That's right, come to think of it; there aren't even any snakes here." More loudly he asked, "What's this about Norm's tank? Is he going into competition with Pacific Fuels?"

"Course not," returned Hay, looking up from his job of bailing. "I cleaned out one of the pools on the reef a little way from the beach and fenced it off, and have been putting things in it to make an aquarium. I did it just for fun at first, but there are some magazines that want pictures of sea life, and I've sent for some color film. Trouble is, nothing seems to live very long in the pool; even the coral dies."

"I suppose you haven't seen it since the boat was out. Let's go over now and have a look."

"I've been swimming over every day or two with Hugh or Shorty. It's still not doing so well. I don't know whether we could get there and back now before supper; we must have been working a long time on the boat, and the sun's getting down a bit." The other boys looked up, noticing this fact for the first time; their parents had long since given up trying to keep them from exploring any part of the island inside the reef, but they had some sort of regulation about meeting mealtimes. Without further remark Rice headed the boat back toward the creek, and the rowers began to take longer strokes.

Bob rowed without thinking much. Everywhere he turned there was lots to see, but none of it seemed to bear on his problem; the Hunter seemed to feel that Teroa should be tested, of course, but even he had no definite suspicion—it was simply that the boy was going out of reach. The thought reminded him of the talk he had had with Charlie that morning; he wondered whether the Polynesian boy had found Rice during the lunch hour.

"Anyone seen Charlie Teroa today?" he asked.

"No." It was Malmstrom who answered. "He comes a couple of days a week for navigation, but this isn't one of them. Think he'll ever use it?"

"Not for anyone who knows him." Rice's voice was scornful. I'd rather hire someone likely to stay awake on the job."

Bob concealed a smile. "He seems to get some work done in that garden of his," he remarked.

"Sure, with his mother watching and his sisters helping. Why, he went to sleep with a boatload of dynamite last fall, when they were clearing the east passage."

"You're crazy!"

"That's what you think. They sent him in alone for a case, and told him to stand by when he got back, and twenty minutes later my father found him moored to a bush on the reef, sound asleep, using the case for a foot-rest. He was lucky there weren't caps aboard and that he wasn't where a wave could have knocked the boat into the reef."

"Maybe that wasn't luck," Bob pointed out. "He knew he didn't have caps, and figured it was safe enough where he was."

"Maybe; but I haven't let him live it down yet." Rice grinned mischievously.

Bob looked at the redhead, who was rather short for his age. "Someday he'll throw you in the drink, if you don't stop riding him. Besides, wasn't that stowaway business *your* idea?"

Rice could have asked with some justice, what that had to do with matters, but he just chuckled and said nothing. A moment later the boat's flat bottom grated on the beach.

Chapter XI. *SLIP!*

BOB REMEMBERED after he got home that he had forgotten to ask Hay about the doctor's book, but reflected that there was plenty of time tomorrow. There probably would not be much of actual help in it anyway. He spent the evening in the house for a change, reading and talking to his parents; and the Hunter perforce did nothing but listen and think. The next forenoon was little better, from the detective's point of view; Bob worked around the house in the morning while his friends were in school, and neither of them thought of any means of getting Teroa long enough for a test. Bob, it is true, suggested leaving the Hunter near the other's home in the evening and coming back the next day, but the alien refused under any and all circumstances to place himself in a situation where Bob could see him either going or coming. He was sure what the emotional effect would be. Bob couldn't see it, but was convinced when the Hunter pointed out that there was no way for him to be sure that the mass of jelly which would return to him after the test was actually the detective. The boy had no desire whatever to let their quarry get at his own body.

The afternoon was distinctly better. Bob met the others as usual, and they repaired immediately to the boat. There was no time problem on this occasion, and they set out northwest, paralleling the shore at a distance of a few rods, with Hay and Colby rowing. The new plank had swelled, and there was very little leakage this time.

They had well over a mile to go, and they had rowed most of it before the Hunter fully understood the geography which he had been picking up in snatches from the conversation. The islet on which Hay had made his aquarium was, as he had intimated, close to the beach; it was the first section of the reef which curved away to the north and east from the end of the sand strip where the boys usually swam. It was separated from the beach itself by a stretch of water not twenty yards wide, a narrow channel which was protected from the breakers by other ridges of coral a little farther out which barely appeared above water. This channel, the Hunter judged, must be the one in which the dog was supposed to have been taken by a shark; and remembering the monster he had ridden ashore and seeing the seething currents among the ridges on its seaward side he shared Rice's doubts about that theory.

The islet itself was composed of coral, which had accumulated enough soil to support some bushes. It was not more than thirty or forty yards long and ten yards wide. The pool was at its widest part, almost circular, and about twenty feet across. It appeared to have no connection with the sea that raged a few yards away; Norman said he had blocked up two or three submarine passages with cement and that waves broke high enough and often enough at high tide to keep it full. As he had said, it was not doing well: a dead butterfly fish was floating near one side, and the coral that composed its walls showed no sign of living polyps.

"I thought it must be some sort of disease," he said, "but I never heard of one that attacks everything alike. Have you?"

Bob shook his head. "No. Was that why you borrowed that book of the doc's?"

Norman looked up sharply. "Why, yes. Who told you about that?"

"The doc. I wanted to find out something about viruses, and he said you had the best of his books on the subject. Are you still using it?"

"I guess not. What got you interested in viruses? I read what it had to say about 'em and couldn't get much out of it."

"Oh, I don't know. It was something about nobody being able to decide whether they were really alive or not I guess. That sounded pretty queer. If they eat and grow, they must be alive."

"I remember something about that——" At this point the conversation was interrupted, sparing Bob the need for further invention.

"For gosh sakes, Norm, give him the book when you get home, but let's not get lost in the upper atmosphere now! Exercise your brains on this pool of yours if you like, or else let's go along the reef and see what we can find." It was Malmstrom who had cut in, and Rice supported him vocally. Colby, as usual, remained silent in the background.

"I suppose you're right." Hay turned back to the pool. "I don't know, though, what I'm likely to think of right now that I couldn't in the last three or four months. I was hoping Bob might have a new idea."

"I don't know much biology—just the school course," Robert replied. "Have you gone down in it to see if you could find anything? Have you brought up anything like a piece of coral, to see what's happened to the polyps?"

"No, I've never been swimming in it. At first I didn't want to disturb the fish I had collected, and later I thought that whatever disease affected so many different things might get me too."

"That's a thought. Still, you must have touched the water a lot before things got really bad, and nothing happened to you. I'll go in if you like." Once again the Hunter came close to losing his temper. "What would you like me to bring up?"

Norman stared at him for a moment. "You really think it's safe? All right, I'll go in if you will."

That gave Bob a jolt; he had, almost without thought, been assuming himself safe from any disease germ that might be around, but Hay, as far as anyone could tell, had no symbiote to protect him.

That thought gave rise to another—*did he?* Would that explain his courage? Bob thought not, since it seemed most unlikely that their quarry's host would have any idea of the alien's presence but it was something to be considered when there was more time. For the moment the question was whether he should make good his offer of entering the questionable water if Hay were going to follow him.

He decided that he would; after all, the argument he had used against the trouble's being a disease seemed sound; and anyway there was a doctor on the island.

"All right," he said, starting to strip.

"Wait a minute! Are you fellows crazy?" Malmstrom

and Rice yelled almost together. "If that water's been killing the fish, you're foolish to go in."

"It's safe enough," said Bob. "We're not fish." He was aware of the weakness of this argument but could not think of a better one on the spur of the moment. The two Kenneths were still expostulating as he slipped feet first into the pool, with Norman beside him—both knew better than to dive into a coral pool, however clear it might be. Colby, who had not contributed to the argument, walked over to the boat, got an oar, came back, and stood watching.

The trouble with the pool manifested itself with remarkable speed. Bob swam out to the middle and did a surface dive, a maneuver which should have taken him without effort to the bottom eight feet down. It did nothing of the sort; his momentum barely got his feet under water. He took a couple of strokes, reached the bottom, broke a sea fan loose, and bobbed back to the surface with remarkable speed. As was his custom, he started blowing out air just before his head broke water, and managed to get some of the liquid into his mouth in the process. That was enough.

"Norm! Taste this water!" he yelled. "No wonder your fish died." Hay obeyed hesitantly, and grimaced.

"Where did all the salt come from?" he asked. Bob swam to the edge of the pool, clambered out, and started to dress before answering.

"We should have guessed," he said. Sea water comes in when the waves are high enough, but the only way it leaves is by evaporation. The salt stays behind. You shouldn't have blocked off all the passages to the sea. We'll have to chip out one of your plugs and find some wire netting, if you still want to take those pictures."

"My gosh," exclaimed Hay, "and I wrote a school report on Great Salt Lake only last year." He started to dress, indifferent as Bob to the fact that he was still wet. "What'll we do? Go back for a crowbar or something, or poke around the reef for a while now that we're here?"

A brief discussion resulted in the adoption of the second plan, and the group returned to the boat. On the way Norman pulled a large, battered bucket out of the bushes, laughing as he did so. "I used to fill up the pool with this sometimes, when I thought it was getting low," he said.

"I guess we can find some other use for Mr. Bucket now."
He tossed it into the bow of the boat after the others,
entered, and shoved off.

For an hour they rowed along inside the reef, occasionally disembarking on one of the larger islets, more
often coasting alongside the ridges and lumps of coral
while using poles to keep them off the more dangerous
sections. They had worked some distance along the reef
away from the island itself and had reached another fairly
large islet—this one actually supported half-a-dozen coconut palms—where they disembarked and pulled the boat
well up on the gritty soil. Their loot up to this time had
not been very impressive, consisting mainly of a few
cowries and a weirdly colored fragment of coral for which
Malmstrom had gone overboard in twelve feet of water.
The Hunter's profit from the expedition had been even less
so far, which annoyed him, since the exploration of the
reef for clues had been largely his idea.

He made the utmost use of Bob's eyes, however. They
were nearing his arbitrary one-mile limit north of the
beach, which meant that about half of the region in which
he expected to find clues of his quarry's landing had been
covered. There was still not very much to see, however.
On one side of the irregular islet the breakers thundered;
on the other was the relatively calm water of the lagoon,
with the bulk of one of the great culture tanks a few
hundred yards away. The scavenger barge was beside
the tank at the moment, and the small figures of its crew
were visible on the catwalks that crossed the paneled
roof; beyond, and dwarfed by a distance of fully three
miles, the houses of the island dwellers were barely
visible.

These, however, could hardly be considered clues, it
seemed to the Hunter, and he brought his attention back
to the immediate surroundings. The present bit of land
was similar to that on which Hay's pool was located,
and like it, had very irregular edges—clefts, walled with
living coral, in which the water gurgled down almost out
of sight and then spurted upward into the watchers' faces
as another breaker came thundering against the barrier.
Some of the openings were narrow at the outer edge and
broadened farther in, so that the water in them was

quieter, though there was always the endless up-and-down wash started by the waves.

It was in these larger openings that the boys did most of their searching—it would have been impossible to get anything out of the others, reckless as some of the youngsters tended to be.

Rice, the first one out of the boat, had run to one of the largest while the others were still pulling the little craft up and making it fast; and dropping into a prone position with his head over the edge, he shaded his eyes and looked down into the clear water. By the time the others came up he was already pulling off his shirt.

"My chance first," he said quickly as the others peered down to see what he had sighted. Before anyone was sure what he was looking at, Rice had slipped into the water, disturbing the surface so that nothing was clearly visible. He stayed down for some time, and finally reappeared asking for one of the poles that were carried in the boat. "I can't work it loose," he said. "It seems to be jammed in place."

"What is it?" several voices asked at once.

"I'm not sure; I've never seen anything like it. That's why I want to get it up." He received the pole which Colby handed down to him and slid under water once more. The object at which he was prying was about five feet below the surface—that is, it varied from about four to six feet as the water level rose and fell in response to the urge of the breakers.

Several times Kenneth came up for breath, without having dislodged the mysterious object; and finally Bob went down to help. He had one advantage over the other boy; thanks to the Hunter's prompt supplementing of the curvature of his eye lenses with some of his alien body material Bob could see much better under water than usual. He could make out easily the shape of the object on which Kenneth was working but did not recognize it. It was a hollow hemisphere of dull metal eight or nine inches in diameter and half an inch thick, with the flat side protected over half its area by a plate of similar material. It was hung on a stubby branch of coral only a few inches from the bottom, rather like a cap on a peg; and another lump of the stuff had either fallen or grown so as to wedge it in place. Rice was prying at the upper lump with a pole.

After a few minutes of futile effort they stopped, got their breath, and planned a more co-operative method of attack. Bob, it was agreed, would go to the bottom and work the end of the pole behind the object; Kenneth, upon receiving his signal, would brace one foot against the steep side of the pool—they both wore their shoes, as any sane person would in a coral pool—and push outward, to get the thing out from under the heavy fragment that pinned it down. The first time the attempt failed; Bob did not have the pole well enough set and it slipped out. The second, however, succeeded—almost too well. The piece of metal popped free and rolled away from the wall into deeper water; Bob, who was approaching the end of his store of breath, came to the surface. He refilled his lungs and started to speak to Rice, and then realized that the redhead was not visible. For a moment he supposed the other boy had taken a quick breath and gone back down for his prize, but as the water sank abruptly Rice's head appeared.

"Help! My foot——" The words were cut off again as the water surged up, but the situation was crystal-clear. Bob immediately dived again, braced his feet on the bottom, and strove to lift the lump of coral, which had been freed by the removal of the piece of metal and had landed on Kenneth's foot. He was no more successful than before, and returned anxiously to the surface just as the water went down again.

"Don't talk! Get air!" Malmstrom yelled superfluously —Rice was too busy to do anything else when the opportunity to gulp air occurred. Bob was looking around for the pole, which had disappeared. He saw it floating a few yards away and went after it. Colby had disappeared toward the boat without saying anything; as Bob came back with the pole and prepared to dive once more, the young boy came back. He was carrying the bucket that Hay had brought from the pool.

Everything had happened so rapidly that Malmstrom and Hay had scarcely realized what was going on. They now looked at Hugh Colby and his bucket in astonishment. Colby wasted no time explaining. He threw himself face downward at the water's edge and reached out and

107

downward to the trapped Rice. As the water receded he placed the inverted bucket over the other's head and spoke his only words during the entire incident.

"Hold it there!"

Rice, for a wonder, got the point, and followed orders; and as the water surged up again over his head he found his face enclosed in a bucket full of air. Bob had not seen this trick, as he was under water again prying at the lump of coral but he came up a moment later, saw, blinked in bewilderment, and then understood.

"Shall we come in?" Hay asked anxiously.

"I think I can get it off this time," Bob replied. "I was worried at first because of his air supply, but he'll be all right now. Just a minute till I get my own breath." He rested a moment, while Hay yelled encouragement to his trapped comrade in the intervals that the latter's head was above water. Robert found time to mutter to the Hunter, "This is why I didn't want to come here alone!" Then he took a firmer grip on the pole, and submerged again.

This time he succeeded in finding a better point of leverage, and applied all his strength. The lump of coral started to shift, and he felt that the work was about done, when the pole broke, the splintered end raking down his own chest. For once the Hunter could raise no objection; the injury was clearly "line of duty," and he closed the scratches without resentment. Bob popped back to the surface.

"I guess you'd better come in at that. I got it started, and the pole broke. Get the other poles, or maybe an oar or two and everyone who can get at it come in."

"Maybe we'd better go for a crowbar," suggested Malmstrom.

"Maybe we'd better do the work ourselves," retorted Bob. "The tide's coming in, and that bucket will be good just so long as the water gets below his head every few seconds. Come on."

Within a few seconds the four boys, armed with poles and oars, were in the water beside their comrade: Bob at the bottom placing the levers, the others supporting them and ready to lift when he gave the word. They knew nothing about his advantage in seeing under water, of course; they accepted his leadership simply because he had started telling them what to do and no one intended to argue at a time like that.

Heavy as the block was, it yielded to this concentration of effort, though the job nearly cost them an oar. For just a moment the fragment of coral lifted, and Kenneth was able to drag his numbed foot from beneath it. With the aid of his friends he scrambled out of the water and sat nursing the foot while the others gathered around.

Rice was remarkably pale, considering his normal tan, and it was some time before his breathing and heartbeat returned to normal and he felt like standing up. The other boys were almost as frightened, and for some time nobody suggested going back into the water for the piece of metal that had started the trouble. After ten minutes or so Rice suggested that it would be a pity if all that work were wasted, and Bob took the hint and went down again; but the thing was not visible among the sea fans and branching corals that covered the pool's bottom, and he stopped groping under things after encountering a sea urchin which believed in passive resistance. Rice had nothing to show for his afternoon's work but fright, which was not the sort of souvenir he had any intention of showing to his parents.

It was now almost half-past four, which left plenty of time before supper, but somehow the prospect of further search on the reef no longer attracted them. They decided, with very little argument, to row the two miles and a fraction that separated them from the big dock. "That ought to be fairly peaceful, with the ship not due for nearly a week," Hay innocently remarked. No one said anything in answer at the time, as all of them probably had some such idea in mind; but he heard a good deal about that remark later.

The Hunter hardly heard the statement, of course; for the past quarter hour his mind had been fully occupied with a generator casing he had just seen and felt and which had definitely not come from the flattened wreckage of his own ship.

Chapter XII. *AND FALL!*

THERE WAS little talk for the first half of the row, for
they had been badly scared; but when Norman Hay passed
a remark about his aquarium the conversation quickly
blossomed full strength.

"Maybe we can find something here to get one of those
cement plugs out of the pool," were his words.

"You'll need something pretty good," remarked Shorty.
"That underwater cement you got is rugged stuff—at least
they used it on the dock, and there's no mark yet where
the tanker comes in."

"The tanker doesn't touch the dock, unless someone
gets careless," pointed out Rice from the bow. "Still,
Norm's right about needing some good tools. There's nothing around our house that'll do, I know."

"What'll we use, anyway—hammer and cold chisel!"

"You can't get much good out of a hammer under water.
We need a long, heavy crowbar with a good point. Who
knows where we can get one?" There was no answer to
that, and Hay continued after a moment. "Well, we'll
ask some of the dock crew, and if they don't know, the
construction gang up on the hill is bound to."

"If we could snaffle a diving helmet we'd get the work
done faster," Rice contributed.

"The only helmets on the island are the rescue rigs on
the dock and at the tanks, and I don't think they'd appreciate our borrowing one of those," Bob said. "We could
never get the suit, and anyway probably Shorty's the only
one who could wear it."

"What's wrong with that?" Malmstrom wanted to know.

"You'd be kicking about doing all the work. Anyway,
they wouldn't let us take it."

"Why don't we make one? There's not much to it."

"Maybe not; but we've talked about that for four or

110

five years and wound up holding our breath every time we worked under water." It was one of Colby's rare contributions to the exchange; as usual, no one could think of an answer.

Rice broke the short silence with another question. "What are you going to use to keep your fish in? Bob said something about wire netting, but where are you going to get any?"

"I don't know that either. If there's any on the island, it ought to be in one of the storerooms on the dock. I'll try to scrounge a piece if there is, and we'll get some heavy wire and make it if there isn't. The hole won't be very big anyway."

They tied up at the foot of a ladder on the landward side of the structure, almost under the causeway leading from the shore; Rice and Bob made both bow and stern painters fast while the others went up to the main level without waiting. Ken had a little trouble with the ladder because of his foot, but managed to conceal it fairly well. Once on the dock, the group looked around, planning.

The dock was a large structure, even as such things go. The weekly production of oil was considerable, and expansion was still going on; storage space had been designed accordingly. Four enormous cylindrical tanks were the most striking features; their auxiliary pumping and control mechanisms looked tiny by comparison. There were no fire walls; the structure was built of steel and concrete, with numerous large drains opening on the water below, and the fire-fighting apparatus consisted principally of high-pressure hoses to wash burning oil into the lagoon.

Between and around the tanks were a number of corrugated-iron sheds similar in structure and function to the storage buildings on shore; and at the end opposite the causeway was a complicated and versatile apparatus which could be used to distill gasoline, heating, or lubricating oils from the crude products of the culture tanks—it was cheaper to make the small quantities of these which were used on the island on the spot rather than to ship the crudes for refining to Tahiti and then bring them back again and store them.

It was the storage buildings which interested the boys at the moment. None of them could think offhand of any normal use for wire netting on the island, but one never could be sure, and they intended to leave no stone unturned. They headed in single file down the narrow space between the tanks.

There was a slight interruption before they reached the storeroom they sought; as they passed the corner of one of the small sheds an arm reached out, attached itself to Rice's collar, and pulled him inside the building. The boys stopped in astonishment for a moment, then grinned understandingly at one another as the voice of Charlie Teroa reached their ears. He was saying something about "stowaways" and "jobs," and seemed quite emphatic; and for once a conversation lasting several minutes took place in Rice's neighborhood without his voice being audible. Bob had wondered whether he ought to give him a hint about Teroa's intentions but had been pretty sure no damage would be done—the older boy was too pleased with himself. Nevertheless, it was a very sheepish-looking redhead who rejoined the group. Teroa was behind him, with a faint grin on his face; he winked as he caught Bob's eye.

"You kids aren't supposed to be out here, are you?" he asked.

"As much as you," retorted Hay, who had no intention of leaving while there was a chance of getting what he wanted. "You don't work here, either."

"You can ask about that," returned Teroa severely. "At least I'm helping. I suppose you're after something." It was a statement, but there was a faint suggestion of question at the end.

"Nothing that anyone will miss," replied Hay defensively. He was going to enlarge upon this theme when a new voice cut in.

"Just how sure can we be of that?" The boys whirled to see the speaker, and discovered Bob's father standing behind them. "We're always glad to *lend* things," he went on, "as long as we know where they're going. What were you needing this trip?"

Hay explained without reluctance—his conscience was clear, as he had every intention of asking for the wire, though he had hoped to exercise a little selection of his own in deciding whom to ask.

Mr. Kinnaird nodded in understanding. "You'll probably have to go up to the new tank car for a crowbar or anything like it," he said. "I think we can do something about your grating, though. Let's look."

Everybody, including Teroa, trailed him across the somewhat slippery steel plates. As they went, Hay explained what had happened to his pool and the way in which they had discovered the cause of the trouble. Mr. Kinnaird was a good listener, but he shot a glance at his son, which that young man fortunately missed, when he heard about the question of entering the possibly disease-laden water. The conversation reminded Bob of the book he wanted, and he asked Hay about it when the latter stopped talking for a moment. Mr. Kinnaird could not restrain a comment.

"My word, are you going to be a doctor now? You don't seem to have been acting like one!"

"No—it's just something I wanted to find out," Bob said lamely (the Hunter's troubles were coming thick and fast; he wondered when he would get a chance to talk to his host—the present background was impossible).

Mr. Kinnaird smiled and turned to the door of one of the sheds they had reached. "There may be something in here, Norman," he said, and unlocked the door. It was dark inside, but a switch in the doorframe lighted a single bulb in the center of the ceiling. All eyes focused on the same thing immediately—a large roll of quarter-inch mesh galvanized wire that might have been made to order for Norman's needs. Hay made a rush for it, while Bob's father stood back looking as though he had invented the stuff.

"How much will you need?"

"A piece eighteen inches square will be plenty," was the reply. Mr. Kinnaird took a pair of cutters from a bench at one side of the shed and went to work on the roll. It was awkward driving the cutters too far, but he handed Norman the desired piece after a few seconds' work and they went outside together.

"I didn't know that stuff was used anywhere on the island," Bob remarked as his father relocked the door behind them.

"Really?" asked the latter. "I thought you'd poked around here enough to rebuild the place if you had to." He led the way to the nearest of the storage tanks and indicated one of the safety drains beside it. "There," he said, pointing down the four-foot-square unguarded opening. The boys crowded around and looked down. A couple of feet below the opening, between them and the water a dozen feet farther down, was a protective net of the mesh that Norman was carrying.

"I shouldn't think that would be strong enough to hold a person who fell down there," remarked Bob.

"People aren't supposed to fall down there," retorted his father. "Or, if they do, they're expected to be able to swim. That's to catch tools, which do skitter around on these plates a good deal. People aren't allowed anywhere near these openings." He turned away from the drain as the boys drew back thoughtfully, and promptly demonstrated the truth of his own words.

He slipped; at least Malmstrom insisted that it was Mr. Kinnaird who slipped first, but no one was really sure. The group acted like a well-struck set of pins in a bowling alley; the only one to keep his feet was Teroa, and he was forced to move with remarkable speed to do so. Malmstrom was knocked against Hay, whose feet went out from under him and caught the ankles of Bob and Colby. Their shoes, in turn, failed to grip on the somewhat oily metal, and Bob gave a yell as he realized he was about to put the strength of the netting to practical test.

His reaction speed had earned him his position on the school hockey team, and that was what saved him now. He fell feet first; and his toes touched the mesh, he spread his arms wide and forward, reaching as far onto the solid part of the dock as he could. The edge of the plating caught his painfully across the ribs, but enough of his weight came on his arms so that the mesh was not overloaded, and it held.

His father, on hands and knees, made a lunge for Bob's hand, but he slipped again and missed his aim. It was Malmstrom and Colby, who had both fallen within reach, who seized his wrists without attempting to rise from their prone positions and gave him enough anchorage to let him work himself back onto solid footing.

Bob wiped sweat from his forehead, and his father appeared to brush something from his eyes as they looked at each other; then the man gave a rather forced smile. "You see what I mean," he said. Then, recovering himself a little, "I think one of us is going to be late for supper. I take it that that boat I saw tied up is yours and has to go back to the creek." The boys admitted that this was the case. "All right, you'd better charge along before something else happens. I'll be going home myself shortly, Bob. Had we better tell your mother? I thought not." There was no pause between question and answer, and they parted almost laughing.

The Hunter was not laughing, however, and could scarcely have felt less like it. He wanted to talk to Bob but had so much to say that he could hardly decide where to begin. He was intensely relieved when his young host took up his station in the bow of the boat rather than at an oar; and the instant Bob was looking away from his friends, the Hunter attracted his attention.

"Bob!" The projected letters were thick, slanted, and underlined. They would have been colored if there had been any way to do it; as it was, the boy got the desired impression of urgency and promptly directed his gaze toward the horizon.

"We will pass over," the Hunter began, "for the moment, at least, your tendency to expose yourself to minor injury because you know I will take care of it. The tendency itself is bad enough, but you have been practically broadcasting your confidence in your immunity. You offered publicly to go into that water this morning without the least hesitation; you have been announcing your new interest in biology in general and viruses in particular to all and sundry. Several times today I felt like forgetting my upbringing and paralyzing your tongue. At first I merely thought you might scare our quarry into a better hiding place; now I am not sure that the matter may not be even more serious."

"But what else could it do?" Bob muttered the question so that none of the others could hear.

"I am not certain, of course, but it seems odd that your near accident should follow so closely all that talk—particularly when the talk was in the hearing of some of our likeliest suspects." Bob absorbed that thought in silence for a minute or two. He had not previously considered that there might be personal danger in this mission. Before he could think of anything to say the Hunter added a point. "Even your examining that dead fish as closely as you did could easily attract the attention of a person as suspicious as our friend is likely to be."

"But Norm was examining the skate as much as I was," pointed out Bob.

"So I noticed." The Hunter did not enlarge upon that point, leaving his young host to derive any implications he might like from it.

"But anyway, what could he do? How could he have caused that fall—you said yourself that you couldn't make me do anything. Is he different from you?"

"No. It is quite true that he could not have forced any of those people to push you, or anything like it. However, he might have persuaded them; you have done much for me, remember."

"But you said he would not have made himself known."

"I didn't think he would—it would be risky for him. Still, he might have decided to chance it, and enlist his host's aid by some story or other—that would not be hard. How could the host prove he was living?"

"I don't see, offhand; but what good would it have done him if I had gone into the drink back there? I can swim, and everyone there knows it; and if I couldn't, and got drowned, that wouldn't stop *you* for long."

"True; but he may have intended that you be slightly hurt, so that I would betray myself by repair activities. After all, no matter what story he told his host, he would be unlikely to persuade one of your friends to do you serious or permanent harm."

"You think, then, that maybe Charlie Teroa is trying to get that job off the island to suit our friend? I thought he was covering up that story about sleeping on the job because he really wanted to start working."

"The possibility exists, certainly. We definitely must find means of checking him before he goes—or keeping him from going." Bob did not pay too much attention to this statement. Not only had he heard it before, but another thought came swelling up into his mind—one that affected him quite enough to have been noticed by his friends had he been facing any of them.

The thought had been started by one of the Hunter's sentences a little earlier and had taken a little while to form; but now it sat there in his mind, glaringly clear. The Hunter had said his quarry would be able to deceive his host by a story and that there would be no way for the host to prove its falsehood. Bob suddenly realized that *he had no means of checking the Hunter's own tale.* For all he *knew,* the being now ensconced in his own body might be a fleeing criminal seeking to rid itself of legitimate pursuit.

He almost said something, but his natural common sense saved him at the last instant. This was something he must check himself; and until it was checked, he must appear to be as trustful and co-operative as ever.

He did not really doubt the Hunter seriously. In spite of communication limitations, the alien's very attitude and behavior had given the boy a remarkably good picture of his personality—as was evidenced by the fact that this was the first time Bob had thought to question his motives. Still, the doubt was there now and would have to be resolved in some way.

He was preoccupied when the boat reached the creek and said little while they were pulling it up and stowing the oars. The fact did not cause remark; all the boys were fairly tired and not a little subdued by two accidents in one afternoon. They splashed up the creek to the culvert, retrieved their bicycles from the bushes, and went their various ways, after agreeing to meet at the same place after breakfast.

Alone at last, Bob could speak more freely to the little detective.

"Hunter," he asked, "if you think my talking and investigating are likely to make our friend suspicious of me, why do they worry you? If he tries anything, it will give us a clue to him! That might be the best way to find him—use me as bait. After all, the only smart way to hunt for a needle in a haystack is to use a magnet. How about it?"

"I thought of that. It is too dangerous."

"How can he hurt you?"

"I don't suppose he can. The danger that bothers me is yours. I don't know whether you are showing the bravery of maturity or the foolhardiness of youth, but understand, once and for all, that I will not expose you to any danger as long as I can see an alternative course of action."

Bob made no answer for a moment, and if the Hunter interpreted correctly the tightening of the muscles as the boy strove to suppress a smile of satisfaction he did not mention the fact. There was one other thing Bob wanted settled, however, so he put the question as he turned up the drive to his home—he had walked the bicycle from Rice's drive, so there would be no danger in the Hunter's talking to him.

"In the boat you said something about paralyzing my tongue. Could you do it, or were you simply shooting off?"

The Hunter was not familiar with that bit of slang, but was able to guess correctly at its meaning. "I could paralyze any muscle in your body by pressing on the controlling nerve. How long the state would last after I stopped I cannot say, as I haven't tried it with you or any of your people."

"Show me." Bob stopped and kicked down the stand of the bike and stood expectantly.

"Go indoors and eat your supper and stop asking foolish questions!"

Bob went, grinning openly now.

Chapter XIII.   *ENGINEERING INTERLUDE*

SATURDAY was not too profitable from the Hunter's point
of view—at least as he judged it then—and even less so
from that of Norman Hay. The boys met at the culvert
as planned, Norman bearing his piece of netting, but
nobody had brought anything that looked capable of doing much to the cement plugs Hay had installed.

It was decided, therefore, to go to the other end of the
island, where a new culture was under construction, to
see what might be available. They rode together down the
road, across the larger creek, and past the school to Teroa's
house. Here, instead of turning down toward the dock,
they continued straight on, past some more corrugated-
iron storage sheds, to the end of the paved surface.
This left them on the shoulder of the islands' highest hill
though still on the lagoon side. Somewhat below and ahead
of them was a row of three small tanks which had been
there for some years; higher and still farther ahead was
a new structure almost as large as the tanks in the lagoon.
This had been completed only a month or two before; and
another, the boys knew, was being built beyond it. This
was their immediate goal.

While the hard-surfaced road stopped at the last of the
sheds, the construction machinery had beaten a very
plain trail which formed a continuation of it. It proved
better, however, to traverse this section on foot, and the
boys soon abandoned the bicycles rather than walk them.
It was not far to go—three hundred yards to the big tank,
seventy more along its lower wall, and as much farther
to the scene of activity.

Like its neighbor, the new tank was on the hillside,
partly cut into the ground and partly above it. The floor
had been laid, reinforced, and the concrete cast; those
portions of the walls that lay against the earth of the

hillside were occupying the attention of the men at the moment. The boys noted with relief that digging seemed to have ended; it should, then, be possible to borrow the tools they needed. They had, as a matter of fact, surprisingly little trouble; they encountered Rice's father almost at once, and he readily located a couple of crowbars and gave permission to take them. He may have had ulterior motives; nearly all the children of the island between the ages of four and seventeen were underfoot at the time—the men were seriously considering having a local regulation passed ordering school to keep seven days a week—and anything that looked as though it might get rid of some of them would have been encouraged. The boys cared nothing about his reasons; they took the bars and returned the way they had come.

It was an encouraging start, but the rest of the morning was less so. They reached the pool without noteworthy delay, and went to work, diving by turns and pecking away at the concrete with the crowbars. They could not even work on the seaward side of the plug; anyone entering the water on that side of the islet would have been cut to pieces against the coral by the first breaker. They had chipped away enough to encourage them by dinnertime but there was yet much to be done.

After the meal, however, meeting at the usual place, they found one of the jeeps parked by the culvert. Standing beside it were Rice and his father and in the back seat was some equipment which the boys recognized.

"Dad's going to blast the gate for us!" called the younger Rice, quite superfluously, as the others arrived. "He got away from the tank for a couple of hours."

"Anything to get you out of my hair," remarked his father. "You'd better stick to your bikes—you, too, Ken. I'll ride the sticks."

"It's safe enough!" remonstrated Bob, who wanted to examine the plunger more closely.

The man looked at him. "No remarks from you," he said. "Your father would have the bunch of you stay here while he laid the charge and come back here with you to fire it! And I don't blame him a bit." He climbed under the wheel without further comment; and Bob, who knew that Mr. Rice had spoken the truth, mounted his bicycle and headed northwest, followed by the others.

At the Hay house the jeep was parked and its load removed. Mr. Rice insisted on carrying the dynamite and caps himself, though Bob thought he had a good argument when he claimed they should not be carried together. The wire and plunger were taken in charge by Bob and Malmstrom, and everybody headed for the beach on foot. They went a little to the left of the course the boys had followed Wednesday and emerged at the southern end of the strip of sand.

Here, as at the pool, the reef reappeared, curving away to the south and east, eventually to circle the island almost completely. On the southern side the lagoon was narrower, the reef never being more than half a mile from the shore, and no attempt had so far been made to build any installations on this side. Where the barrier started at the south end of the little beach was a passage from open sea to lagoon similar to that isolating the islet of the pool; but this was much narrower, offering at the base barely passage for a rowboat.

This was the "gate" to which Rice had referred. It looked, from a little distance, as though it were perfectly clear; but a closer inspection showed, as Rice had said, that there was an obstruction. The end of the passage toward the beach, which was exposed to the waves from the open sea to the west, had been neatly plugged by a brain coral about six feet in diameter, which had been dislodged from some point farther out in the reef and rolled about, probably by successive storms, until it had wedged securely where the waves could drive it no farther. Even the boys had not had to look twice to know they could never shift the huge thing by hand labor, though they had made some half-hearted attempts to break away enough coral to clear a passage around it.

It was possible, obviously, to reach the southern lagoon in a boat by rowing around the other end of the island, but it was generally agreed that clearing the gate would be worth the trouble.

Mr. Rice unbent sufficiently to allow Colby to place the charge—he did not want to go under water himself—after careful instruction; but he made everyone follow him back to the palm trees and take shelter behind the sturdy trunks before he fired it. The results were very satisfactory: a column of spray and coral chips fountained into the air, accompanied by a moderate amount of noise —dynamite is not particularly loud stuff. When the rain of fragments seemed to be over, the boys raced back to the gate and found that there would be no need of a second blast. About a quarter of the original piece was visible, rolled some distance from its original site; the rest had completely disappeared. There was ample room for the boat.

The boys controlled their exuberance sufficiently to help Mr. Rice pack the blasting equipment back into the jeep; but from that point their opinions were divided. Hay and Malmstrom wanted to go back to work on the pool; Bob and Rice wanted to take advantage of the newly opened gate to explore the southern reef. Colby, as usual, cast no vote. None of them thought of splitting up; and, oddly enough, Hay won the argument, his main point being that it was already well along in the afternoon, and it would be much better to start in the morning and spend the entire day on the reef.

Bob would have been considerably more insistent, in order to let the Hunter examine the rest of his "probable landing" area, but the detective had informed him the night before of the nature of the piece of metal that had indirectly caused Rice's accident.

"It was a generator casing from a ship similar to mine," he said. "And it certainly was not from my own. I am certain of my facts; if I had merely seen it, there might be a chance of error—I suppose your people might have apparatus that would look like it from a little distance— but I felt it while you were pulling at it barehanded. It had line-up marks etched into the metal, indicated by letters of my own alphabet."

"But how did it get there, when the rest of the ship isn't around?"

"I told you our friend was a coward. He must have detached it and carried it with him for protection, accepting the delay such a load would have caused. It was certainly good armor, I will admit; I cannot imagine any living creature breaking or piercing that metal, and he would have to stay so close to the bottom that there would be no chance of being swallowed whole. It was a rather smart move, except that it left us evidence not only of the fact that he has landed on the island, but also where."

"Can you judge what he would do then?"

"Exactly what I said before—pick up a host at the first opportunity, anyone he could catch. Your friends are still definitely under suspicion, including the young man who went to sleep near the reef with a boatload of explosive."

In consequence of this information, Bob was willing to forego the examination of the southern reef, and to spend an afternoon at dull work. It would give him time to think; and thought seemed necessary. He was rewarded during the afternoon with one idea, but he was unable to speak clearly enough with the others around to get it across to Hunter. He finally gave up trying for the time being and concentrated on chipping concrete.

By the time they were ready to go home for supper they had actually penetrated the plug—at least a hole large enough to accommodate one of the crowbars was all the way through. The trip back to the creek was chiefly occupied with an argument whether or not this hole would be sufficient. The discussion was still unsettled when the boys separated.

Once alone Bob promptly put his suggestion up to the Hunter.

"You've been saying all along," he said, "that you would never leave or enter my body when I was awake—that you didn't want me to see you. I don't think I'd mind, but I won't argue the point any more.

"But suppose I put a container—a can, or box, or almost anything big enough—in my room at night. When I was asleep—I couldn't possibly fool you on that—you could come out and get in the box; if you like, I'll promise not to look inside. Then I could plant it next to the house of each of the fellows in turn and leave it there overnight. You could come out, do all the inspecting you wanted at that house and get back to the can by morning. I could even put some sort of indicator on the can that you could move to tell me whether you wanted to come back to me or go on to the next house."

The Hunter thought for several minutes. "The idea is good, very good," he finally answered. "Its big disadvantages, at least as far as I can see, are only two: first, I could examine only one house each night, and would then be even more helpless than usual until the next night. Second, while I am making those examinations, you will be left unprotected. That might not ordinarily be too bad, but you must remember we now have reason to suspect that our quarry has identified you as my host. If he sprang a trap of some sort while I was away, it might be very bad."

"It might also convince him that I am not your host," pointed out Bob.

"And that, my young friend, might not do either of us the least good." As usual, the Hunter's implied meaning was plain.

At home, Bob found his father already eating, somewhat to his surprise.

"I'm not that late, am I?" he asked anxiously as he entered the dining room.

"No, it's all right, son; I came home to grab an early bite. I have to go back to the tank; we want to get the last of the forms for the back wall in place and pour tonight, so that the concrete can set over Sunday."

"May I come along?"

"We don't expect to be done till midnight anyway. Well, I guess it won't hurt. I expect if your mother were asked politely she would give her consent, and perhaps even double the sandwich order she's preparing at the moment."

Bob bounced toward the kitchen but was met halfway by his mother's voice.

"All right this time; but after you're back in school this sort of thing is out. Bargain?"

"Bargain." Bob seated himself opposite his father and began asking for further details. Mr. Kinnaird supplied them between mouthfuls. It had not occurred to Bob to wonder where the jeep was, but he understood anyway when its horn sounded outside. They went out together, but there was room for only one more in the vehicle. The fathers of Hay, Colby, Rice, and Malmstrom were already aboard. Mr. Kinnaird turned to Bob.

"I forgot to mention—you'll have to take your bike. You'll also have to walk it home, unless you have that light fixed, which I doubt. Still want to come?"

"Sure." Bob turned to the space under the porch where he stored the machine. The other men looked at Kinnaird with some surprise.

124

"You going to take a chance on having him around w' 'e we pour, Art?" asked the senior Malmstrom. "You'll be fishing him out of the cement."

"If he can't take care of himself by now, it's time we both found out," replied Bob's father, glancing in the direction his son had vanished.

"If there's anything in heredity, you won't find him in much danger," remarked the heavy-set Colby as he shifted to make room in the jeep. He spoke with a grin that was meant to remove the sting from the words. Mr. Kinnaird was apparently unaffected by the remark.

The red-haired driver turned the jeep and sent it down the drive, Bob pedaling furiously behind. Since the distance to the road was not great and the curve at that point sharp, he held his own down the drive; but once in the main road the men quickly drew ahead. Bob did not care. He rolled on through the village to the end of the road, parked the bicycle, and proceeded on foot along the path the boys had taken that morning. The sun had set during the ride, and darkness was closing in with typical tropic speed.

There was no lack of light at the scene of construction, however. Wherever there seemed the slightest need big portable fluorescents blazed. They were all powered from a single engine-driven generator mounted on a dolly parked at one side of the already smoothed floor; and for some time Bob occupied himself finding out all he could about this installation without actually taking it apart. Then he wandered over to the rear wall where the forms were going up, and, applying the principle the boys had long since found best, helped for a while carrying the two-by-fours that were being used to prop the great, flat, prefabricated sections in place. He met his father several times, but no word either of approval or censure was passed.

Like the rest of the men, Mr. Kinnaird was far too busy to say much. He was a civil engineer by training, but, like everyone else on the island, he was expected to turn his hand to whatever job needed doing. For once the work came very near to his specialty, and he was making the most of it. The Hunter saw him occasionally, when Bob chanced to be looking somewhere near the right direction, and he was always busy—clinging precariously (it seemed

125

to the alien) to the tops of ladders gauging the separation of the molds; stepping across the thirty-foot-deep chasm which the concrete was to fill, to climb the slope beyond and check the preparations of the men at the mixers; freezing over a spirit level or a theodolite as he gauged location or angle of stance of some newly positioned part; checking the fuel tank on the generator engine; even taking a turn at the power saw where the ends of the props were cut to the proper angles—jobs which would each have been done by a different man anywhere else, and jobs which sometimes scared even the watching Hunter. The alien decided that he had been overhasty in condemning the man for letting his son do dangerous work. Mr. Kinnaird just didn't think of that phase of the matter. Well, so much more work for the Hunter. Maybe someday he could educate the boy to take care of himself; but if he had had fifteen years of this example the chances were smaller than the detective had hoped.

The man was not completely ignoring his son, however. Bob succeeded in concealing one yawn from everyone but his guest; but his father spotted the second and ordered him away from work. He knew what lack of sleep could do to a person's coordination and had no desire to see the elder Malmstrom's prediction fulfilled.

"Do I have to go home?" asked Bob. "I wanted to see them pour."

"You won't be able to see if you don't get some sleep. No, you needn't go home; but stop working for a while and catch a nap. There's a good place up at the top of the hill there where you can see what's going on and lie down in comfort at the same time. I'll wake you before they pour, if you insist."

Bob made no objection. It was not yet ten o'clock, and he would never have ordinarily dreamed of sleeping so early; but the last few days had been a tremendous change in activity from the routine of the school, and even he was beginning to feel the results. Anyway, he knew that objecting would do him no good.

He climbed the hill accordingly, and on the very top found a spot which answered to his father's description. He stretched out on the soft grass, propped his head up on his elbows, and regarded the brilliant scene below him.

From here he could see almost everything at once. It

was as though he looked down from a balcony onto a lighted stage. Only the area at the very foot of the wall to be was hidden by the molds; and there was plenty to watch elsewhere in the work area. Even outside this something could be seen; there was the faint glow from the water of the lagoon, with the nearer tanks silhouetted against it and the brighter band of luminosity that limned the outer reef. Bob could hear the breakers if he listened for them; but, like everyone else on the island, he was so accustomed to their endless sound that he seldom noticed it. To his left a few lights were visible, some on the dock and some in the half-dozen houses not hidden from his gaze by the shoulder of the hill. In the other direction, to the east, there was only darkness. The machines used to mow the lush vegetation grown there to feed the culture tanks were abandoned for the night, and the only sound was the rustling among the pithy stalks caused by small animals and vagrant breezes. There were a few mosquitoes and sand flies as well, but the Hunter also believed his host needed sleep, and frightened off with tiny pseudopods any that landed on the boy's exposed skin. It may have been listening to these faint noises which proved to be Bob's undoing, for in spite of the firmest determination merely to rest and watch he was sound asleep when his father came up the hill to find him.

Mr. Kinnaird approached silently and looked down at the boy for some time with an expression that defied interpretation. At last, as the sound of the mixers below swelled abruptly, he nudged the prone figure with his toe. This proving ineffective, he bent over and shook his son gently; and eventually Bob emitted an audible yawn and opened his eyes. It took him a second or two to take in the situation, then he got to his feet at once.

"Thanks, Dad. I didn't think I'd go to sleep. Is it late? Are they pouring?"

"Just starting." Mr. Kinnaird made no comments about sleep. He had only one son but knew the minds of boys. "I'll have to go back to the floor; I suppose you'll want to watch from the top. Just to be sure someone's around to see you if you fall in." They started downhill together without further talk.

At the mixers Mr. Kinnaird bore off to the left, continuing down past the cut made for the tank, while Bob stayed by the machinery. It was already in action, and more of the lights had been moved up to the scene, so that every operation was clearly visible. The upper ends of the machines received apparently endless supplies of sand and cement from stock piles previously built up and of water pumped up from one of the big desalting units at the edge of the lagoon. A smooth, gray-white river of concrete poured from spouts at the lower end and into the chasm between the carefully placed mold boards. The scene of activity was gradually being obscured under a haze of cement dust. The men were protected from it by goggles, but Bob was not, and presently the penetrating stuff began to get into his eyes. The Hunter made a half-hearted attempt to do something about it, but it meant putting tissue on the outside of the boy's eyeballs which would interfere with sight from both their proper owner and himself, so he let the tear glands do the job. He had no particular ulterior motives, but was far from disappointed when his host moved a little way up the hill to get out of the dust cloud; for, as usual, Bob had been watching things with an annoying disregard for his own safety and had had to be ordered out of the way several times by some of the men.

Just before midnight, with the pouring almost done, Mr. Kinnaird reappeared and located Bob, who was asleep again. He did not fulfill his promise of making the boy ride home on his bicycle.

Chapter XIV. ACCIDENTS

SUNDAY morning the boys met as planned, bringing
lunches with them. The bicycles were cached as usual,
and the group splashed down the creek to the boat, where
all but Bob changed to bathing suits. He kept on shirt
and slacks, as his sunburn was not quite at the stage
where another layer would be advisable. He and Malmstrom took the oars, and they rowed along the shore
toward the northwest. They stopped for a moment at
Hay's tank and tasted the water, which seemed now to be
ordinary sea water; then they headed the small craft between the islet and the north end of the beach. They
were forced ashore at the seaward end of the passage, as
the surf was too heavy for rowing; they splashed overside
in water that one moment was knee deep and the next
barely reached their ankles, and towed the boat for the
half mile that lay between them and the gate. Here they
reembarked, and the exploration of the southern reef began.

This barrier ran much closer to the island than did that
on the northern side, the stretch of water enclosed by it
usually only a few hundred yards wide and never more
than half a mile. The islets were fewer as well, the reef
consisting for the most part of a forest of branching corals
that appeared above water only at low tide, though it
was wide enough to block even the heaviest breakers. It
was a harder place to loot, from the boys' viewpoint, since
the flotsam in which they were apt to be interested frequently lodged in the midst of a jagged, marble-hard
labyrinth. The boat could not possibly be taken among
those growths, and someone had to wade, wearing heavy
shoes.

Bob, of course, was no longer seeking clues. but Hay had
a box of wet seaweed and a number of jars which he hoped

would accommodate specimens for his pool, and the others all had their plans. The section had not actually been deserted since the boat and gate had been out of commission, for other youngsters on the island had boats, and not all were too lazy to row around the long way; but these would have worked the east end of the reef first. It was very likely that the day might be profitable, and everyone was in high spirits.

They had worked their way a mile or so along the reef, and Hay in particular had had very good luck. His jars were all filled with sea water and specimens, and he was talking about going back early to establish them in the pool and get the screening in place—they had decided that the small hole would be enough. The others, naturally, wanted to continue with the original program. They thrashed the problem out while they ate their lunch on one of the few soil-covered islets available, and the result was a draw. The exploration was not continued, and they did not take the specimens to the pool.

The solution was taken out of their control quite unintentionally by Rice, who stood up in the bow of the boat after all were aboard, with the intention of shoving off from the coral ledge to which it was moored. It had not occurred to the boys that where one board had been rotten enough to yield to a fourteen-year-old's weight others might be in like state. They were reminded of the possibility when Rice's left foot, with a loud crack, went through the plank adjacent to the new one and he saved himself from falling overboard only by a quick snatch at the gunwales. He might as well have let himself go, for in a matter of seconds the craft had filled and left them sitting waist deep in the lagoon.

For a moment everyone was too startled for any reaction. Then Colby laughed, and the others, except Rice, joined in.

"That'll be the last I hear about stepping through the bottom of a boat I hope," Hugh finally got out between chuckles. "At least I did it near enough to home so there was no trouble getting it there."

They waded to the shore only a yard or two away, taking the boat with them. There was no question of procedure. All could swim, all had had experience with swamped boats, and all knew that, even full of water, their craft was perfectly capable of supporting their weight if they kept their bodies low in the water. They simply made sure all their property was accounted for—most of Hay's specimens had escaped—reentered the water, and pushed off across the narrow lagoon toward the main island. Once away from the reef and in water deep enough for swimming they removed their shoes and placed them in the boat. Each clung to the gunwales with one hand, pushing it along as he swam. No particular difficulty was encountered, though somebody cheerfully pointed out, when they were about halfway across, that they had just finished eating.

Once ashore another disagreement arose, the question this time being whether they should leave the boat here and bring the wood and tools across the island, or take it around to the creek. The actual distance to their homes directly across the ridge was not great, but most of it was jungle; and carrying heavy loads through that would be no joke. The things could, of course, be brought around by the beach, but that involved extra distance. Since the next day was Monday, with school, they could not hope to do the job in one trip, and it was finally decided to take the boat back to the creek.

There was plenty of time before them, however, and before starting they pulled the craft up on the shore to examine the damage in more detail. Obviously the entire plank would need replacing. It had rotted away from the screws that held it to the sidepieces near the bow and cracked right in two midway between that point of attachment and the first crosspiece, opening downward like a double trapdoor. If Rice had tried to pull straight up without working his way loose carefully, the two pieces would probably have clamped firmly on his legs. It was fortunate, the boys agreed, that their craft was not a larger one carrying ballast.

It finally occurred to them to examine the rest of the woodwork; and the fact gradually forced itself upon them —that satisfactory repair of the boat was going to amount almost to a rebuilding job. A good deal of scavenging was going to be necessary before the craft would once more be seaworthy, for the big plank they had been using would never be sufficient.

Bob came forth with a suggestion. "Why don't we leave

it here for now and go over to the new tank? There's lots of scrap lumber there, and we can pick up what we need, take it to the creek, and bring the boat around either tonight or tomorrow."

"That would mean an extra trip over here," pointed out Malmstrom. "Why not do what we planned, and go up to the tank afterward?"

"Besides, there'll be no one there," added Colby. "We're going to need more than scraps, and we can't take the big stuff without permission."

Bob admitted the justice of this, and was willing to relinquish his suggestion, when Rice had another thought.

"I'll tell you what we might do," he said. "We're apt to be a long time finding just what we want. Why don't one or two of us go up like Bob says and pick out what we could use, and sort of put it to one side, while the others take the boat around—that won't need very many hands. Then after school tomorrow we can just ask for the stuff we've put aside all at once and be able to go to work without wasting time."

"That's O.K., if you think we can get it all at once. Sometimes it's better to ask for one thing at a time," Hay pointed out.

"Well, we can make more than one pile and ask different people. Who'll go up to the tank and who pushes the boat?"

It was eventually settled that Bob and Norman would set out at once for the construction site and the others would work the rowboat back to the creek. No one was in a hurry to start, but at last they dragged the wreck back into water deep enough to float it, and the two emissaries returned to shore, with Rice's voice behind them grunting the song of the Volga boatmen.

"I'm going home first and get my bike," said Norman as they headed away from the water. "It's easier, and'll save time."

"That's a thought," agreed Bob. "We'll lose a little cutting through the jungle, but the bikes should make up for it. I'll wait for you at my drive, shall I?"

"O.K., if you get there first. I know your place is closer to here, but the jungle is narrower up my way. I'll go up the shore till I'm opposite my house before I cut over."

"All right."

The boys separated, Norman walking rapidly along the beach in the direction taken by the others—whom he speedily overtook and passed—while Bob headed uphill into the heavy growth he had already shown to the Hunter. He knew the island as well as anyone, but no one could say he knew that jungle. Most of the plants were extremely fast-growing varieties and a path had to be in constant use to remain in existence. The larger trees were more permanent and would have made satisfactory landmarks had it been possible to proceed directly from one to the other; but the thorny undergrowth usually prevented it. The only really reliable guide was the slope of the ground, which enabled one to take a straight course with the assurance that he would come out somewhere. Bob, knowing where he was in relation to his house, was reasonably sure of reaching the road within a short distance of the dwelling—or even hitting it exactly if he bore enough to the right to cross the comparatively well-used trail he had employed a few days before. He plunged into the undergrowth without hesitation.

At the top of the ridge they paused, more to let Bob get his breath than his bearings. Ahead of them, down the slope where the houses should be, was a wall of brush. Even Bob hesitated at the sight and looked to each side; the Hunter cringed mentally and prepared himself for action. For the first time the boy went down on his hands and knees to thread his way through the barrier. It was a little better close to the ground, since the worst bushes tended to grow in clumps and spread as they rose, but it was still far from clear, and the scratches began mounting up. The Hunter had thought of something really biting to say on the subject of just how much time and effort were being saved by the short cut, when his attention was taken by something he saw from the corner of Bob's eye.

To the right of their line of travel was an area that, except for the thorns, looked more like a bamboo thicket than a lilac bush—the plants were separate stalks thrusting individually from the ground a few inches apart and shooting straight up. Like nearly everything produced in the first year or two of the island laboratory's existence, they possessed horns—iron-hard, needle-sharp specimens an inch and a half long on the main stems and only a trifle shorter on the stubby, horizontal, thin-leafed branches that commenced within a foot of the ground. The object that had attracted the Hunter's attention lay at the edge of this patch of vegetation. He could not make it out exactly, since its image was well off the optical axis of Bob's eye lenses, but he saw enough to arouse his curiosity.

"Bob! What is that?" The boy turned his eyes in the direction indicated, and both recognized the pile of white objects instantly—Bob because he had seen such things before and the Hunter from his general knowledge of biology. Bob wormed his way over to it as quickly as he could, and then lay prone looking at the skeleton which lay partly in and partly out of the thicket of straight-growing shrubs.

"So that's what became of Tip," the boy said at last slowly. "Hunter, can you offer a guess at what killed him?"

The Hunter made no answer at first, but looked carefully over the bones. As nearly as he could tell from his memory of the dog's structure they were arranged naturally—even to the claws and the tiny bone that seemed to correspond to the hyoid in his host's tongue. The animal had apparently died in one piece and been undisturbed afterward.

"He doesn't seem to have been eaten, at least by any larger or medium-sized creature of his own general type," the Hunter advanced cautiously.

"That seems true enough. Ants, or something of the sort, could have cleaned the bones like that after he died, but we have none on this island that could have killed him first. Are you thinking what I am?"

"I'm no mind reader, though I've learned to know you well enough to predict your actions occasionally. I think I know what you mean, though. I admit that it is perfectly possible that the dog was killed and eaten by our friend after being ridden here from some part of the shore. I would point out, however, that I can see no reason for killing the dog *here* of all places; there could hardly be a less suitable place on the island for finding a new host. Also, the dog had flesh enough to last for weeks. Why should he stay here long enough to consume it all?"

"Panic. He might have thought you were right on his trail, and picked this for a hiding place." The Hunter had not expected such a prompt answer to what he had meant as a rhetorical question, but he had to admit that Bob's suggestion was distinctly possible. The boy had another idea before he could say any more.

"Hunter, couldn't you tell by examining these bones whether the flesh had been taken by one of your people or not? I'll hold one as long as you like, if you want to go over it thoroughly."

"Do that, please. Something might be learned."

Bob gingerly picked a femur out of the collection. The neighboring bones tended to adhere slightly; there were apparently traces of cartilage remaining in the joints. The boy held it firmly in his clenched hand, knowing how the Hunter would make his examination. It was the first time he had an opportunity actually to see part of his guest's body, but he nobly resisted the temptation to open his hand. As a matter of fact, it would have done him no good: the Hunter used exploratory filaments fine enough to reach through the pores in his host's skin and much too thin to be visible. The search took several minutes.

"All right; you may put it down."

"Did you find anything?"

"A little. Such evidence as there is suggests that our friend was not responsible. The marrow in the bone had decayed normally, as did blood and other organic material in the bone tubelets. It is hard to see why our friend should have remained long enough to consume the greater part of the available flesh but leave what I found. The evidence indicates that your suggestion of ants is a very likely one."

"But not certain?"

"Of course not. It would be a most remarkable coincidence, but if you wish to believe that our arrival scared the fugitive away before he had time to finish his meal, I could not disprove it."

"Where would he have gone?"

"*I* am not defending this wild supposition. However, if we must dispose of it, then his most likely goal would be your body, and I can guarantee he has not tried that!"

"Maybe he guessed you were here." Bob could be irritating at times, the Hunter reflected, much as he liked the youngster.

"Maybe he did. Maybe he's flowing at top speed through this thicket to get away." The Hunter's voice would have been weary had it been audible. Bob smiled and headed downhill once more, but the detective noticed that he kept to the edge of the stand of plants he had mentioned. However improbable an idea might be, Bob was not going to leave it unchecked if checking were so easy!

"You have a friend waiting for you, you know."

"I know. This won't take long."

"Oh. I thought you might be planning to go entirely around this patch of spikes. I was going to point out that, if all the things we have been saying are true, you might also be walking into what I believe you call a booby trap. You don't have to be logical, but you might at least be consistent."

"Did I ever read those words?" countered Bob. "You'd better start teaching me English. If you'd listen, you'd realize we were coming to the creek, which should lead to the path we used the other day, which should lead to my house. I know it's not straight, but it's sure." He stopped talking and jumped as a small animal sprang out from almost underfoot and vanished into the thicket. "Darned rats. If there were a few million more of you, Hunter, you could do this island—not to mention a lot of other places—considerable good. They're too smart for any other animal small enough to catch 'em."

"In places like that I suppose you mean," the other supplemented. "We have similar pests where I come from. We work on them when they get too troublesome, or when there is nothing better to do. I'm afraid there is a rather serious problem facing us just now. It begins to look as though we would have to employ your idea, at least to check young Teroa, in the next few nights."

Bob nodded thoughtfully and occupied his mind with details of this possibility as they traveled. The bush had opened out a little on their left, and it was possible to walk erect again as they approached the creek. The stream was already two or three feet wide, even this far up the hill; it had its origin in a spring surprisingly close to the top of the ridge, which occasionally dried up during prolonged rainless spells. These, as it happened, were rare. The creek itself had cut deep into the soil without spreading very wide; the roots of the thick vegetation held the steep and sometimes undercut banks. In many places saplings that had been unable to meet the fierce competition for soil had fallen over so that they made bridges across the stream or moss-draped inclines sloping from the banks into the water. Occasionally larger trees had fallen and damned the creek, making little dark pools with tiny waterfalls at their lower ends.

Such a pool was located a few yards above the spot where Bob and the Hunter reached the stream. The tree which formed it had fallen years before, and most of its few branches had fallen away or become buried in the soft soil as rain, insects, and worms did their bit. The water escaped from the pool on the side from which Bob and the Hunter had approached and had deeply undercut the bank at that point, and the buried branches—perhaps—aggravated the situation. There was no warning. Bob started to turn downstream at what should have been a perfectly safe distance from the bank even if he had had a thought of danger in his mind. As his weight came on his right foot the ground suddenly gave way and let him down, and something struck his ankle a heavy blow. He reacted rapidly enough to catch himself with his hands and the other leg as his right knee disappeared, then he paused to recover his wits.

As he did so he became aware of a severe pain in his leg; and as he started to stand up again the Hunter spoke urgently.

"Wait, Bob! Don't try to move your right leg!"

"What's happened? It hurts."

"I'm sure it does. Please give me opportunity to work. You have taken a bad cut from a buried branch and you cannot move without injuring yourself further." The Hunter had understated the matter, if anything. A comparatively thin piece of wood, buried almost vertically in the ground, had split diagonally under Bob's weight and the splintered end had been driven completely through his calf from a point about four inches above the ankle on the inside to one just below the knee, scraping along the rear side of the lower leg bones and severing the main artery at that point. Without the Hunter, as far as he was from help, the boy could easily have bled to death long before anyone would have missed him.

As it was, the only blood lost was carried out by the stick itself. The Hunter was on the job instantly, and there was plenty of work to be done. Much of it was routine—

sealing leaks in the circulatory system, destroying the host of micro-organisms which had been carried into his host's flesh, and fighting off shock. There was also the fact that the stick extended apparently much farther into the ground below, and Bob was perforce pinned in one spot until it could be removed either from the ground or from his leg. The job was not going to be easy, and the alien sent an exploring tentacle down into the earth to find just how firmly the stick was lodged.

The results were not encouraging. He encountered water first. Then for six or eight inches the branch went nearly straight into hard earth; at that level it had been broken almost completely across and the tip section bent sharply upward again, still underground. It was as though the branch had been jabbed forcibly into the earth, bent and broken, and then pushed a little farther—which might, the Hunter realized, be exactly what had happened. In any case, there was no possibility of getting it out of the ground; he himself lacked the strength, and Bob was pinned in a position from which he could not work very well.

He believed in sparing his host as much physical damage as possible but knew that ignorance was seldom very helpful, so he now explained the situation completely to the boy.

"This is about the first time I've really been sorry I could do nothing about the pain without injuring your nervous system, or, rather, risking injury to it," he concluded. "This will hurt, I know. I will have to pull your muscle tissue away from the stick while you pull your leg out. I will try to tell you when and how much to pull."

Bob's face was pale, even though the alien was holding his blood pressure up. "Right now I think I'd take the chance of damage, if you were willing," he said.

The Hunter realized in a dim fashion just how much the youngster was standing, and decided some help was needed. "As a last resort, Bob, I will do it," he said. "Please try to hold on, though, for even if my work on your nerves does no permanent damage, it will interfere with your ability to control your leg at the moment; and I cannot possibly lift your leg out of this hole myself."

"All right; let's get it over with."

The Hunter set to work, forcing as much as possible of

his body material around the splintery stick to prevent further tearing of his host's flesh as it was withdrawn. Bit by bit, tight-lipped with pain, Bob withdrew his leg, pulling when the Hunter indicated it was safe, waiting when he had to. It took many minutes, but at last the job was done.

Even Bob, knowing what he did, was a little startled at seeing his trouser leg stained only with dirt. He was going to roll up the cloth to see the injury, but the Hunter stopped him.

"A little later, if you must; but right now lie down and rest for a few minutes. I know you don't feel the need of it, but I assure you it is advisable."

Bob realized the alien probably knew what he was talking about and complied. By rights he should have fainted, for will power means nothing in the face of such an injury, but he did not, thanks to his guest; and as he relaxed obediently, he thought.

Things had been happening just a little too fast for Bob, but it was dawning on him that the events of the last half-hour had followed with remarkable fidelity the outline he and the Hunter had discussed, half-jokingly, just before they started—an outline based on one particular contingency. And even he was impressed by the coincidence.

Chapter XV. *ALLY*

TO THE HUNTER, who had examined in detail both the
bones of the unfortunate Tip and the splintered stick
which had injured his own host so badly, the whole thing
was coincidence. It was so obvious to him that his quarry
had nothing to do with the matter that he never thought
of saying so to Bob. The boy's line of thought, therefore,
at this point began to diverge widely from the detective's
—a fact that turned out to be extremely fortunate.

Bob had been lying motionless for some time when they
were disturbed by a voice calling his name. The boy
started to spring to his feet and almost collapsed as the
injured leg sent a furious protest.

"I forgot we were meeting Norman!" he said. "He must
have gotten tired waiting, and is coming uphill after us."
More gingerly this time he put weight on the injured
limb—a thing no doctor would have recommended and to
which the Hunter also objected. "I can't help it," said
Bob. "If you write me off as a cripple, they'll put me in
bed and we can't do a thing. I'll favor it as much as I
can—it can't get infected with you there and will just have
more trouble growing together, won't it?"

"Isn't that enough? I admit that no permanent damage should result, but——"

"No buts! If anyone learns how bad this is they'll send
me to the doctor; and he simply won't believe I made it
home without bleeding to death. You've done too much to
remain concealed from him now if he gets a chance to
look me over!" The boy began limping downhill, and
the Hunter pondered over the sad fact that the active
member of a partnership was too apt to take control,
regardless of qualifications.

Somewhat later it occurred to him that there might be
worse things than the doctor's learning of his presence;

it might even give them a most valuable ally. There was certainly enough evidence at the moment to prove to a stupider person than Dr. Seever that the Hunter was more than a figment of Bob's imagination. Unfortunately, by the time the thought occurred to him, it was too late to mention it—Bob and Hay had met.

"Where have you been?" was the greeting of Norman. "What happened to you? I got my bike and have been waiting in front of your house long enough to grow a beard. Did you get hung up on the thorns, or what?"

"I had a fall," Bob replied with perfect truth, "and hurt my leg a bit. It was a while before I could use it."

"Oh, I see. Is it all right now?"

"No, not quite. I can get around, I guess. I can ride a bike, anyway. Let's get back down to the house and pick mine up."

The meeting had taken place at no great distance from the Kinnaird house, since Hay had not dared go very far into the jungle for fear of missing Bob altogether. It took them only a minute or two to reach the dwelling, in spite of Bob's limp, and, once there, it proved fairly easy to ride the bicycle provided Bob mounted from the left and pedaled with the instep of his right foot instead of the toe.

They made their way up to the construction site, amusing each other the while with speculation on the troubles the others would be having getting the swamped boat through the breakers at the beach, and began prowling for materials. These proved fairly plentiful, and well before suppertime they had placed the articles of their choice in a number of inconspicuous places, to insure their remaining unused until after school the next day. They were honest youngsters, in their way.

Two things happened to prevent Bob's getting back to the site immediately after school. One of them occurred Monday morning, when his father saw him limping as he descended to breakfast, and demanded the cause. Bob repeated the story he had given Hay; but the next demand was a little awkward.

"Let's see it." Bob, thinking fast, pulled his trouser leg halfway to the knee, exposing the entry wound. This, of course, did not look nearly so bad as it should have, since the Hunter had held the torn skin in place all night and was still on duty. To the boy's vast relief Mr. Kinnaird did not ask about the depth of the injury, taking for granted that nothing so obviously free from blood clots and infection could have been very deep. The relief was short-lived, however. The man turned away, saying, "All right. If you're still limping the next time I see you, you'd better be able to tell me you've seen Doc Seever." The Hunter's respect for Mr. Kinnaird was increasing daily.

Bob set out for school with that problem on his mind —nothing was more certain than the fact that his torn calf muscle would keep him limping for days to come, Hunter or no Hunter; and his father would certainly be at the construction site that afternoon. At the end of school another cause for delay materialized: the teacher who handled the older pupils requested that he remain for a time, so that his proper position in the group might be discovered. Bob requested a moment's excuse, hastily explained to the others, and saw them started for the new tank; then he returned to the schoolroom for the inquisition. It took some time. As frequently happens when a pupil changes from one school to another, the difference in programs had put him a year or so ahead in some subjects and as far behind in others. By the time a mutually satisfactory program had been worked out, Bob was pretty sure his friends would have obtained what they needed and taken it to the creek.

Even so, there remained the problem of the limp and his father's ultimatum. He had been trying all day to walk as though nothing were the matter, and had succeeded only in attracting more attention. He stood at the doorway of the school for some minutes, pondering this problem, and finally put it up to the Hunter. He was distinctly startled at the alien's answer.

"I suggest that you do exactly what your father said— go to Dr. Seever."

"But how can we get away with that? He's no dumbbell, and you won't make him believe in miracles. He won't be satisfied just to see one of those holes, either—he'll check the whole leg. How will I account for the shape it's in without telling about you?"

"I have been thinking about that. Just what, would you say, is wrong with the idea of telling him about me?"

"I don't want to be written off as cracked, that's what. I had trouble enough believing in you myself."

"You'll probably never have better evidence for your story than you have right now, if the doctor is as thorough as you say. I will back you up; and *I* can prove I am here to anyone's satisfaction, if necessary. I know we have been making strenuous efforts all along to keep my presence secret, and the reasons for that are still sound; I don't mean to broadcast the story. I think, however, that a doctor might be a remarkably good associate in our work. He has knowledge neither of us possesses and should be willing to use it—it is certainly no exaggeration to describe our quarry as a dangerous disease."

"And if he turns out to be the host of our quarry?"

"He is certainly one of the least likely candidates on the island. However, if that should be the case—— I think I can find out very quickly and certainly. There is certainly a precaution we can take." He outlined this precaution at length to his host, and Bob nodded slowly in understanding.

The doctor's office was not far from the school. It would hardly have been worth using the bicycle had it not been for Bob's injury. There was a slight delay caused by the presence of another patient, then Bob and his invisible guest entered the pleasant room which Dr. Seever had turned into a consulting room and dispensary.

"Back again so soon, Bob?" greeted the doctor. "Is that sunburn still giving trouble?"

"No, sir, I'd forgotten about that."

"Not entirely, I hope." The two grinned in sympathy.

"This is something else. I had a fall in the woods yesterday, and Dad said I'd better either see you or stop limping."

"All right, let's see the damage." Bob seated himself in a chair facing the doctor and rolled up his trouser leg. At first Dr. Seever did not see the exit wound, but after a moment he did. He examined both openings carefully and at considerable length, then he sat back and eyed the boy.

"Let's have the story."

"I was up in the woods, near the head of the first creek. The bank had been undercut farther than I thought, and I broke through, and a sharp-pointed branch underneath went into my leg."

"'Through' is the word you want. Go on."

"There's not much else. It hasn't bothered me too much, so I didn't come to you until Dad made me."

"I see." The doctor was silent for another minute or two. Then, "Did something like this happen at school back in the States?"

"We-e-ll——" It never occurred to Bob to pretend not to know what the doctor meant. "There was this." He extended the arm that had been cut the night the Hunter had made his first attempt at communication. The doctor silently examined the thin, barely visible scar.

"How long ago?"

"Three weeks about." Another period of silence, while Bob wondered what was going on in the other's mind. The Hunter thought he knew.

"You've discovered, then, that there's something unusual about you—something you couldn't understand; something that made injuries which should need stitches behave like scratches and punctures that should put you flat on your back 'not bother you much'; and you've been worried about it? Was that what got into you at school?"

"Not exactly, sir. You're almost right, but—I know what causes it." With the Rubicon crossed, Bob went ahead quickly and clearly with his story, and the doctor listened in rapt silence. At the end he had some questions.

"You have not seen this—Hunter yourself?"

"No. He won't show himself to me. Says it might disturb my emotions."

"I think I can see his point. Do you mind being blindfolded for a little while?" Bob made no objection, and the doctor found a bandage and tied it over his eyes. Then: "Please put your hand—either one—on the table here, palm up; let it relax. Now—Hunter, you understand what I want!"

The Hunter understood clearly enough and acted accordingly. Bob could see nothing, of course, but after a moment he felt a faint weight in the palm of the extended hand. His fingers started to close on it instinctively, and the doctor's hand promptly descended to pin them in place. "Hold on a moment, Bob." For a short time the weight could be detected, then the boy began to doubt whether or not it was actually there—it was rather like a pencil stowed behind the ear, which can be felt after it is gone. When the blindfold was removed, nothing was visible, but the doctor's face was even more sober than before.

"All right, Bob," he said. "Part of your story appears to be true anyway. Now, can you enlarge on this mission of your friend?"

"First, there is something I have to say," replied Bob. "This is really his speech, and I'll try to give it in his own words, as near as I can remember.

"You have been convinced, at least in one essential, of the truth of this story. You must be able to see why the secret has been kept so far and the risk we chose to face in telling you. There is certainly a chance, however small, that you are actually the person harboring our quarry.

"In that event, we see two possibilities. Either you know of his presence and are consciously co-operating with him because he has convinced you of the justice of his position, or you do not know. In the first case, you are now planning means to get rid of me. Your guest would be perfectly willing to do anything to my host in the process, but I know you would not; and that presents you with a problem that will take time to solve and will probably betray the truth to me in your attempts to solve it.

"In the second case, Doctor, your host now knows where I am. He also knows that you are a doctor, and will find some means to detect his presence in your body if anyone can. That, I fear, will mean that we have placed you in danger, for he will have no hesitation in doing whatever he thinks necessary to escape. I cannot suggest any precautions to you; you should be able to think of some yourself. Don't mention them aloud, though.

"I am sorry to have exposed you to this risk, but it seems to me to be one that falls within your normal duty as a doctor. If, however, you are not willing to take it, simply say so. We will leave at once. We will, of course, test you at the first opportunity; but with the fear of immediate discovery no longer pressing, he may at least leave your body without harming you, since he will be in no hurry. What is your decision?"

Dr. Seever did not hesitate an instant.

"I'll take any risks there may be. I think I can see how to test myself too. According to your story, you have been

145

in Bob's body nearly six months; and your quarry, if he is in mine at all, is likely to have been there for several weeks at least. That is long enough for the formation of specific antibodies—you say you are, in effect, a virus. I can make a serum test with a sample of Bob's blood and my own that should give us an answer at once. Have you learned enough medical English to gather what I mean?"

Bob replied slowly, reading off the Hunter's answer as it came. "I know what you mean. Unfortunately, your plan won't work. If we had not long ago learned how to prevent the formation of antibodies for our particular cells, our way of life would never have been possible."

The doctor frowned at this. "I should have thought of that. I suppose there's no use expecting your friend to let any of his own tissue be caught in a section or a blood sample, either." He looked up sharply. "How did you plan to make identification? You must have some method."

Bob explained the Hunter's difficulty in that direction, then the alien finished: "I intended, when reasonably certain, to make a final check by personal inspection. He certainly could not hide for any length of time if I went into the same body in search of him."

"Then why not check me that way? I know you have no particular reason to suspect me, but it would be just as well to know one way or the other. You would know then that you could trust me; and, frankly, I should like to know myself. I've been rather afraid these last few minutes that I might find out the hard way as soon as you two leave the office."

"Your point is a good one," relayed Bob. "But the Hunter will not enter or leave any human body while its owner is awake. You seem to sympathize with him on that." The doctor nodded slowly, looking thoughtfully at his visible guest.

"Yes. Yes, I understand his reason. However, that situation can be arranged also." Dr. Seever left his chair and went to the front door, taking a small placard from a wall stand as he passed it. This he placed on a hook outside the door, closed and locked the latter, and returned to the office. He looked at Bob again, then went over to one of the numerous small cabinets.

"How much do you weigh, Bob?" he asked over his shoulder. The boy told him, and he made a brief calculation in his head, then he reached for a bottle of clear liquid. With this in his hand he turned back to the visitors.

"Hunter, I don't know whether this stuff will affect you as well. I would suggest that you get out of Bob's alimentary and circulatory systems before we take it. We will sleep for from one to two hours—I suppose that's longer than necessary, but I can't guarantee that any smaller dose would put us out at all. You can make your test while we're unconscious and get back to tell us the result—or maybe do something else, if necessary. All right? We won't be disturbed—I've seen to that."

"I'm afraid it is not quite all right," was the answer. "It means that my host would be helpless before I know for certain about you. However, I will concede that the test should be made, and I will relax my demand somewhat to get it over with. If you and Bob will sit side by side, holding hands tightly, and guarantee that you will not separate those hands for twenty minutes, I will shift enough of myself into your body to make the inspection and return."

The doctor agreed instantly—he had intended to use the drug only because of the Hunter's insistence that the hosts be insensible, and this alternative was both safer and pleasanter. He moved his chair out beside Robert's, therefore, took one of the boy's hands in his own, dropped the bandage that had served as a blindfold over the two hands as an added safeguard for the Hunter's peace of mind, and relaxed.

It took a little more than the promised twenty minutes, but to their relief the Hunter was able to give a negative report. Discussion for the first time flowed freely—at least between Bob and the doctor—and the general conditions of the problem were thrashed over so thoroughly that Dr. Seever almost forgot about Bob's injured leg. It was only at the end of the visit that he mentioned it.

"As I understand it, Bob, your friend can do nothing to speed up the processes of healing; he simply prevents bleeding and infection. My advice is to stay off that leg— you gave the muscle an awful beating."

"The only trouble is," said Bob, "I seem to be transportation division for this army and am vehicle for the commander in chief. I can't be immobilized."

"Well, it will certainly slow up the healing; I can't see

that any other damage will result, under the circumstances. Use your own judgment; I know the situation is serious for someone. Just keep off it as much as possible." The doctor closed the door behind them and returned to his study, where he speedily immersed himself in a work on immunology. Maybe the Hunter's people knew what to do about antibodies, but there were other tricks to the medical trade.

It was not quite suppertime, and Bob and the Hunter made their way to the creek, where the boys should be. A sound of sawing gave evidence well before Bob was close enough to see that they were there; but work stopped as he came in sight.

"Where have you been? You've certainly ducked out of a lot of work this afternoon. Look at the boat!"

Bob looked. There was very little boat to see, as a matter of fact, for the removal of the bad timber had accounted for a remarkable percentage of the total, and very little replacement had as yet been accomplished. There was a reason for this, Bob noticed: there was very little replacement material on hand.

"Where's the stuff we picked out last night?" he asked Hay.

"A good question," said the other dryly. "Some of it was where we put it, and that's right here now. The rest had disappeared. I don't know whether the young kids cleaned it out or the men found it and used it. We didn't stay to get more; we thought we'd better get what was left down here and use it before it disappeared too. We'll have to go back for more—there isn't nearly enough here to finish."

"You're telling me," said Bob, looking at the rather forlorn framework lying on the beach before them. Its state reminded him of something else, and he turned to Rice.

"Red, I'm afraid I found Tip yesterday." The others laid down the tools with which they had been about to resume activity and listened with interest.

"Where?"

"Up in the woods, near the head of the creek. I had my fall just afterward and forgot everything else, or I'd have told you this morning. I don't really know it was Tip, since there wasn't much left, but it was a dog about his size. I'll show you the place after supper if you like—there isn't time now."

"Could you tell what killed him?" Rice had long since accepted the fact of the dog's death.

"No. Your guess is as good as mine when you've seen him. I think Sherlock Holmes himself would have trouble finding clues, but you can try."

The news put a final stop to work on the boat for that afternoon. As Bob had said, suppertime was approaching, anyway, and presently the group drifted back up the creek to the road, and its members went their ways. Rice, before vanishing, called after Bob a reminder that they were to visit the woods after the meal.

As it happened, everybody was there. Their curiosity had been aroused by Bob's extremely sketchy description of what he had found, and they all wanted to see. Bob led the way slowly along the path to the creek and up the watercourse to the point where he had had his accident, which he pointed out. Hay, groping curiously down the hole, encountered the branch which had caused so much trouble, and after considerable effort got the vertical part out.

"You just missed some bad trouble with this," he remarked, holding it up to view. Bob indicated his leg—the boys had all seen the lower puncture; as he had done with his father, he had avoided mentioning the other.

"I didn't quite miss it," he said. "I suppose that's what did this." Hay looked more closely at the stick. The sun was on the point of setting and the woods were already rather dark, but he saw the stains left from the accident.

"I guess you're right at that," he said. "You must have been a while pulling out: blood has gone down this thing a foot or more from the sharp end. I wonder why I didn't notice it on your pants leg when I met you yesterday."

"I don't know," Bob lied hastily, and began leading the way from the creek along the edge of the thicket. The other three followed, and Hay, after a moment, shrugged his shoulders, dropped the branch, and trailed along.

He found the others grouped around the skeleton of the dog exchanging theories. Bob, who had brought them here with a definite purpose in mind, was watching all the others sharply. He himself was quite sure, in spite of what the Hunter had said about the bones, that Tip had been killed by their quarry, who had then rigged the trap into which he had fallen. He even had an explanation for the

149

fact that there had been no attempt to enter his body while he was helpless—the alien had found another host first: a host who used the creek as a highway through the jungle, as Bob and his friends used it. That implied, of course, that one of those friends had been in the neighborhood and motionless for some reason long enough for the creature's purpose. Bob had not heard of such an incident, but was hoping that here and now, if ever, someone might refer to it.

It was rapidly growing dark now, and the only conclusion reached by the boys was the obvious one that nothing much larger than insect life had disturbed the dog's body. No one had actually touched the bones as yet, but with seeing growing more difficult by the moment Malmstrom decided to get a closer look. The skull was inside the thicket, but it was this he chose to examine, and he reached very gingerly among the thorns to pick it up.

Getting in gave little trouble, but it developed that the thorns on the short side branches pointed back in toward the main stems. This furnished about as efficient and unpleasant a trap as one could well hope not to encounter, and Malmstrom picked up several very nasty scratches as he withdrew hand and skull. He handed the latter to Colby and shook the injured member.

"There's something that would make a good fish spear," he remarked. "The darned thorns fold back against the branches easily enough, but they spring out again when you pull the other way. I bet that's what happened to Tip —he chased something in here and couldn't pull out."

The theory was a reasonable one, and even Bob was impressed by it. He suddenly remembered that he had not told his other idea to the doctor; what would Seever's opinion be? Perhaps by now he had worked out some medical test, and there would be no difficulty for him in finding an excuse to use it. Bob had hoped to give him some line on whom to test first; now he did not know what to think. He led the way back downhill in the darkness, his brain working furiously.

Chapter XVI. *PROSPECTUS*

TUESDAY WENT as usual until the end of school, except for the fact that the Hunter was growing progressively more anxious about Charles Teroa. That one was due to leave the island on Thursday, and as far as the Hunter could see Bob had done nothing toward testing him or delaying his departure. There were only two more nights . . .

The boys, who had no such worries, departed on a search for more boatbuilding materials as soon as they were dismissed. Bob started with them, but stopped off at the doctor's office, ostensibly to have his leg checked. Here he told in full the story of the preceding evening and of his theory; and the detective realized for the first time that his host had been working along a line of thought radically different from his own. He hastily attracted the boy's attention and gave his own views, together with the evidence supporting them.

"I'm sorry I didn't realize the trend of your thoughts," he concluded. "I remember telling you that I didn't think the dog had been killed by our friend, but perhaps I did not mention the fact that your 'booby trap' also seemed to be entirely natural. I should say that the branch was driven into the ground that way when the tree fell. Is this why you have been ignoring the matter of Charles Teroa?"

"I guess so," Bob replied. He gave a brief summary of the Hunter's silent speech to the doctor.

"Young Teroa?" asked Seever. "He should be coming to me for shots tomorrow. Have you reason to suspect him?"

"At first it was simply the fact that he was to leave the island," replied the Hunter. "We wanted to be sure before he was out of reach. However, we learned later that he had slept at least once in a boat moored at the reef, which gives definite opportunity for our quarry to get at him. He was also present when we nearly went through the drain on the dock, but that hardly involves him alone."

"That's right," mused the doctor. "We have quite a list of what you might call first-class possibles, with the whole island following right behind as slightly less probables. Bob, did nothing happen last night to give you ideas, one way or the other, about any of your friends?"

"Just one," replied the boy. "When Shorty Malmstrom pulled Tip's skull out of the thicket he got several gashes from the thorns; they bled like nobody's business. I kind of thought we needn't worry too much about him."

Seever frowned slightly, and addressed his next remark to the detective. "Hunter, just what sort of conscience has this friend of yours anyway? Could he or would he, for example, let an injury of that sort bleed just to make someone reach Bob's conclusion—that there was no one of your race there?"

"His conscience is non-existent," returned the alien. "However, the sealing of such minor injuries is so much a habit with us that he might have done it anyway if he were there. Certainly if he had any reason to believe his host were under suspicion, and if he thought of it, he would refrain from helping him regardless of the seriousness of the injury—he is looking out for just one creature's health. Bob's point is no positive proof either way, but we can list it as a minor point in Malmstrom's favor."

The doctor nodded. "That's about what I thought from your earlier story," he said. "Well, we seem to be left with the immediate problem of testing young Teroa. It would be nice to know what yellow-fever vaccine does to your people, Hunter. He's getting a dose of it tomorrow."

"I would gladly let you find out if the stuff will not harm Bob. However, I can guarantee that our friend will simply withdraw from the limb in which you inject the stuff and wait till it attenuates. Besides, the chances of its being harmful to us are very remote. I still think I had better examine him myself. Once we locate our quarry, we can find something that will damage him."

"Once you locate your quarry, you'd better be *ready* with something that will damage him," retorted the doctor. "All I can offer that may do it without harming his host are a few antibiotics and vaccines; and we can't test them all at once on Bob. We should have started this business days ago." He thought tensely for a moment. "I'll tell you. Suppose we start now, one substance at a time, with the things I know will not harm Bob. You can tell us the effect they have on you—we'll arrange things so you can leave his body in a hurry until he eliminates the particular substance you couldn't stand. We'll leave testing Teroa until we find one of them that works. If none of them do, we're no worse off anyway."

"But, as you say, that will take days, and Teroa leaves this island in less than forty-eight hours."

"Not necessarily. I don't like to do it, because I know how eager the fellow is to get going, but I can hold him on the island for observation until the next visit of the boat if necessary.

"That will give us ten days, with two drugs a day, and should give us a fair chance of finding something. We'll start with antibiotics, since vaccines are usually pretty specific in their likes and dislikes."

"Very good indeed, if you are willing, Bob," was the reply. "It is a pity we did not get you into the fight before, Doctor. Shall we make one test now?"

"Sure," replied Bob. He seated himself, and the doctor draped a cloth over his legs.

"I don't know whether it's worth the trouble to take your shoes off," he said as he was swabbing the boy's arm with antiseptic. "From what I gather about your friend, he can get out if he has to without their bothering him. All set?" Bob nodded, and Seever held the hypo syringe against his arm and pressed the plunger. The boy kept his eyes on the wall and waited for the Hunter's report.

"Just another kind of protein molecule to me," was the sentence that finally appeared. "You might ask the doctor if I should consume the stuff or if it's all right to leave loose in your system."

Bob relayed the message.

"It doesn't matter, as far as anyone knows," replied the doctor. "In fact, he would be doing me a favor if he let it go and reported any effect on your tissues to me. We believe it's harmless. Well, it's probably best not to try another today; you might as well get back to your friends. Keep your eyes open; Teroa isn't our only suspect, even if your own idea wasn't so good."

The boys were still at the construction site—Bob had

153

kept an eye on the road to be sure of that. His leg gave a twinge as he mounted his bicycle. He realized with amusement that the doctor had forgotten the injury entirely. He wished he could himself. The ride did not take long, and he noted with satisfaction that there was already a fair-sized stack of loot at the point where the other machines had been left. He parked his own at the same point and sought his friends.

The four boys, it turned out, had called a temporary halt in the search for materials. They were on the hillside at the top of the wall which Bob had seen poured. The concrete had set and the forms were now being placed in preparation for the side walls; the boys were leaning over and looking down the smooth expanse of concrete. Bob, joining them, saw that the attraction was a crew of men busy with some peculiar apparatus at the bottom. They all wore breathing masks, but the man in charge was recognizable as Malmstrom's father. They seemed to have a pressure pump connected by flexible tubing to a drum of some liquid, which, in turn, was fed to a nozzle. One of the men was spraying the liquid on the concrete and the others were following with blowtorches. The boys had a rough idea of what was going on—many of the bacteria used in the tanks produced extremely corrosive substances, either as intermediate or final waste products. The glaze being applied to the wall was meant as protection from these. It consisted, actually, of one of the fluorine-bearing "plastics" developed a few years previously as a by-product of uranium isotope separation research; it was stored in the drum with one of the standard inhibitors and polymerized into a glassy varnish almost at once when this was boiled out. The fumes of the inhibitor were rather unhealthful, which was why the men were masked.

The boys, thirty feet above the scene of action, got an occasional whiff of the fumes. Not even the Hunter recognized the danger, but others did, and did something about it.

"First a sunburn that nearly toasts you alive and now this. You don't care much what happens to you any more, do you?" The group turned and looked up in surprise, to see the tall form of Bob's father looming over them. They had last noticed him well out on the floor of the tank, apparently busy, and none of them had seen him head their way. "Why do you suppose Mr. Malmstrom and his crew are wearing masks? You'd better come along with me. You may be safe enough at this distance, but there's no sense taking a chance on it." He turned and led the way along the wall, and the boys followed silently.

At the end of the finished section Mr. Kinnaird waved a hand at the far section of mold. "I'll meet you down there in a couple of minutes. I have to drive home to pick up something, and if you'd care to load up your loot in the jeep I'll drive it down to the creek with you." He watched the youngsters head downhill at top speed and descended to the floor himself via one of the diagonal braces.

He picked up the T-shirt he had removed for comfort and stowed by one of the power saws, donned it, and walked down to the point he had indicated, where the jeep was parked. Only his son awaited him there, the others had gone on to the pile of material they had collected. Mr. Kinnaird sent the jeep along their trail, coasting most of the way.

The loading was quickly accomplished; the boys already had their hands full of the smaller scraps, and Mr. Kinnaird himself managed the longer stuff in a single armload. Then he headed on down the road, the five bicycles following. The boys, of course, made a race of it; the distance being short, they were not very far apart at the end, and even the jeep had not had to wait long for them.

Mr. Kinnaird, seeing the boys doff shoes and roll up their trouser legs, followed suit, and, with the same load of lumber under his arm, splashed behind them down the creek to the scene of operations. He looked over the skeleton of the boat, made a few constructive suggestions, and returned the way he had come, slapping as he went. "I think you kids keep trained bugs around, to discourage company," he said. The boys answered in the same vein, and finally got to work.

They paused to swim more than occasionally, and it was during one of these swims that the Hunter learned why human beings avoided jellyfish. Bob failed to do so at one point, and his guest became intimately acquainted with the nettle cells of the Coelenterata. He blocked the spread of their poison, not because he felt that his host should be encouraged to ignore the creature, but in a half-sentimental recollection of the mistakes of his first day on earth. He felt that he was paying for knowledge.

In spite of sundry interruptions a good deal of work was accomplished in the first hour or so. Then another boat made its appearance, and Charles Teroa was with them, to the intense interest of the detective and his host.

"Hi, sleepy!" Rice greeted the newcomer boisterously, waving a saw in welcome. "Having a last look around?"

Teroa eyed him in none too friendly a fashion. "It's a pity that built-in danger signal of yours can't be seen by your tongue," he remarked. "You fellows having boat trouble again? Seems to me you got it fixed once." Four eager pairs of lungs vied in giving him the story, Rice suddenly fading into silence. The visitor simply looked at him when they had finished, and the expression on his brown face changed from annoyance to amusement. Nothing he could have said would have conveyed his thoughts more clearly, or made Rice feel sillier. Relations were a little strained between the two for the half-hour Teroa remained.

There was much talk and little work during that half-hour—Teroa enlarging on his future in great detail, with Hay and occasionally Colby contributing remarks in between times. Bob, whose knowledge of the doctor's intentions made him rather uncomfortable, said little; he spent most of the time reminding himself that it was for Teroa's own good. Rice had had his batteries silenced in the first exchange, and even Malmstrom was less talkative than usual. Bob put it down to the fact that he had always been on closer terms with Teroa than the others, and didn't like the idea of his friend's leaving. Sure enough, when Teroa returned to his boat, Malmstrom went with him, asking Colby to take home the bicycle he had left where the creek and road met.

"Charlie says we're going to meet the barge and get a tow around to the fields. He wants to see the fellows on the barge and then come back over the hill by the new tank and see the folks there. I'll go with him and walk home. I may be late, but what the heck."

Colby nodded, and the two departed, pulling strongly out into the lagoon to intercept the scavenger barge, which was making one of its periodic trips around the tanks. The others watched silently until contact was made.

"It's fun to ride him, but I'm sorry to see him go," remarked Rice at length. "Still, he'll be back every so often. Shall we get back to the boat?"

There was muttered agreement, but enthusiasm for the work seemed to have died out for the time being. They pottered around for a while, went swimming again, sawed a couple of boards to length, and eventually startled their parents by appearing at home well in advance of the evening meal.

Bob, instead of settling down to schoolwork after supper, went out again. To his mother's casual question he replied that he was going "down to the village." It was true enough, and he had no intention of worrying his parents by telling them he wanted to see Dr. Seever. The doctor had said that the next drug would not be tried until tomorrow, and Bob himself had nothing specific to tell or ask; but he was uneasy about something, and could not himself decide just what. The Hunter was a good and trustworthy friend, no doubt, but he was not even at the best of times an easy being to converse with; and Bob simply had to talk.

The doctor welcomed him with some surprise.

"Good evening, Bob. Are you getting impatient for another test, or do you have some news? Or are you just being sociable? Come in, whichever it is." He closed the door behind his young guest and motioned him to a seat.

"I don't exactly know what it is, sir. At least I do partly: it's this trick we're playing on Charlie. I know we have good reason, and it won't hurt him permanently, but I don't exactly feel right about it."

"I know. I don't pretend to like it myself—I'm going to have to lie, you know, in a way that goes very much against the grain. When I give a wrong diagnosis, I'd like it to be an honest mistake." He smiled wryly. "Still, I see no alternative, and deep down I know we are doing no wrong. You must realize that too. Are you sure there's nothing else on your mind?"

"No, I'm not," was the reply, "but I can't tell you what it is. I just can't seem to relax."

"That's natural enough; you are involved in a tense situation—more so than I, and I can certainly feel it. Still, it is possible that there is something of importance you have seen and can't bring back to mind—something you didn't notice at the time but which has some connection with our problem. Have you thought over carefully everything that has happened since you came home?"

"Not only that, but everything that's happened since last fall."

"Have you just *thought,* or have you talked it over with your friend?"

"Thought mostly."

"It might be a good idea to talk—it frequently gets one's thoughts in better order. We can at least discuss the cases against your friends, to see whether you've considered all the points. We have covered young Teroa pretty thoroughly, I should say—the fact that he slept near the reef and was present at your accident on the dock seem to be all we have against him. Besides, we already have a plan of action covering him.

"You mentioned a minor point in favor of Malmstrom, when he cut himself on those thorns. Have you anything else that could be given, either for or against him? He has not slept near the reef, for example?"

"All of us were sleeping on the beach the day the Hunter arrived, but come to think of it Shorty wasn't there that day. Anyway, that doesn't matter. I told you about finding that piece of the ship; it was a mile from the beach, and anyway the Hunter says it would have taken a long time for this creature to bring it ashore. He couldn't have landed until later." He paused. "The only other thing I remember noticing about Shorty was that he left us and went off with Charlie this afternoon; and they were always good friends, so there's nothing funny about his wanting to talk to him before he goes." The doctor was able to untangle this mess of pronouns, and nodded.

"Yes, I should say that everything you've dredged up on young Malmstrom is either immaterial or in his favor. How about the redhead—Ken Rice?"

"Pretty much the same as the rest, as far as haunting the reef and being there on the dock. I haven't seen him get injured, so—— Wait a minute; he did get his foot pretty badly bruised by that chuck of coral. He had his heavy shoes—the kind we always wear on the reef—on, though, so there's no reason to suppose he got any cuts. I suppose the bruise wouldn't mean any more than Shorty's scratches, though."

"When did all this take place? I don't recall your telling me about it."

"Out on the reef, the same time we found that generator shield—same place, in fact; I should have thought of that." He went on to tell the story in detail. "We've kept quiet about it, of course; after all, he did come pretty close to getting himself drowned."

"That is a very interesting little tale. Hunter, would you mind enlarging once more on your reasons for suspecting people who have *slept* on the outer reef?"

The alien could see what the doctor was driving at, but answered the question as it was asked.

"He must have come ashore somewhere on the reef; he could not possibly catch a human being who saw him first; and he would be too obsessed with the need for secrecy to waylay an intelligent host and enter his body regardless of objection—which would, of course, be physically possible. He would not mind terrifying his host, but he would not want to have anyone with the desire and ability to report his whereabouts to, say, a medical specialist. I think, Doctor, that if a lump of jelly had swarmed onto any one of these island people and soaked into his skin, you would have heard about it in very short order."

The doctor nodded. "That's what I thought. It occurs to me, however, that young Rice could very easily have been invaded without his own knowledge while his foot was trapped under water. Between the natural fear and excitement of the situation and the pain caused by the weight of the block on his foot any sensations incident to such an attack would have passed unnoticed."

"That is perfectly possible," agreed the Hunter.

Bob transmitted this speech as he had the other, but continued with a remark of his own. "We can't have it both ways. If this creature entered Red's body only that afternoon, he couldn't have had anything to do with the trouble at the dock a few minutes later—first, because it would probably take him days, like the Hunter, before he would be well enough set up to look around; second, because he wouldn't have any reason for it—he could not possibly have begun to suspect that the Hunter was with me."

"That's true enough, Bob; but the dock affair might really have been an accident. After all, *all* these things that keep happening to you and your friends can't have been planned. I've known you all your lives, and if someone had asked me before you told me about this situation I would have had to admit that I was not the least surprised at the things that had been happening to you. The other kids on the island are pretty much the same. There are falls and cuts and bruises every day, and you know it."

Bob had to admit the justice of this point. "It was Ken who wrecked the boat this time too," he said, "though I can't see how that would connect with this business."

"Nor do I, at the moment, but we'll remember it. So far, then, young Rice has one of the best grounds for suspicion against him that we've dug up to date. How about the others? Norman Hay, for example? I've had a thought or two about him myself since you came up with this yarn."

"What's that?"

"Not being completely brainless, I now see why you were digging information about viruses from me the other day. It has occurred to me that Hay might have had a similar motive—you remember he had one of the books I wanted to lend you. I admit his sudden interest in biology might be natural, but it might be as much of a sham as yours. How about it?"

Bob nodded. "That's an idea. He had lots of opportunity too; he was often on the reef working on that pool of his, I understand. I don't know whether he ever took a nap on the job, but it's possible. He was willing to go in the water with me, too, that time we thought there might be some peculiar disease in his pool."

The doctor raised his eyebrows interrogatively, and Bob took time out to give the details of that occurrence.

"Bob," the doctor said when he had finished, "I may know more medicine, but I'd be willing to bet there's enough data right now in your memory to solve this problem if you could evaluate it properly. That's a darned interesting point. It would imply, of course, that Norman was in communication with his guest, as you are with the

Hunter, but we've assumed that before without straining any of the known facts. The creature could easily have told a phony story to enlist Hay's sympathy."

It was at this point that Dr. Seever was first struck by the idea that the Hunter might have done just that; like Bob, he thought fast enough to keep the idea to himself; and, like Bob, he resolved to test the possibility at the first opportunity.

"I suppose Norman, like the others, was around on the dock that time, so he is even with them in opportunity there," the doctor went on without a perceptible pause. "Can you think of anything else about him—for or against? Not at the moment? All right, that leaves, I believe, Hugh Colby in your particular crowd, though we mustn't forget that there are plenty of others on the island who work or play around the reef."

"We can count out the workers," insisted Bob. "And none of the kids play around it—at least on that side of the island—anywhere near as much as we do."

"Well, granting that for the moment, what about Colby? I don't know him too well myself—I don't think I've exchanged more than about two words with him. He's never here professionally, and I don't think I've had to work on him since he was vaccinated."

"That sounds like Hugh all right," replied Bob. "We've heard more than two words, but not much more. He doesn't talk much and is always in the background. He thinks fast, though. He had gone after that bucket for Red's head before anyone else could figure out what was going on. He was at the dock, of course, but I can't think of anything else about him either way. I'm not too surprised, either; he's just not the sort of fellow you think much about, though he's a good enough guy."

"Well, we have Rice and Hay to think about anyway, and Charlie Teroa to work on. I don't know whether this has brought any of your worries into the open or not, but at least I have learned a lot, Bob. If you remember anything else, come around and we'll talk it over.

"I hadn't expected to see you again today, but it's several hours since we tested that last drug; it's probably out of your system by now. Do you want to try another?"

Bob was perfectly willing, and the preparations of the

afternoon were repeated. The result were the same, except that the Hunter reported the new drug to be rather more "tasty" than the previous sample.

WEDNESDAY MORNING Bob left for school early and got another drug tested before appearing at that institution. He did not know just when Teroa was to appear for his shots and did not particularly want to meet him, so he wasted as little time as possible at the doctor's office. The school day went much as usual; afterward the boys decided to omit boat work for the afternoon and visit the new tank once more. Malmstrom was an exception to this; he vanished by himself without being very specific as to his plans, and Bob watched him go with considerable curiosity. He was tempted to follow, but he had no legitimate excuse for doing so, and anyway Rice and Hay rated higher on the suspect list.

Construction, it appeared, was not going quite so rapidly. The walls for which molds were now being set up were not only not backed on one side by the hill for the greater part of their length, but started from a floor which was itself some fifteen feet from the ground at its northern extremity. This involved the setting of diagonal braces considerably longer than had previously been necessary; and since none of the two-by-fours or two-by-sixes was long enough, piecing was required. The slope of the hill meant, further, that no two braces were of identical length; and Mr. Kinnaird was hustling from hillside to power saw with a slide rule in his hand and a steel tape popping in and out of his pocket.

Heavy boards were making rapid trips from lumber pile to saw to wall: and Bob, more or less indifferent to splinters, and Colby, who had borrowed a pair of work gloves, helped with these for some time. Hay and Rice equipped themselves with wrenches, and the persuasive redhead managed to get permission for them to tighten bolts on the conveyor troughs leading from the mixers up the hill down to the molds. These troughs ran on scaffolding, and much of their length was well off the ground, since some of the spouts delivered their contents at the end of the wall farthest from the mixers. Neither of the boys minded the height particularly, but some of the men did and were quite willing to have more active individuals take care of those sections. The scaffolding was solid enough to reduce risk of falling to a minimum.

The coating of the completed south wall was still under way and the boys were not allowed near this activity; but Bob was permitted once to drive down to the dock to re- fill the drum of fluor varnish. This material could not be kept for any length of time near the scene of the work, since it tended to polymerize at ordinary temperatures even with the inhibitor present. The reserve was stored in a refrigerated chamber near the diminutive cracking plant. The drive took only two or three minutes, but he had to wait nearly half an hour while the drum was cleaned and refilled; to leave any of the former contents in it was asking for trouble. There was literally no solvent known that could clean it out, once it hardened, without dissolving the metal of the drum first.

When he got back to the tank Bob found Rice no longer aloft; instead, he was about as low as he could get, driving stakes to butt the diagonal braces. Asked what had caused the change of occupation, he seemed more amused than otherwise.

"I dropped a bolt and nearly beaned Dad, and he told me to get down before I killed somebody. He's been lec- turing me most of the time you were gone. He told me either to work down here or get away altogether; he said if I could drop anything on anyone from here he'd give up. I've been wondering what he'd say if the head came off this sledge on the upswing, which it seems to want to do."

"If he's in the way, he won't say a word. You'd better tighten it—that's a little too risky to be funny."

"I suppose you're right." Rice stopped swinging and busied himself with the wedges, while Bob looked around for something else to interest him. He held an end of the steel tape for his father for a while, was sternly for- bidden to carry hundred-pound bags of cement to the stock pile near the mixers, and finally settled down at the top of a light ladder checking with a spirit level the trueness of each section of form before its braces were finally set. The work was important enough to make him satisfied with himself, easy enough so he could keep it up, and safe enough to keep his father from interfering.

He had been at this task for some time when he suddenly remembered that he should have seen the doctor immediately after school for another test. Now he was stuck here; as to most conspirators, however good their motives, it did not occur to him that there was no need for him to account for his movements. He stayed at the job therefore, trying to devise an excuse that would let him leave without arousing question in anyone's mind. The men might not notice, but there were his friends; and even if they didn't, there was a horde of smaller fry around who would be sure to want to know where he was going. Bob thought they would, anyway.

His reverie on these matters was interrupted by Colby, who was still working on the trough sections and happened to be nearly overhead.

"Say, there comes Charlie all by himself. I thought Shorty had probably gone to see him."

Bob looked down the hill toward the road extension and saw that Hugh was right. Teroa was coming slowly up toward the tank; his facial expression was hard to make out at that distance, but Bob was pretty sure from the aimless way he walked and his generally listless air that he had seen the doctor. Bob's own face tightened, and a pang of conscience went through him; for a moment he considered going up his ladder and out of sight over the forms. He managed to restrain the impulse and held his position, watching.

Teroa was now close enough to be seen clearly. His face was nearly expressionless, which in itself was something of a contrast to his usual good humor; he barely answered the greetings flung at him by the envious youngsters he passed. Two or three of the men, seeing that something must be wrong, tactfully said nothing; but tact was a word missing from the vocabulary of Kenneth Rice.

That young man was working perhaps thirty yards downhill from the foot of Bob's ladder. He was still driving stakes, using the sledge which he had repaired; it looked ridiculously large beside its wielder, for Rice was rather small for his age. He looked up from his work as Teroa approached, and hailed him.

"Hi, Charlie. All set for your trip?"

Charles did not change his expression, and answered in a voice almost devoid of inflection. "I'm not going."

"Weren't there beds enough on board?" It was a cruel remark, and Rice regretted it the instant it passed his lips, for he was a friendly and kind-hearted, if sometimes thoughtless, youngster; but he did not apologize. He was given no opportunity.

Teroa, as Bob had judged, had just seen Dr. Seever. For months the boy had been wanting the job; for nearly a week he had been planning his departure; and, what was worse, he had been announcing it to all and sundry. The doctor's statement that he must wait at least one more trip had been a major shock. He could not see the reason for the delay, which was not too surprising. He had been walking aimlessly for more than an hour since leaving the doctor's office before his feet had carried him to the construction site. Probably, if he had been giving any thought to his destination, he would have avoided the spot with its inevitable crowd of workers and children. Certainly he was in no fit mood to meet company; the more he thought, the less just the doctor's action seemed and the angrier the young man grew. Kenny Rice's raillery, quite apart from considerations of tact or courtesy, was extremely ill-advised.

Charles did not even pause to think. He was within a yard or two of Rice when the latter spoke, and he reacted instantly—he leaped and swung.

The smaller boy had quick reactions, and they were all that saved him from serious injury by that first blow. Teroa had put all his strength into it. Rice ducked backward, dropping his sledge and raising his arms in defense. Teroa, losing whatever shreds of temper that might have remained to him as his blow expended itself in empty air, recovered himself and sprang again with both fists flailing; and the other, with the molds forming an effective barrier to further retreat, fought back in self-defense.

The man whom Rice had been assisting was far too startled to interfere at first; Bob was too far away, as were all the other workers on that side of the tank; Colby had

166

no ready means of descending from the scaffold. The fight, therefore, progressed for some moments with all the violence of which the combatants were capable. Rice stayed on the defensive at first, but he lost his own temper when the first of Teroa's blows got past his guard and thudded solidly against his ribs, and from then on he pulled no punches.

The fact that the other boy was three years older, a full head taller, and correspondingly heavier had considerable bearing on his success, of course. Neither belligerent was a scientific fighter, but some effective blows landed in spite of that. Most of them were Teroa's, who found his adversary's face on a very convenient level; but his own ribs sustained a heavy assault, and at least once the elder boy was staggered by a blow that landed fairly in the solar plexus.

Quite involuntarily he stepped back and dropped his guard over the afflicted region. For Rice, the fight reached a climax at that instant. He was not thinking and was not an experienced boxer, but he could not have reacted more rapidly or correctly if he had trained for years in the ring. As Teroa's arms went down momentarily, Rice's left fist jabbed forward, backed by the swimming-and-rowing-muscles of his shoulders, waist, and legs, and connected squarely with his opponent's nose. It was a nice blow, and Rice, who had little to be pleased or proud about in connection with the fight, always remembered it with satisfaction. It was all the satisfaction he got. Teroa recovered his wind, his guard, and his poise, and responded with a blow so nearly identical in placement that it formed an excellent measure of the true effectiveness of Rice's guard. It was the last of the fight. The man with the other sledge had recovered his wits, and he flung his arms about Teroa from behind. Bob, who had had time to leap from his ladder and dash to the scene, did the same to Rice. Neither combatant made any serious effort to escape; the sharp action had winded them, the pause gave them a chance to evaluate the situation, and both presented rather shame-faced expressions—or what could be seen of their expressions—to the crowd which was still gathering.

The children, who formed the greater part of the group, were cheering both parties indiscriminately; but the men who appeared and shouldered their way through

167

the smaller spectators showed no such enthusiasm. Mr. Rice, who was among them, bore a look on his face that would have removed any lingering trace of self-righteousness from his son's manner.

The son himself was not much to look at. Bruises were already starting to take on a rich purple color, which contrasted nicely with his red hair, and his nose was bleeding copiously. The bruises his adversary had collected were mostly concealed by his shirt, but he, too, had a nosebleed that said something for Rice's ability. The elder Rice, stationing himself in front of his off-spring, looked him over for some time in silence, while the chatter of the crowd died down expectantly. He had no intention of saying what he had in mind where anyone but the intended recipient could hear it, however, and after a minute or so he simply said:

"Kenneth, you'd better get your face washed and the worst of the stains out of that shirt before your mother sees you. I'll talk to you later." He turned around. "Charles, if you'd go with him, and perhaps take the same advice, I'd appreciate it. I should like very much to hear exactly what caused this nonsense."

The boys made no answer, but started down toward the lagoon, now very much ashamed of themselves. Bob, Norman, and Hugh followed them. Bob and Hugh had heard the start of the trouble but had no intention of telling anyone until the principals of the affair had decided what should be told.

Mr. Kinnaird knew his son and the latter's friends well enough to guess this, and it was only that knowledge which enabled him to keep quiet as he rounded the lower end of the tank and came face to face with the party.

"I have some salt-water soap in the jeep," he remarked. "I'll get it, if one of you will take this blade up to Mr. Meredith at the saw." He moved as though to scale the disk-shaped object, which the boys had not noticed he was carrying, at Colby, who automatically slipped to one side. Recovering himself, Colby hooked a finger through the center hole of the blade and turned back uphill with it, while Mr. Kinnaird headed around the corner of his vehicle. The boys accepted the soap gratefully—Rice, in particular, had been worrying about his mother's reaction to the sight of his bloodstained shirt.

Half an hour later, the stains gone, he was worrying about her reaction to a pair of beautifully blacked eyes. He had kept his teeth by some miracle, but Bob and Norman, who were administering first aid, admitted that it would be some time before casual observers would quit asking him about his fight. Teroa was considerably better off in that respect; his face had been reached just once, and the swelling should go down in a day or two.

All animosity had vanished by this time; both combatants had spent much of the time apologizing to each other while their injuries were being worked on. Even Bob and Norman were amused to see them walking side by side back up the hill to face Mr. Rice.

"Well," Hay remarked at last, "we told Red he was asking for it. I hope he doesn't get into too much trouble, though; Charlie gave him enough. Those peepers are going to take a long time to forget, I'd say."

Bob nodded in agreement. "He certainly picked a bad time for his wisecracks—right after Charlie said he wasn't going. He must have been feeling pretty bad."

"I didn't hear that. Did he say why he wasn't going? It's news to me."

"No." Bob remembered in time that he was not supposed to know, either. "No, there wasn't time for explanations after that; things happened too fast. I don't suppose it would be smart to ask now, either, though he may have told Red by this time. Shall we go back up and see?"

"I don't think it would do much good. Besides, I still haven't put the grating in that pool of mine—we've been spending so much time fixing the boat and working up here. What say we go out and do that? We don't need the boat; the stuff is out there, and we can swim across from the beach."

Bob hesitated. This seemed a good opportunity of seeing the doctor and getting another drug written off the list—he was not very optimistic on this point, as may be seen—but he was still not quite sure how to get away from his friend; he still had an exaggerated fear of betraying his real motives.

"What about Hugh?" he asked. "He hasn't come down from delivering that saw blade yet. Maybe he'd like to go."

"He's probably found something else to do up there. I

think I'll go back myself, if you don't want to work on the pool. You coming, or have you something else to do?"

"I did think of something," Bob replied. "I think I'll look after it now."

"O.K. I'll see you later." Hay went back up the hill after the still-visible fighters without a backward glance, while Bob, wondering how much the other suspected, turned along the shore toward the big dock. He walked slowly, since he had much to think about; but he said nothing, and the Hunter forbore to disturb him. The alien had thoughts of his own, in any case.

At the shoreward end of the dock they turned up the road past the Teroa house, turned right there, and presently reached the home of the doctor. Here his plans, such as they were, were interrupted by the sight of a sign on the door which said the doctor was out on professional business, time of return uncertain.

The door was never locked, as Bob well knew. After a moment's consideration he opened it and went into the office. He could wait, and the doctor was bound to be back before too long. Besides, there were other books there, books which he had not read and which might prove interesting or useful. He investigated the shelves, helped himself to several promising titles, and sat down to deal with them.

He made heavy weather of the job: they were technical works, intended for professional readers, and they pulled no punches when it came to medical terms. Bob was far from stupid, but he simply did not have the knowledge needed to interpret very much of what they said. In consequence, his mind wandered frequently and far from the printed matter.

Naturally much of his thinking was about the afternoon's rather unusual events. More of it dealt with his problem. He had even asked the Hunter point-blank what he thought about the conclusions reached the night before—the strong suspicions Bob and Seever had developed toward Hay and Rice. He did so now.

"I have avoided criticizing your efforts," replied the Hunter, "since it seems to me that, however wrong your conclusions appear, you still have reason for them. I prefer not to tell you my opinions about Rice and Hay, or even about the other boys, for if I were to discourage your ideas on the grounds that they disagreed with mine, I might as well be working alone."

It was an indirect speech, but Bob suspected that the alien disagreed with their ideas. He could not see why— the logic used by the doctor and himself seemed sound —but he realized that the Hunter must have more knowledge about the creature they were seeking than he could impart in a lifetime.

Still, what could be wrong? Strictly speaking, they had reached no actual conclusions—they knew their limitations and had spoken only of probabilities. If the Hunter objected to that, then he should have a certainty!

"I have nothing certain," was the answer, however, when this line of reasoning was expounded to the detective, and Bob settled back to think some more. He got results, but this time he had no chance to discuss them with the Hunter, for just as the idea struck him, he heard the doctor's step on the front porch. Bob sprang to his feet, concentrating tensely; then, as the door opened, he turned to the entering figure.

"I've got some news," he said. "You can let Charlie go tomorrow, after all, and we can forget about Red too!"

Chapter XVIII. ELIMINATION

THE DOCTOR had stopped as he heard Bob's excited voice; now he finished closing the door behind him and moved to his usual chair.

"I'm glad to hear it," he said. "I have some news also. Suppose you give me the details first. Has the Hunter been making tests on his own?"

"No, I have. I mean, it's something I saw. I didn't realize what it meant until just now.

"Charlie and Red had a fight up by the new tank. It started when Red kidded him about not going away tomorrow—I suppose he must have seen you just before. Any way, they both went right up in the air; they were swinging for all they were worth. They both picked up a lot of bruises—Ken has a beautiful pair of shiners—and they both had first-class nosebleeds when we got 'em apart!"

"And you feel that this display of injury means none of the Hunter's race can't be present? I thought we decided that our fugitive would refrain from stopping blood flow for fear of betraying himself. I don't see what your story proves."

"You don't get my point, Doc. I know that a cut or scratch bleeding wouldn't prove anything, but don't you see the difference between that and a nosebleed? There's no cut out in the open for the world to see; there'd be nothing surprising if a fellow got hit on the nose and it didn't bleed. Those two were regular fountains—he'd have been bound to stop 'em!" There was a pause, while the doctor considered this point.

"There's one objection remaining," he said at last. "Would our friend *know* what you have just mentioned —that a blow on the nose does not necessarily cause bleeding? After all, he hasn't had a lifetime of human experience like you."

172

"I even thought of that." Bob was triumphant. "How could he be the sort of thing he is, and be where he is, without knowing? He just would have to know what causes a nosebleed and whether it's necessary or not. I haven't asked the Hunter yet, but how else could it be? How about it, Hunter?" He awaited the answer, at first with complete confidence, then with mounting doubt as the alien considered the wording of his response.

"I should say that you are quite right," the Hunter replied at last. "I had not considered that possibility before, and there was the chance that our friend had not, either; but even in that case he would certainly have seen that there was no danger in stopping the bleeding at any time. The boys who were fighting kept it up long after you were applying nose pressure and cold water and other odd remedies. You score first, Bob; I am willing to forget those two."

Bob repeated this to Dr. Seever, who received the information with a grim nod.

"I have an elimination candidate also," he answered. "Tell me, Bob, didn't you say your attention had been attracted to Ken Malmstrom yesterday?"

"Yes, a little. He didn't work so hard as usual on the boat and he seemed quieter, but I figured it was because Charlie was going away."

"And today?"

"I don't know. I haven't seen him since school."

"I'll bet you haven't," said Seever dryly. "You shouldn't have seen him in school, either. He had a temperature of a hundred and three right afterward, when he finally decided to tell his parents he wasn't feeling well."

"What——?"

"Your friend is down with malaria, and I'd like to know where in blazes he picked it up." The doctor glared as though Bob had been personally responsible.

"Well, there are mosquitoes on the island," pointed out that young man, uneasy under the glare.

"I know, though we keep 'em down pretty well. But where did *they* get it? I keep track of the people who leave this island or visit it; the crew of the tanker—some of 'em —come ashore for short periods. They're out, I'm sure; I know their medical histories. You've been away long enough to get anything and come back, but you can't be the one, unless the Hunter has been preserving the disease in your blood for fun."

"Is it a virus disease? The Hunter wants to know."

"No. It's caused by a flagellate—a protozoan. Here"—the doctor found a book with appropriate microphotographs —"look at these, Hunter, and see if anything like 'em were or are still in Robert's blood."

The answer was prompt.

"They are not now, and I really do not recall all the types of micro-organisms I destroyed months ago. You should recall whether or not he has ever shown symptoms of the disease. Your own blood contains many creatures that bear a superficial resemblance to that inert state illustrated, as I noticed yesterday, but with only those pictures to go by I could not say whether they were identical or not. I should be glad to help you more actively, if my problem were not so pressing."

"Bob," said the doctor when this had been transmitted, "if you don't hang onto that friend of yours after he finishes his job, and go to medical school yourself, you'll be a traitor to civilization. However, that's not germane to either of our problems. I don't like what you implied, Hunter, but I won't deny its possibility without further tests. That's my job. The point I started to make is that your friend cannot be inside Malmstrom's body; everything you've just said about nosebleed goes double for germ disease. You can't suspect anyone for *not* getting sick, and our fugitive must know it."

There was a silence of general agreement after this statement. This appeared ready to lengthen indefinitely; Bob broke it with the remark, "That leaves Norman and Hugh of our original top-priority list. I would have voted for Norm without question this afternoon; now I'm not so sure."

"Why not?"

The boy repeated the Hunter's words of a few minutes before and the doctor shrugged them off.

"If you have your own ideas and won't tell us, Hunter, you can only expect us to act on ours," he said.

"That is just what I want," pointed out the detective. "You both have a tendency to regard me as all-knowing in this matter. That is not true. We are on *your* world, among your people. I will develop and test my ideas, with your help when necessary, but I want you to do the same with yours. You won't, if you let yourselves be influenced to any great extent by my opinions."

"A good point," agreed Seever. "All right, then, my present idea is the same as Bob's—that you make a personal examination, with the least practical delay, of Master Norman Hay. The only other candidate on our list always did seem the least likely. If this were a detective story, I suppose I'd be advising you to work on him. Robert, here, can take you up to a point near Hay's home as he planned before, and you can make the check tonight."

"You have forgotten your own argument—that I should be ready to do something about it if I find our friend there," responded the detective. "It seems to me that the testing of drugs had better go on, while you, Robert, and I keep our eyes open for evidence such as turned up today."

"I'm darned if I'll spread a malaria epidemic just for that," said the doctor. "Still, I suppose you're right. We'll try another drug—and don't tell me you like the taste; it's too expensive for candy." He set to work. "By the way"— he looked up from loading the gun—"wasn't Norman one of the stowaways a while back? How would that fit in?"

"He was," Bob replied, "but I couldn't tell you how it fits. The whole idea was Red's, and he backed out at the last minute from what I hear."

Seever applied the hypo thoughtfully. "Maybe that thing *was* with Teroa for a while and shifted to Hay. They must have slept at least once fairly close to each other while they were hiding on the ship."

"Why should he change?"

"He might have thought that Hay's chances of getting ashore were better. Remember Norman wanted to see the museum on Tahiti."

"That would mean that it had been with Charlie long enough to learn to understand English; and it would also mean that Norm's interest in biology had nothing funny about it, since it developed before he was invaded," pointed out Bob. The doctor was forced to concede this.

"All right," he said, "it was just an idea. I never claimed to have evidence for it. It's a pity we can't find the drug we're looking for. This malaria business would give me

175

an excuse to administer it wholesale, if I had enough, which I probably wouldn't."

"You're no closer to finding it so far," reported the Hunter at that point. The doctor grimaced.

"We probably won't, either. Your structure is too different from that of any earthly creature, I suppose. I wish you would give us some of your own ideas; this seems too haphazard to me."

"I discussed my ideas with Bob a long time ago," the Hunter replied. "I have been following them. Unfortunately, they lead to such a wide field of possibilities that I am afraid to start testing them. I'd rather exhaust your field first."

"What, in Heaven's name, did you discuss with him that you haven't mentioned to me?" Seever asked the boy. "This is a fine time to learn that you have more clues."

"I don't think I have." Bob was frowning in perplexity. "All I remember discussing with the Hunter was the method of search; that was to guess the probable movements of our quarry and look for clues along those routes. We did that, and found the generator shield; it seems to me we're still doing it."

"Me too. Well, if the Hunter wants us to run our ideas dry before he explains his any further, I suppose we'll have to do it. His reasons are good enough—except that one about the other field being too big. That's no excuse not to get started on it, it seems to me."

"I am started," pointed out the Hunter. "I just see no need of diverting your checking activities as yet. I am strongly in favor of observing Hay and Colby very closely indeed. I never did think very much of the case against Rice."

"Why not?"

"Your principal point against him was that he was helpless enough to be invaded for a time at the place our quarry came ashore. It seemed to me, however, that our friend would never enter the body of a person in the very considerable phyical danger that was facing Rice at that moment."

"It would not be danger for him."

"No. But what use would a drowned host be to him at that point? I am not in the least surprised that your redheaded friend has been shown to be innocent—or unin-fected, as I suppose Dr. Seever would put it."

"All right. We'll get the other two settled as quickly as possible, so we can really get to work," the doctor said, "but it still seems illogical to me."

Bob felt the same, but had come to develop a good deal of trust in the Hunter—except on one point. He made no further attempt to sway the alien's decision and went out from the doctor's office into the late-afternoon sunshine. Hay and Colby must be found and watched; that was all he could see to do.

He had left them at the tank. They might still be there; in any case, his own bicycle was. He would have to walk up there to get it, and could tell at the same time whether or not they had found something else to do.

Passing the Teroa house, he noticed Charles at his old occupation of gardening, and waved to him. The Polynesian boy seemed to have recovered his temper; Bob remembered that there had been no talk of letting him go, after all, and hoped the doctor would remember. Certainly there was no need for keeping him around now.

His bicycle was lying where he had left it. The other boys' bicycles had disappeared, which left him with the problem of just where they were likely to have gone. He remembered Hay's desire to work on his pool, and decided that that was as likely a probability as any, so he mounted his machine and headed back along the road he had come. At the doctor's he turned aside to make sure Seever had not forgotten about releasing Teroa; at the second creek he stopped to look for bicycles, though he was reasonably sure the others would not be working on the boat. Apparently he was right.

Norman had, of course, said that they would swim to the islet if they went at all. That would mean their machines would be, most probably, at Hay's home, at the end of the road. Bob remounted and headed in that direction. The Hay residence was a two-storied, large-windowed building rather like that of the Kinnairds'. The principal difference was that it was not surrounded by jungle. It was situated at the end of the ridge, where the high ground sloped down to meet the beach, and the soil was already too sandy to accommodate so many of the heavy thorn growths of the higher ground. There was still vegetation enough to give ample shade, but walking around the house was not quite such a major undertaking. There was a spot in back where a rack had been constructed to accommodate a large number of bicycles—many of the adults on the island used them—and Bob automatically looked there first. He was pleased to see that his deductions had been at least partly right: the machines of Rice, Colby, and Hay were there. Bob racked his own beside the others and headed toward the beach. At the north end, where the reef recommenced, he was not surprised to see the trunk-clad figures of his three friends on the islet across the narrow strip of water.

They looked up at his hail, and waved him back as he started to strip.

"Don't bother to come over! We're all done here!" Hay called. Bob nodded in understanding and stood waiting. The others looked around as though to make sure they had left nothing and made for the water. They had to pick their way gingerly among the coral growths that rimmed the islet and studded the passage before the water was deep enough to swim, and the few yards of swimming was rather awkward in shoes; but the beach side was clearer, and they presently waded out beside Bob.

"You got the wire in place?" Robert opened the conversation.

Hay nodded. "We made the hole a little bigger. It's about six or eight inches across now. I got some more cement and a piece of ordinary copper screening, and I cemented them both in together. The big mesh will serve as a support and the screening will keep practically anything in the pool."

"Do you have any specimens yet? And how about that color film?"

"Hugh got a couple of anemones in. I suppose I owe him a vote of thanks; I'm darned if I'd touch them."

"Neither would I, again," replied Colby. "I thought they always folded up when something big came near. One of 'em did, and I didn't have any trouble with it, but the other—wow!" He held up his right hand, and Bob whistled in sympathy. The inside of the thumb and the first two fingers were dotted with red points, where the stinging cells of the sea anemone had struck; and the whole hand up to the wrist was visibly swollen and evidently painful

—the care with which Hugh moved the hand demonstrated that.

"I've been stung by the things, but never that bad," commented Bob. "What kind was it?"

"I don't know. Ask the professor. It was a big one. But big or little, he collects his own from now on!"

Bob nodded thoughtfully. It seemed peculiar, even to him, that everything should be happening on the same day; but it was hard to see around the apparent fact that four of the five chief suspects were now eliminated. Certainly if Hugh had transported one of the flowerlike creatures without injury or trouble, his hypothetical guest would have no reason for not acting on the stings of the second. Even if he were indifferent to his host's pain, he certainly would not want the hand disabled even temporarily.

It looked as though Norman Hay, by elimination, held star position. Bob resolved to put the point to the Hunter at the first opportunity.

In the meantime appearances had to be maintained.

"Did you fellows hear about Shorty?" he asked.

"No. What's happened to him?" returned Rice.

Bob promptly forgot his worries in the pleasure of bringing startling news. He told at great length, detailing their friend's illness and the doctor's mystification as to its source. The others were properly impressed; Hay even seemed a trifle uneasy. His biological interests had given him some knowledge of malarial mosquitoes. "Maybe we ought to look through the woods and drain or oil any still-water pools we find," he suggested. "If there is malaria on the island, and any mosquitoes get at Shorty now, we're in for trouble."

"We could ask the doc," replied Bob; "but it sounds good to me. It will be an awful job, though."

"Who cares? I've read what that stuff is like."

"I wonder if we can see Shorty," put in Rice. "I suppose we'd have to ask the doctor about that too."

"Let's go ask him now."

"Let's see what time it is first. It must be getting pretty late." This was a reasonable suggestion, and they waited at Hay's house, holding their bicycles, while he went inside to determine this important matter.

After a moment his face appeared at a window, "My

folks are just starting supper. I'll see you afterward, in front of Bob's. O.K.?" And without waiting for an answer he disappeared again. Rice looked serious.

"If he's just on time, then I'm late," he remarked. "Let's go. If I'm not there after supper, fellows, you'll know why." He had approximately a mile to go, almost as far as Bob. Even Colby, who lived nearest to Hay, wasted no time, and the three machines rolled swiftly down the road. Bob had no means of telling how the others made out, but he had to get his own meal from the refrigerator and wash his dishes afterward.

Only Hay was waiting for him when he finally got out; and, though they remained for some time, neither of the others appeared. There had been ultimatums dangling over their heads for some time on the late-for-meals matter, and apparently the ax had fallen.

Eventually Norman and Robert decided there was no use waiting any longer and set out for the doctor's. He was in, as usual, though they had half-expected he might be at the Malmstroms'. It had not occurred to Hay to look up their drive to see whether his vehicle was present.

"Hello, gents; come in, Business is getting really brisk today. What can I do for you?"

"We were wondering if it was all right for Shorty to have visitors," replied Hay. "We just heard he was sick a little while ago and thought we'd better ask you before we went to his house."

"This was a good idea. I should think there would be no harm in your seeing him—you can't catch malaria just by breathing the same air. He's not very sick now—we have drugs that knock out our friend the plasmodium quite thoroughly these days. His temperature was down some time ago; I'm sure he'd be glad to see you."

"Thanks a lot, Doctor." It was Bob who spoke. "Norm, if you want to start along I'll be with you in a minute. There's something I want to check here."

"Oh, I don't mind waiting," replied Hay disconcertingly. Bob blinked, and for a moment found himself at a loss. The doctor filled the gap.

"I think Bob means that work has to be done on that leg of his, Norman," he said. "I'd prefer to work on that without witnesses, if you don't mind."

180

"But—well, I was sort of—that is, I wanted to see you about something too."

"I'll wait outside till you're done," said Bob, rising.

"No, that's all right. It may take a while. Maybe you'd better know anyway; I might have done the same thing to you. Stick around." Hay turned back to Dr. Seever. "Sir, could you tell me just what malaria feels like?"

"Well, I've never had it myself, thank goodness. It shows a period of chills. Then those die away, and usually alternate with fever and sweating, sometimes bad enough for the patient to be delirious; the whole thing has a fairly definite period, caused by the life cycle of the protozoan responsible for the disease. When a new batch of the organisms develop, the whole business starts over."

"Are the chills and fever always bad—that is, bad enough to make a person really sick?—or might he have it a long time without noticing it much?" The doctor frowned as he began to get an inkling of what the boy was driving at. Bob tightened up as though it were the last period of a tied hockey game—it was worse for him, since he had a piece of information not yet known to the doctor.

"Sometimes it seems to remain dormant for a long time, so that people who have had the disease once break out with the symptoms again years later. There's been some argument about how that happens, though, and I don't recall hearing of a person who was a carrier who had not had the symptoms at some time or other."

Hay frowned also, and seemed undecided how to phrase his next remark.

"Well," he said at last, "Bob said something about your not being sure where Shorty picked up the germ. I know it's carried by mosquitoes, and they have to get it from someone who already has malaria. I'm afraid that's me."

"Young man, I was around when you let out your first squall, and I've known you ever since. You've never had malaria."

"I've never been sick with it. I can remember having chills-and-fever sessions like you described, but they never lasted long and were never bad enough to bother me much —I just sort of felt queer. I never mentioned 'em to anyone, because I didn't think much of 'em, and didn't want to complain about something that seemed so small. Then, when Bob told us the story this afternoon, all the things

I'd read and the things I remembered sort of ran together, and I thought I'd better see you. Can't you check some way to see if I really have it?"

"Personally, I think your idea is all wet, Norman, my boy; of course, with malaria so nearly wiped out, I don't pretend to be an expert on it, but I don't recall any case such as yours would be. However, if it will make you happy, I can take a blood specimen and have a look for our friend the plasmodium."

"I wish you would."

The two listeners did not know whether to be more worried or astonished at Norman's words and actions. Not only did they promise, if the boy were right, to remove him from the list of suspects, they also seemed out of character. The sight of a fourteen-year-old boy displaying what amounted to adult powers of analysis and social consciousness startled the doctor exceedingly and seemed odd even to Bob, who had always been fully aware of the fact that Norman was younger than he.

As a matter of fact, it was out of character; had the victim of the disease not been one of his best friends, Hay probably would not have devoted enough thought to the matter to recall his childhood chills; and if he had, it is more than doubtful whether he would have reported them to the doctor. At the present his conscience was bothering him; it is very probable that if he had not seen the doctor that night he would have changed his mind about doing so at all before morning. However that may be, he was now almost as eager as Seever drew the blood sample—whether or not he *was* responsible for Malmstrom's illness, he could feel that he was doing something to help.

"It will take quite a while to check," said the doctor. "If you have it at all, it must be very mild, and I might have to do a serum test as well. If you don't mind, I'd like to look over Bob's leg before I get to work on it. All right?"

Norman nodded, with a rather disappointed air, and, remembering the earlier conversation, got up and went reluctantly out the door. "Don't be too long, Bob," he called back. "I'll go slow."

The door closed behind him, and Bob turned instantly to the doctor. "Never mind my leg, if you ever meant to do anything to it. Let's find out about Norman! If he's right, it scratches him too!"

"That had occurred to me," replied Seever. "That's why I took so much blood—that serum-test story I told Norman was simply an excuse, though I suppose it wasn't necessary. I may want the Hunter to do some checking too."

"But he doesn't know the malaria parasite, at least not first-hand."

"If necessary, I'll get some from Malmstrom for him to compare. However, I'll do a microscopical right now. The trouble is, I wasn't kidding about the probable mildness of his case; I might look over a dozen slides or a hundred without seeing the parasite. That's why I wanted the Hunter—he can check the whole sample, if necessary, much faster than I can. I remember that trick of his you mentioned, of neutralizing the leucocytes in your body. If he can do that, he can look over every last one of these blood cells—or smell them, or whatever he does—in jig time." The doctor fell silent, brought out microscope and other apparatus, and set to work.

After two or three slides he looked up, stretched, and said, "Maybe one reason I'm not finding anything is because I don't expect to." He bent to his work again. Bob had time to think that Norman must long since have grown tired of waiting and gone on to pay his visit alone, when Seever finally straightened up once more.

"I find it hard to believe," he said. "But he may be right. There are one or two red cells which seem to be wrecked the way the plasmodium does the job. I haven't seen the brute himself, though there's everything else. I never cease to marvel!"—he sat back in his chair and assumed a lecture-hall manner, oblivious of Bob's abrupt stiffening at his words—"at the variety of foreign organisms present in the blood stream of the healthiest individuals. If all the bacteria I have spotted in the last half-hour or so were permitted to reproduce unchecked, Norman would be down with typhoid, two or three kinds of gangrene, some form of encephalitis, and half-a-dozen types of strep infection. Yet there he walks, with mild chills at long enough intervals for him to need outside stimulation to recall them. I suppose you——" He stopped, as though the thought that had been striving to get from Bob's mind to the open air struck him.

"For Pete's sake! Malaria or no malaria, there's certainly *one* infection he doesn't have! And I've been straining my eyes for the last hour. With all that stuff in his blood—Bob, boy, tell me I'm an idiot if you like—I can see you've been on to the idea ever since I mentioned the critters." He was silent for a moment, shaking his head. "You know," he said at last, "this would be a beautiful test. I can't imagine our friend leaving a normal crop of germs in his host's blood just to meet this situation; that would be carrying caution just a mite too far. If I just had an excuse for making blood tests of everyone on the island—— Well, anyway, that leaves only one suspect on the list. I hope the principle of elimination is good."

"You don't know the half of it," said Bob, finding his voice at last. "It leaves no one on the list. I scratched off Hugh before supper." He gave his reasons, and the doctor had to admit their justice.

"Still, I hope he brings that hand to me. I'll get the blood smear if I have to lie like Ananias. Well, there's at least one good point: our ideas have run dry, and the Hunter will finally have to come across with some of his. How about it, Hunter?"

"You would seem to be right," the detective replied. "If you will give me the night to work out a course of action, I will tell you what I can tomorrow."

He was perfectly aware that the reason for delay was rather thin, but he had a strong motive just then for not telling his friends that he knew where their quarry was.

Chapter XIX. *SOLUTION*

THOUGH BOB had no share in the turmoil of thoughts that were boiling through the Hunter's mind, he was a long time going to sleep. Hay had still been at Malmstrom's house, and they had chattered at the invalid's bedside until his mother had suggested that Kenneth could use some sleep; but very little of Robert's mind had been on the conversation.

The Hunter claimed to have carried their line of thought further and to be able to work out another line of action from it; Bob couldn't, and was wondering how stupid he must be compared to his guest. It bothered him, and he kept trying to imagine how the other alien's probable course could have been traced any further than the piece of metal on the reef—if Rice and Teroa were to be left out of consideration.

The Hunter felt stupid too. He himself had suggested that line of thought to Bob. True, he had not expected much to come of it, but it had contained possibilities for action on his host's part and should have left him free to work out ideas more in line with his training and practice. These last, however, had failed miserably, as he might have expected so far from the civilization which gave them technical backing; and he was now realizing that he had deliberately ignored the answer to his problem for some days, even with the diverse arguments of Bob and the doctor endlessly before him.

It was fortunate that Bob had been working on his own in the matter of the "trap" in the woods, of course; had he not been, the plan of having the Hunter check Teroa and the other boys individually would have been put to work before the doctor was in the secret. That would have meant that the Hunter was not with Bob for stretches of at least thirty-six hours at a time, and he would, he now

185

realized, have missed clues that had been presented to him practically every day. Most of them meant little or nothing by themselves, but taken together . . .

He wished his host would go to sleep. There were things to be done, and done soon. Bob's eyes were closed, and the alien's only contact with his surroundings was auditory; but the boy's heartbeat and breathing proved clearly that he was still awake. For the thousandth time the detective wished he were a mind reader. He had the helpless feeling of a movie patron as the hero walks into a dark alley; all he could do was listen.

There was enough sound to give him a picture of his surroundings, of course: the endless dull boom of the breakers a mile away across the hill and even farther over the lagoon; the faint whine and hum of insect life in the forest outside; the less regular rustle of small animals in the undergrowth; and the much more distinct sounds made by Bob's parents as they came upstairs

They had been talking, but they quieted down as they approached. Either Bob had been the subject of the conversation, or they just didn't want to disturb him. The boy heard them, however; the sudden ceasing of his restless motion and the deliberate relaxation that followed told the Hunter that. Mrs. Kinnaird glanced into her son's room and went on, leaving the door ajar; a moment later the Hunter heard another door open and close.

He was tense and anxious by the time Bob was definitely asleep, though not nearly enough to impair his judgment on that important matter. Once certain, however, he went instantly into action. His gelatinous flesh began to ooze out from the pores of Bob's skin—openings as large and convenient for the Hunter as the exits of a football stadium. Through sheet and mattress he poured with even greater ease, and in two or three minutes his whole mass was gathered into a single lump beneath the boy's bed.

He paused a moment to listen again, then flowed toward the door and extended an eye-bearing pseudopod through the crack. He was going to make a personal check of his suspect—or certainty, for he was morally certain he was right. He had not forgotten the argument of the doctor in favor of postponing such an examination until he was prepared to take immediate measures in disposing of what he found; but he felt that there was now one serious flaw in those arguments—if the Hunter's belief was correct, Bob must have betrayed himself time and again! There would be no more delay.

There was a light in the hall, but it was not nearly bright enough to bother him. Presently he was extended in the form of a pencil-thick rope of flesh along several yards of the baseboard. Here he waited again, while he analyzed the breathing sounds coming from the room where the elder Kinnairds slept; satisfied that both were actually asleep, he entered. The door of the room was closed, but that meant nothing to him—even had its edge been sealed airtight, there was always the keyhole.

He knew already the difference in rate and depth that served to distinguish the breathing of the two, and he made his way without hesitation to a point beneath the suspect's bed. A thread of jelly groped upward until it touched the mattress and went on through. The rest of the formless body followed and consolidated within the mattress itself; and then, cautiously, the Hunter located the sleeper's feet. His technique was polished by this time, and, if he had cared to do so, he could have entered this body far more rapidly than he had made himself at home in Bob's, for there would be no exploring to be done. However, bodily entry was not in his plans; and most of him remained in the mattress while the exploring tentacle started to penetrate. It did not get far.

The human skin is made of several distinct layers, but the cells which make up these are all of strictly ordinary size and pattern, whether they be dead and cornified like those in the outer layer or living and growing like those below. There is not, normally, a layer—or even a discontinuous network—of cells far more minute, sensitive, and mobile than the others. Bob had such a layer, of course—the Hunter had provided it for his own purpose; and the detective was not in the least surprised to encounter a similar net just beneath the epidermis of Mr. Arthur Kinnaird. He had expected it.

The cells he encountered felt and recognized his own tentacle. For an instant there was a disorganized motion, as though the web of alien flesh were trying to avoid the Hunter's touch; then, as though the creature of which it

187

formed a part realized the futility of further concealment, it relaxed again.

The Hunter's flesh touched and closed over a portion of that net, bringing many of his own cells into contact with it; and along those cells, which could act equally well as nerves or muscles, sense organs or digestive glands, a message passed. It was not speech; neither sound nor vision nor any other normal human sense was employed. Neither was it telepathy; no word exists in the English language to describe accurately that form of communication. It was as though the nervous systems of the two beings had fused, for the time being, sufficiently to permit at least some of the sensation felt by one to be appreciated by the other—nerve currents bridging the gap between individuals as normally they bridged that between body cells.

The message was wordless, but it carried meaning as well and feeling much better than words could have done.

"I am glad to meet you, Killer. I apologize for wasting so much time in the search."

"I know you, Hunter. You need not apologize—particularly when you conceal a boast by it. That you have found me at all is of minor importance; that it took you half a year of this planet's time to do so amuses me exceedingly. I did not know just what had become of you; I can now picture you sneaking about this island for month after month, entering houses one after another —for no purpose, since you can do nothing to me now. I thank you for giving me information of such amusing character."

"I trust you will be equally amused to know that I have been on the island searching for seven days, and that this man is the first I have tested physically. I might have been faster if you had carried a sign, but not much." The Hunter was human enough to possess vanity and even to let it override normal caution. It did not occur to him until afterward that the other's speech had shown that it had not suspected Bob, and that his own answer had furnished far too much information for safety.

"I do not believe you. There are no tests you could have used on a human being from a distance; and this host has suffered no serious injuries or diseases since my coming. Had he done so, I should have found another rather than betray myself by helping."

"That I believe." The Hunter's nerves carried clearly the contempt and revulsion he felt at the other's attitude. "I did not say anything about *serious* injuries."

"The only ones I have worked on were those too minor to be noticed—if another human being was in a position to see the injury acquired, I left it alone. I even let parasitic insects take blood unobstructed while others were around."

"I know that. And you *boast* of it." The disgust was deeper, if possible.

"You know? You certainly don't like to admit you were beaten, do you, Hunter? But do you expect to fool me with your boasts?"

"You have been fooling yourself. I knew you had been letting mosquitoes bite your host when he had company, and not at other times; I knew you were in the habit of repairing unnoticeably small injuries which he received. I suppose you might be given credit for it, although you probably did it to save yourself from complete boredom. It was that, or attempt to control this host as you did with your last; and that would certainly betray you. No intelligent creature can spend its time doing nothing whatever without going mad.

"You were bright, in a way, to handle only inconspicuous injuries. However, there was one being who was bound to notice your activities, whether he attributed them to the true cause or not, and that was *your host himself!*

"I heard conversation—by the way, did you bother to learn English?—that described this man as a cautious individual who would take few chances himself and permit members of his family even fewer. Those words were spoken by men who have known him for years—two different men, my friend. Yet I have seen him running blindly in a container of sharp-edged tools for something he wanted; I have seen him climb down an inclined piece of wood full of splinters, and carry similar pieces in his hands and under his arm next to unprotected skin; I have seen him cut a piece of woven-wire mesh which could easily have taken the skin off his bare hand had it slipped at the pressure he was using; I have seen him carrying a sharp, toothed blade by the *edge* when even an adolescent, notoriously careless in matters pertaining to personal safety, held it at the center. You may have been concealing yourself from most of the human race, my friend, but your host knew you were there—whether he was aware that he knew it or not! He must have noticed subconsciously that nothing was apparently happening when he made minor slips in such matters and grew progressively more careless. I have evidence enough that human beings tend to act that way. I also heard your host mention on one occasion something to the effect that other people kept trained insects around to bother him; apparently he noticed that he was not bothered when he was alone.

"Really, you see, you never had a chance of staying hidden. You must either try to dominate and betray yourself, do a minimum of your duty and betray yourself, or do nothing at all except think for the rest of your life, and in that case you might as well surrender. Even on earth, without skilled assistance, experience, or natives to help me, you were bound to be caught if only I came to the right neighborhood. You were foolish to run in the first place; at home you would simply have been restricted; here, I have no alternative but to destroy you."

The other might have been impressed by most of the Hunter's speech, but the last part aroused him to ridicule.

"Just how do you propose to do that? You have no selective drugs to drive me out of this body and no means of making—or at least of testing—any. Being what you are, you will not consider sacrificing this host to get rid of me; and I assure you I will have no such scruples about yours. It seems to me, Hunter, that finding me was a serious mistake on your part. Before, I was not even sure that you were on the planet; now I know you are here and cut off from home and help. I am safe enough, but watch out for yourself!"

"Since there is nothing I could or would say to disabuse you of that impression, I will leave you with it," replied the Hunter. Without further communication he withdrew, and in a few minutes was flowing back toward Bob's room. He expected momentarily to hear Mr. Kinnaird awaken, but the other apparently had decided there was too little chance of his host's doing the right thing even if he were aroused.

The Hunter was furious with himself. He had been sure, once he had decided that Mr. Kinnaird was the host of his quarry, that the accident on the dock had been deliberate—caused by the alien's interference with his host's eyesight and co-ordination. That would mean that Bob's secret was known, and there was no point in the doctor's plan of concealment until they were ready to strike. It had turned out that he was wrong—the fugitive had apparently not even suspected his pursuer's whereabouts; and the Hunter had certainly given enough data in the conversation to tell the other alien pretty accurately where he himself was. He could not even leave Bob now—the criminal would take no chances, and the Hunter must stay with the boy he had endangered, to protect him as far as possible.

The question now, he thought, as he re-established himself in Bob's still-sleeping body, was whether or not the boy should be told of the situation and of his danger. There was much to be said on both sides; knowledge that his father was involved might operate seriously against Bob's efficiency, but, on the other hand, ignorance was even more likely to do so. On the whole, the Hunter was inclined to tell the boy everything; and he relaxed into a state as close to sleep as he could come in that environment, with that intention in mind.

Bob took the information remarkably well, on the whole. He was shocked and worried, naturally, though his anxiety seemed greater for his father's plight than for his own danger. He was quick-minded enough, as the Hunter had long since realized, to perceive the situation in which he and his guest were caught, though he did not blame the Hunter for letting the cat out of the bag. He fully appreciated also the need for rapid action, and perceived one point which the Hunter had not considered—the extreme likelihood of their enemy's shifting his abode at any time, or at least at night. They would have, Bob pointed out, no assurance on any given day as to which of his parents would be harboring the creature.

"I don't think we need worry about that," the Hunter replied. "In the first place, he seems too sure of his safety to bother shifting; and, in the second, if he does, the fact will quickly become evident. Your father, suddenly deprived of the protection he has been enjoying for some months, is certainly going to provide plenty of notice of the fact, if he stays as careless as he has been."

"Speaking of that 'month's' business, you still haven't told me how you settled on Dad as prime suspect."

"It was the line of reasoning I gave you. Our friend landed on the reef, as we know. The nearest sign of civilization was one of the culture tanks only a few hundred yards away. He would swim to that—at least I certainly would have, in his position. The only people who visit those tanks regularly are the operators of the fertilizer barge.

"He would have no opportunity to invade one of those men, but he would certainly go with the barge. That brings us to the field on the hill where the tank fodder is grown. I had to find someone who slept in that vicinity.

"There was a chance, of course, that he had made his way alone over the hill to the houses; in that case, we had the whole island to search. However, your father made a remark the other evening that showed he must have slept, or at least rested, at the hilltop above the new tanks. He was, therefore, the best suspect yet uncovered, to my way of thinking."

"It certainly seems obvious enough now," said Bob, "but I couldn't work it out. Well, we'll have to do some fast thinking today. With luck, he will stay with Dad until he's sure where you are—Dad is more suitable for research, since he moves around more. The trouble is we don't have any drugs yet. Isn't there anything else that would force one of your people out of a host, Hunter?"

"What would force you to leave home?" countered the detective. "There are probably lots of things, but they will have to be of earthly origin this time. You have at least as good a chance of hitting upon something as I. Certainly if I were our friend, I would stay right there—it's the safest possible place for him."

Bob nodded gloomily and went down to breakfast. He tried to act his normal self, even when his father appeared; he had no means of knowing how well he succeeded. It occurred to him that the other alien might not appreciate the fact that he was consciously aiding the Hunter; that might be one point in their favor, anyway.

He set out for school, still thinking. Actually, though he did not tell the Hunter so, he was trying to solve two problems at once, and that meant accepting quite a handicap.

Chapter XX. *PROBLEM TWO—AND SOLUTION*

AT THE foot of the driveway a thought occurred to Bob and he stopped to put a question to the Hunter.

"If we do make it impossible, or impossibly uncomfortable, for this thing to stay with Dad, how will it get out? I mean, is it likely to hurt him?"

"Definitely not. If he goes into such a situation, or we find a drug, it will simply leave. If he heads for something our friend thinks it won't like, it may thicken up the eye film to prevent him from seeing, or paralyze him in the manner I mentioned earlier."

"You say you are not sure of the aftereffects of this paralysis?"

"Not entirely, with your people," the Hunter admitted. "I told you why."

"I know you did. That's why I want you to try it on me right now, as soon as I get into the woods here so we can't be seen from the road." Bob's manner was utterly different from the half-humorous one in which he had made the same request a few days before, and the Hunter was not surprised at the futility of his objection.

"I told you long ago why I didn't want to do that."

"If you don't want to risk me, I don't want to risk Dad. I'm getting an idea, but I won't do a thing about it until I'm sure on that point. Let's go." He seated himself behind a bush out of sight from the road as he spoke.

The Hunter's reluctance to do anything that might harm the boy remained as great as ever, but there seemed to be nothing else to do. The threat not to continue with his own plan was minor; but he might also refuse to cooperate with the plans of the Hunter, and that would be serious. After all, the alien told himself, these people weren't too different from his former hosts, and he could be careful. He gave in.

194

Bob, sitting expectantly upright, quite suddenly experienced a total loss of sensation below the neck. He tried to catch himself as he went over backward, and found that his arms and legs might as well have belonged to someone else. The weird situation persisted for perhaps a minute, though it seemed longer to the victim; then, without the pins-and-needles feeling he had rather expected, sensation returned to his limbs.

"Well," he said as he arose, "do you think I'm any worse off?"

"Apparently not. You are less sensitive to the treatment than my former hosts and recover faster. I cannot tell whether that is a peculiarity of your own or a characteristic of your species. Are you satisfied?"

"I guess so. If that's all he does to Dad, I guess there's no objection. It still seems to me that he could kill him, but——"

"He could, of course, by blocking a major blood vessel or tightening up further on the nerves I just handled. Both methods are more work, though, and would take a little more time, at least from our friend's viewpoint. I don't think you need worry about them."

"All right." The boy emerged onto the road once more, remounted the bicycle he had left at the corner of the drive, and resumed his way to school. He was almost too deeply buried in thought to steer.

So the alien, if intelligent, would remain in his father's body because it was the safest possible refuge. Then what would it do if that refuge ceased to be safe? The answer seemed obvious. The difficulty was, of course, how to create a situation dangerous for the alien but not for Mr. Kinnaird; and that problem seemed, for the moment, at least, insuperable.

There was also the problem Bob had carefully refrained from mentioning to his guest. Strictly speaking, Bob did not actually *know* even now that the Hunter was what he claimed to be. The statement made earlier, to the effect that the criminal might have revealed himself to his host and enlisted his help with a false story, was too plausible to be considered with comfort. Something about whatever plan Bob finally devised must give him an answer to that question also—a better answer than the vague tests he had used a few days ago, when he had asked to be paralyzed.

The whole attitude shown by the detective had been convincing, of course, but it just might be acting, whatever Bob wanted to believe. It must be seen whether he would carry that attitude into practice.

The Kinnaird record was not noticeably improved by that day's school session, and he very nearly alienated his friends during the lunch period. In the afternoon session he was as bad, until the threat of having to remain after dismissal time to complete some assignments focused his attention for the time being. He had reached a point in his cogitations where he very much wanted to be free as early as possible.

He certainly did not delay when school was dismissed. Leaving his bicycle where it was, he set out rapidly on foot toward the south across the gardens. He had a double reason for leaving the machine: not only would it be useless in his present project as he visualized it, but its presence would make his friends assume he would return shortly, so that they would be less likely to follow him.

Threading his way along the paths between garden patches until several houses hid him from the school, Bob began to work his way eastward. He was seen, of course—there were few people on the island who didn't know all the other inhabitants; but the ones to whom the boy nodded greeting as he passed were merely casual acquaintances, and there was no fear of their following him or becoming interested in his activities. Twenty minutes after leaving the school he was a mile from it and fairly close to the other shore, almost directly south of the dock. At this point he turned northeast, along the short leg of the island, and quickly put the rising ground of the ridge between himself and most of the houses. The unused ground on this side had not grown up into jungle quite so badly as the other leg; the brush was fairly heavy, but there were no trees. This section was narrow, and his original course would have carried him eventually into the fields of what the Hunter had aptly called "tank fodder."

However, as he came to a point directly south of the highest point of the ridge Bob turned straight uphill, and consequently he did not emerge from the undergrowth until almost at the top. Here he dropped face downward and wriggled his way to a point where he could look down the other side—almost the same point where he had slept for a time on the night the south wall of the tank had been poured.

Activity was much as usual, with men working and children getting underfoot. Bob looked carefully for his friends, and finally decided they must either have gone to work on the boat or to stock the pool. They did not appear to be on the scene below. His father was there, however, and on him the boy kept a careful eye while he waited for the opportunity that was sure to come. He was sure, from the amount of wall still unfinished the day before, that the glazing crew must still be at work; and sooner or later they were going to need a refill. It was not absolutely certain that Mr. Kinnaird would drive down for it, but the chances were pretty good.

The uncertainty about the matter affected Bob noticeably; the Hunter, who was in a uniquely good position to observe, realized that his host was more excited than he had been since they had met. The expression on his face was utterly serious; his eyes steadily roved over the scene as the few missing or weak details of his plan were filled in or repaired. He had not said a word to the Hunter since leaving school, and that individual was curious. He reminded himself that Bob was far from stupid, and his earthly experience might very possibly make him more fit for the present activity than the Hunter. The detective had been just a little smug about his ability to think out the probable course of the fugitive when Bob had been unable to do so; now he realized that the boy was off on a line of thought at least as far ahead of him. He hoped it was equally well founded.

Suddenly Bob started to move, though the Hunter could see no change in the scene below. Without obviously trying to hide, he went downhill inconspicuously. On the ground near the mixers were scattered a number of shirts which had been left there by the workmen; and Bob, indifferent to watchers, proceeded to go through the pockets of these. Eventually he came across a folder of matches, which appeared to be what he wanted. He cast his eyes around, met the gaze of the owner of the shirt, held up the folder, and raised his eyebrows interrogatively. The man nodded and turned back to his work.

The boy pocketed the matches and strolled a little way

back up the hill, where he could see the greater part of the tank floor once more. There he seated himself, and once more concentrated his attention on the actions of his father.

At last the event he had been waiting for occurred. Mr. Kinnaird appeared with a metal drum on his shoulder, and as Bob stood up to see more clearly, he disappeared below the far edge of the flooring, at the point where the jeep was usually parked.

Bob began strolling toward the neighboring tank as casually as he could, keeping a careful eye downhill. He had been in motion only a few seconds when the little car appeared with his father at the wheel and the drum visible beside him. There was no question of his destination; and, as Bob remembered, he was sure to be gone at least half an hour. He disappeared almost at once below the neighboring tank, and, owing to Bob's nearness to this structure, did not reappear at all.

Bob himself used the same tank for concealment. He kept with difficulty, to his casual pace until he had put the tank between himself and the scene of activity; then he turned slightly downhill and began running at the top of his speed.

A few moments brought him to the end of the paved road. Here the line of corrugated-iron storage sheds began; and, to the Hunter's bewilderment, Bob began inspecting them closely. The first few were normally used for construction machinery, such as mixers and graders; some of these were empty, their normal contents being in use. Several more, closer to the residential district, contained cans of gasoline and fuel and lubricating oils. The boy examined them all, stood looking around for a moment as though to get something straight in his mind, and then once more plunged into furious activity.

Choosing one of the empty sheds—he did not actually go in, but looked over about half the floor area from a point outside the door—he began carrying vast armfuls of five-gallon cans and stacking them beside the entrance. Even the Hunter wondered at the number he was able to carry, until the sound as he put them down disclosed the fact that they were empty. When the stack was built to his satisfaction, in a broad pyramid taller than the boy himself, he went to another shed and began reading very carefully the stenciled abbreviations on another set of cans. These, it turned out, were far from empty. They contained a fluid that would have passed anywhere for kerosene, although it had never been in an oil well. Two of these Bob placed at strategic points in his pyramid; another he opened, and began pouring the contents onto the stack of cans and over the adjacent ground. The Hunter suddenly connected this maneuver with the matches.

"Are you making a fire or not?" he asked. "Why the empties?"

"There'll be a fire, all right," was the reply. "I just don't want to flatten this part of the island."

"But what's the point? A fire can't hurt our friend without doing considerably worse to your father."

"I know it. But if he just thinks Dad is in a position where he can't escape the fire, I expect he might be tempted to leave. And I'm going to be standing by with another oil can and more matches."

"Fine." The sarcasm could not be described. "Just how do you expect to get your father into such a situation?"

"You'll see." Bob's voice went grim again as he spoke, and the Hunter began seriously to wonder just what was in his youthful ally's mind. As an afterthought, Bob dumped one more can of oil on the pyre, this time using a heavier fluid normally employed as a lubricant. Then he obtained a can of the kerosene, loosened its screw cap, and stationed himself across the road from his incipient bonfire at a point where he could see the dock between the sheds. He kept his eyes glued on this point, except for an occasional uneasy glance up toward the new tank. If anyone came down and found his handiwork just now, it would be embarrassing.

He had not bothered to check the time when his father went down on the errand, and had no idea how long the construction of his bonfire had taken, so he did not know how long he was likely to have to wait. Consequently, he dared not move from his station. The Hunter had asked no further questions, which was just as well; Bob had no intention of answering them until a time of his own choosing. He did not like to act in this way toward the alien, whom he liked, but the idea of killing an intelligent creature had begun to bother him now that the deed was imminent, and he wanted to be sure he attacked the right one. For a boy of his age Robert Kinnaird had a remarkably objective mind.

At last, to his immense relief, the jeep reappeared, far out on the dock. As it turned onto the causeway, the boy rose slowly to his feet and moved gradually across the road toward his fire, keeping the jeep in view; as it finally became hidden, close to shore, behind the nearer sheds, he took the last few steps to the pile of dripping cans and drew the folder of matches from his pocket. As he did so, he uttered his carefully prepared and carefully timed answer to the Hunter's question.

"It won't be difficult at all, Hunter, to make him come. You see, I'm going to be just inside the shed!" He twisted a match from the folder as he finished speaking. He rather expected to lose the control of his limbs about that time; certainly if the Hunter were not what he seemed but what the boy had feared he might be, Bob would never be allowed to strike that match. He had deliberately refrained from going where he could see the back windows of the shed, which he well knew existed; his guest should not know of them. The idea that a criminal of the sort which had been described to him would have the speed of mind to recognize his actual safety, or the courage to call the boy's bluff, did not occur to Robert. He had so timed his speech that the other should have no time to think; either he trusted the boy, which almost certainly no criminal could bring himself to do, or he would paralyze him instantly. The scheme had flaws, of course. Bob may even have recognized some of them; but, on the whole, it was a very promising one.

He struck the match without interference.

He bent over and touched the flaming tip to the edge of the pool of oil.

The match promptly went out.

Almost trembling with anxiety—the jeep would turn the corner at any moment—he lit another, and this time touched a place where the liquid had soaked into the ground, leaving a thin film instead of a deep pool. This time it caught, with a satisfactory "whoosh" of flame, and an instant later the pile was blazing merrily.

Bob leaped into the shed before the flames spread over

the pool in front of the door and stood back from the already fierce heat, watching the road.

For the first time the Hunter spoke. "I trust you know what you're doing. If you suddenly can't breathe, it'll be me keeping smoke out of your lungs." Then he left his host's vision unobstructed. Bob was satisfied; things were moving too fast for him to find fault with the alien's reaction.

He heard the jeep before he saw it; Mr. Kinnaird had evidently seen the smoke, and stepped on the gas, as the little engine was whining merrily. He had no extinguisher in the vehicle capable of handling a blaze such as this appeared to be, and Bob realized, as the vehicle was almost level with the flame-blocked door, that his father was going up the hill for help. That, however, he was able to modify.

"Dad!" He said nothing else—if his father wanted to conclude that he was in danger, that was all right, but Bob was not going to lie about it. He was sure that the sound of his son's voice coming apparently from inside the inferno would induce Mr. Kinnaird to stop the car and come on foot to investigate or rescue; he underestimated both his father's reaction speed and resourcefulness. So, evidently, did someone else.

At the sound of Bob's voice from within the apparently blazing shed the driver took his foot from the gas pedal and cut the steering wheel hard to the left. His intention was at once obvious to Bob and the Hunter: he meant to bring the vehicle's hood right up to the door, gaining momentary protection for both the boy and himself from the blazing pool beneath, and back out again the instant his son could leap aboard. It was a simple plan, and a very good one. It should have worked, and in that event Bob and his guardian angel would have to devise a new plan—and some rather detailed explanations.

Fortunately, from their point of view, another factor entered the situation. Mr. Kinnaird's hidden guest grasped the situation, or at least his host's plan, almost as rapidly as the two watchers; but that creature had no intention of risking itself any closer to a pile of flaming oil containers which, from all appearances, might be expected to blast a rain of fire all over the surrounding landscape at any moment. They were already within twenty yards of

201

the blaze, and man and symbiote alike could feel the heat. There was literally no way on earth by which the latter could force his host to turn the jeep around and drive in the opposite direction. There was, likewise, no way by which he could be forced to stop the vehicle; but the creature did not realize this in the tension of the moment. At any rate, it did what seemed best.

Mr. Kinnaird took one hand from the wheel and brushed it across his eyes, which told the watchers in the shed more clearly than words what had happened; but he no longer needed eyes to hold a searingly clear mental picture of his son in the flames ahead, and the jeep neither swerved nor slowed. The symbiote must have realized almost instantly that blindness was insufficient, and a dozen yards from the shed Mr. Kinnaird collapsed over the wheel.

Unfortunately for his guest, the jeep was still in gear, as anyone who had paid normal attention to earthly matters would have foreseen unless utterly panic-stricken; and the little car continued its course, still turning slightly to the left, and thudded into the corrugated-iron wall of the shed several yards from the door. The fact that his foot had slipped off the gas pedal when he was paralyzed probably saved Mr. Kinnaird from a broken neck.

Things had been moving a little too fast for Bob; he had expected his father to be overcome while on foot and somewhat farther from the fire. He had intended using the oilcan in his hand to control the spread of the flames so that the fugitive would believe his helpless host in immediate danger of immolation. Now he could not fulfill this plan, since he could no longer get close enough to the pool of fire in the doorway to see the jeep, to say nothing of splashing oil in its neighborhood. To make the situation rather more awkward, one of the full cans that Bob had placed on the pile chose at this moment to let go. Since he had had the intelligence not to use gasoline, the container simply ruptured along a seam and let a further wave of liquid fire spread down the pile and over the ground; but that wave came closer to the stalled jeep than the boy could tell with certainty.

Almost frantic with his own anxiety, the boy suddenly remembered the windows whose existence he had so carefully concealed from the Hunter while the trap was being set. He whirled and dashed for the nearest, still clutching the oilcan and yelling at the same time in island French: "Don't worry! There's a window!" He managed to wriggle through the unglazed opening and drop to the ground outside. He landed on his feet and raced around the corner of the shed. What he saw as he made the turn brought him up short and restored the thought of his original purpose in his mind.

The fire had not yet reached the jeep, though it was spreading momentarily closer; but that was not the fact that drew the boy's eyes like a magnet.

His father was still slumped over the wheel, outlined clearly against the blaze beyond; and beside him, shielded by his body from the fierce, radiant heat, was something else. The Hunter had never allowed Bob to see him, but there was no doubt in the boy's mind what this was—a soft-looking mass of nearly opaque greenish jelly, swelling momentarily as more of its substance poured out of the man's clothing. Bob instantly drew back behind the corner, though he could see nothing resembling an eye, and peeked cautiously.

The alien creature seemed to be gathering itself for a plunge of some sort. A slender tentacle reached out from the central mass and groped downward over the side of the jeep. It seemed to cringe momentarily as it passed below the protection of the metal and felt the radiation; but apparently its owner felt that a little now was preferable to more later, and the pseudopod continued to the ground. There its tip seemed to swell coincidentally with the shrinking of the main mass on the seat, and Bob gathered himself for action. It took nearly a minute for the whole weird body to reach the ground.

The instant its last contact with the jeep was broken Bob acted. He sprang from the concealment and sprinted toward the car, still bearing his oilcan. The Hunter expected him to pour its contents over the creature now flowing desperately away from the flames, but he passed it with scarcely a glance, pushed his father away from the steering wheel, got under it himself, started the jeep, and backed it a good thirty yards from the building. Then, and only then, did he give attention to the Hunter's main job.

The fugitive had covered a little distance during this

203

maneuver. It had kept close to the wall of the shed and made the best possible time away from the heat, the disappearance of the shelter provided by the jeep spurring it to greater efforts. Apparently it saw Bob coming, however, for it stopped its flowing motion and gathered into a hemispherical mass from which a number of fine tendrils began to reach out toward the approaching human being. Its first idea must have been that this would be a satisfactory host, at least until it got away from this neighborhood. Then it must have realized the Hunter's presence in this purposeful and unswerving approach and tried for an instant to resume its flight. Realizing its limitations in speed, however, it humped together again; and even Bob could see, from his recollection of the Hunter's story of his own actions, that the creature must be trying to go underground.

There was a difference, however, between the well-packed, much-traveled ground by the shed and the loose sand of the beach. The spaces between grains were smaller, and most of them were full of water, which is soft only when there is somewhere to push it. Long before there was any appreciable diminution in the creature's size it was being drenched by the stream of oil from the can Bob was carrying.

The boy poured until the container was almost empty, soaking the ground all about the thing for several feet; then he used the last of the oil to form a trail from the pool he had made toward the blaze. This accomplished, he stood back for a moment and watched the finger of fire reach slowly out toward its new playground.

It was too slow to satisfy Bob, and after a moment he took out the matches again, ignited the entire folder, and tossed it as accurately as he could onto the semifluid lump in the center of the oil pool. He had no reason for complaint this time; he barely got away from the sheet of flame himself.

Chapter XXI. *PROBLEM THREE*

THE HUNTER wanted to stay until the fire had burned out, to make certain of results, but Bob, once he had done all he could, turned his attention at once to his father. A single glance at the inferno surrounding the fugitive's last known position was enough for him. He ran back to the jeep, glanced at his father's still motionless form, and sent the vehicle whirling toward the doctor's office. The Hunter dared make no remark; interference with his host's eyesight at this speed would have been a serious error.

Mr. Kinnaird had been able to see ever since the alien had left his body; he had been conscious the whole time. The paralysis, however, had endured considerably longer than the dose given to Bob by the Hunter, and he had not been in a position to see very well what went on by the shed. He knew Bob had stopped at what seemed to him dangerous proximity to the fire and had gone back for something, but he did not know what. He struggled all the way down the road to get the question past his vocal cords.

He recovered enough to sit up before they finished the short ride to the doctor's office, and the questions were beginning to pour forth as the jeep pulled up at the door. Bob, of course, was relieved to see the recovery, but he had developed another and rather serious worry in the meantime, and he merely said, "Never mind about what happened to the shed and me; I want to find out what happened to you. Can you walk in, or shall I help?"

The last sentence was a stroke of genius; it shut the elder Kinnaird up with a snap. He emerged with dignity from the car and stalked ahead of his son to the doctor's door. The boy followed; normally, he would have been wearing a grin of amused triumph, but an expression of worry still overcast his face.

Inside, the doctor finally got a more or less coherent idea of what had happened from their two stories, and from Bob's expression and a number of meaningful glances made a guess at the underlying phenomena; he ordered Mr. Kinnaird onto the examination table. The man objected, saying that he wanted to find out something from Bob first.

"I'll talk to him," Seever said. "You stay put." He went outside for a moment with the boy, raising his eyebrows interrogatively.

"Yes." Bob answered the unspoken question. "But you won't find anything now except maybe a lack of germs. I'll tell you all about it later; but the job's done."

He waited until the doctor had disappeared once more, and then spoke to the Hunter.

"What are your plans, now that your job is finished here? Go back to your own world?"

"I can't. I told you that," was the silent answer. "My ship is totally wrecked, and even if the other were not, I could never find it. I have a rough idea of how a space ship works, but I am a policeman, not a physicist or construction engineer. I could no more make a space ship than you could build one of the airliners we traveled on together."

"Then——?"

"I am on earth for life, except for the ridiculously small chance of another ship's arriving from my old home. You can guess the likelihood of that if you will look at an astronomical picture of the Milky Way. Just what I do here and who my host is—and even if I have a host at all —depend on you. We do not thrust ourselves on those who do not want our company. What do you say?"

Bob did not answer at once. He looked back across the village to the pillar of smoke that was now thinning above the hill, and thought. The Hunter assumed that he was considering the pros and cons of the suggestion, and felt a little hurt that there should be any hesitation, even though he had begun to appreciate the human desire for privacy at certain times; but for once he had misunderstood his host.

Bob was intelligent for his age, as was evident enough,

but he was still far from adult, and was apt to consider his immediate problems before indulging in long-term planning. When he spoke at last the Hunter did not know whether to be relieved, overjoyed, or amused; he never tried to find the words to describe his feelings.

"I'm glad you're staying around," Bob said slowly. "I was a little worried about it, particularly the last few minutes. I like you a lot, and was hoping you could help me out on another problem. You see, when I set up this booby trap we just sprung, there was one point I didn't consider; and it's one that has to be met awfully fast.

"In a few minutes Dad is going to come out that door with his mouth full of questions and his eyes full of fire. One of the questions is going to be, 'How did that fire get started?' I don't think my being fifteen will make any difference in what'll happen if I don't have an awfully convincing answer. I didn't stop to think of one before, and I can't seem to now, so please get your mind to work. If you can't do that, start toughening up that protective net of yours under my skin; I can tell you where it'll be needed most!"